reckless ABANDON

ALSO BY STUART WOODS

FICTION

Capital Crimes°
Dirty Work+
*Blood Orchid**
The Short Forever+
*Orchid Blues**
Cold Paradise+
L.A. Dead+
The Run°
Worst Fears Realized+
*Orchid Beach**
Swimming to Catalina+
Dead in the Water+
Dirt+
Choke
Imperfect Strangers
Heat
Dead Eyes

L.A. Times
Santa Fe Rules
New York Dead+
Palindrome
Grass Roots°
White Cargo
Deep Lie°
Under the Lake
Run Before the Wind°
Chiefs°

TRAVEL

The Romantics Guide to the Country Inns of Britain and Ireland (1978)

MEMOIR

Blue Water, Green Skipper

* A Holly Barker Book
+ A Stone Barrington Book
° A Will Lee Book

STUART WOODS

DOUBLEDAY LARGE PRINT HOME LIBRARY EDITION

G. P. PUTNAM'S SONS

NEW YORK

reckless
ABANDON

This Large Print Edition, prepared especially for Doubleday Large Print Home Library, contains the complete, unabridged text of the original Publisher's Edition.

ιⅅP

G. P. Putnam's Sons
Publishers Since 1838
a member of
Penguin Group (USA) Inc.
375 Hudson Street
New York, NY 10014

ISBN 0-7394-4235-X

Printed in the United States of America

This Large Print Book carries the
Seal of Approval of N.A.V.H.

THIS BOOK IS FOR HARRY AND GIGI BENSON

reckless ABANDON

Elaine's, early.

Stone Barrington had just walked through the door when his cell phone vibrated in his jacket pocket. He dug it out, while Gianni led him back to his usual table. Dino wasn't there yet.

"Hello?"

"Stone?" An unfamiliar female voice.

"Yes."

"It's Holly Barker."

It took only a nanosecond for Stone to display her image on the inside of his eyelids—tall, light brown hair, sun-streaked, well put together, badge. "Hello, Chief, how are you?"

"Confused."

"How can I help?"

"I'm in a taxi, and I don't know where to

tell the driver to take me. Can you recommend a good hotel, not too expensive?"

"In what city?"

"In New York. I'm headed for the Midtown
Tunnel, I think."

"Why don't you stay at my house?
There's a guest room."

"I have a friend with me."

"Male or female?"

"Female."

"My secretary is there right now, working
late. I'll call and tell her to expect you." He
gave her his Turtle Bay address. "There are
three guest rooms—two with king beds and
one with twins, all on the top floor. You
choose."

"Are you sure? I don't want to put you to
any trouble."

"No trouble at all. That's what the guest
rooms are for."

"When will I see you?"

"Have you had dinner?"

"No."

"Drop your luggage, freshen up, and
meet me at Elaine's—Second Avenue, between Eighty-eighth and Eighty-ninth."

"Sounds great. We're at the tunnel now.
How long should it take me?"

"If you're quick, half an hour, but you're a woman . . ."

"Half an hour it is, and don't ever put a 'but' in front of that statement." She hung up.

Gianni put a Knob Creek on the rocks in front of him, and Stone took a sip. "Better get him something, too," Stone said, pointing at Dino, his partner when he had been an NYPD detective. Dino spoke to a couple of people at the front tables, then came back and pulled up a chair. His drink had already arrived.

"How you doing?" Dino asked.

"Not bad. You?"

"The same. You're looking thoughtful."

"I was just trying to remember everything about my trip to Vero Beach, Florida, last year, when I was picking up my Malibu at the Piper factory."

"Why?"

"I was in a bank in the next town, a place called Orchid Beach, getting a cashier's check to pay for the airplane, when a bunch of guys wearing masks walked in and stuck the place up."

"Oh yeah, you told me about that. They shot a guy, didn't they?"

"Yes. A lawyer with a funny name—Oxblood, or something like that."

"Oxenhandler."

"How did you remember that?"

Dino tapped his temple. "I do *The New York Times* crossword every day. Calisthenics for the brain."

"Funny, it doesn't seem to have muscled up."

"I remembered the name, didn't I? While your brain has apparently turned to mush. Why were you thinking about the bank robbery?"

"Not the robbery so much, the woman."

"Ah, now we're getting to the nub of things. I'll bite. What woman?"

"She's the chief of police down there, name of Holly Barker. She was supposed to marry Oxenhandler that very day. I met her at the police station."

"You went to the police station?"

"I was a witness, and I didn't have a shirt."

"You're losing me here."

"I took off my shirt and held it to Oxenhandler's chest wound, not that it did much good. He died shortly after reaching the hospital."

"So you were bare-chested in Orchid Beach, and you met this girl?"

"Woman. We're not supposed to call them girls, remember?"

"Whatever."

"A cop loaned me a shirt. Holly arrived and took over the case. I remember how cool she was under the circumstances."

"Pretty bad circumstances."

"Yeah. After I came home I called her with some information, and we had a couple of phone conversations after that."

"So why are you thinking about this . . . person?"

"She's in town. In fact, she's at my house right—Jesus, I forgot to call Joan." Stone dialed his office number and got his secretary on the phone. "There are a couple of women coming to the house—one is named Holly Barker; I don't know the other one. Will you put them in whichever of the guest rooms they want, and give them a key?"

"You're doing two at a time now, Stone?" Joan Robertson asked.

"I should be so lucky. Just get them settled. I'll explain later."

"Whatever you say, boss." She hung up.

"What's she doing up here?" Dino asked.

"She didn't say. She called from a taxi on the way in from the airport."

"Nice of you to offer her a bed," Dino said slyly.

"Oh, shut up."

"Did you offer the two of them your bed?"

"I offered them a guest room; that's it."

"So far. Well, I guess it's how you keep your weight down, isn't it?"

"Dino . . ."

Gianni put some menus on the table.

"We'll be two more," Stone said. "And we'll order when the ladies arrive."

Gianni brought two more menus and a basket of hot bread. Stone tore into a slab of sourdough.

"Carbing up for later?" Dino asked.

"Get off it. I just want to get something in my stomach with the bourbon."

"Mary Ann and I worry about you, you know."

"Mary Ann has enough to worry about with you on her hands."

"We want to see you settled with some nice, plain girl."

"You just want to drag everybody down

with you," Stone said. "And what do you mean, 'plain'?"

"A beautiful woman demands too much of a man."

"You're married to a beautiful woman."

"I speak from experience. Their care and feeding is a full-time job."

"Mary Ann cares for and feeds both of you, and without the slightest help from you, as I recall."

"She's an exceptional woman," Dino said. "You'll never do that well."

"Thanks a lot."

They finished their drinks and had just ordered another round, when Dino nodded toward the front door. "I'll bet that's your lady cop," he said.

Stone looked up to see a tall woman, more striking than he remembered, striding toward them, smiling.

"Hey, there," Holly said, offering her hand.

Stone and Dino were on their feet, getting her chair.

"This is my friend Dino Bacchetti, my old partner. He runs the detective squad at the Nineteenth Precinct."

"Hey, Dino."

"Hey, Holly."

"Where's your friend?" Stone asked.

"Oh, Daisy's exhausted," Holly replied. "I put her to bed."

"Can I get you a drink?" Stone asked.

"What are you drinking?"

"Bourbon."

"That will do nicely," she said.

Gianni brought her the drink.

"So what brings you to the big city?" Stone asked.

"I'm in hot pursuit of a fugitive," Holly said.

Stone handed her a menu. "Let's order dinner, then you can tell me about it."

They were halfway through their first course, a salad of French green beans, mushrooms, and bacon.

"Tell us about your fugitive, Holly," Dino said. "Maybe I can help."

"That would be nice, Dino," Holly replied. "First, a little background: Not long ago, I wrapped up a case in my jurisdiction that involved a man named Ed Shine; his history is interesting. He came to the U.S. from Italy, as a teenager, and his original name was Gaetano Costello."

"Costello?"

"Second cousin to Frank. The Mob changed his name to Edward Shine, planted a birth certificate in the county records, and put him through high school and college, ostensibly the son of some people named Shine, who just happened to live in the same apartment building as Mr. and Mrs. Meyer Lansky. Right out of college, Ed starts building office buildings, and he never has any trouble arranging financing; he's laundering money for the mob. He continues doing this for forty years or so, and very successfully. In the meantime, he's visiting Florida on a regular basis, and he has a brief affair with a Latino woman and fathers a son out of wedlock, naming the boy Enrico. The kid takes his mother's maiden name, Rodriguez, and is called Trini.

"Trini Rodriguez grows up his father's son and is trained in all the little arts required of a Mafia-made man. His favorite is killing people. I thought I had killed him, but he bounced back."

"Why did you think you had killed him?" Stone asked, putting down his fork.

"Because I stuck a steak knife in his neck and wiggled it around, and he was pumping blood at a great rate the last time I saw him."

Stone gulped. "And why, may I ask, did you stick a steak knife in his neck?"

"He was trying to kill an FBI agent at the time, and I was trying to stop him."

"Oh."

"Apparently, though, his people got him to a hospital in time, and he recovered."

"Wasn't he arrested?"

"Yes, but there were complications."

"He was trying to kill an FBI agent, but there were complications?"

"Right. Turns out Trini had been an FBI informant all the time he was killing people, and the Miami agent in charge, a guy named Harry Crisp, took him out of the hospital and put him in the Witness Protection Program, saying that he needed his testimony in the big case—*my* case. All this without mentioning it to me, and I wanted the guy for mass murder."

Dino spoke up. "So the guy you've come to New York to find is in the Federal Witness Protection Program?"

"Right."

"Well," Dino said, wiping his mouth and taking a sip of his wine, "that's going to make it just a little difficult to arrest him."

"Hang on," Stone said. "You said you wanted him for *mass murder*?"

"Right. I had a witness in protective custody, and he killed two of her relatives, trying to get at her. She insisted on going to the funeral, and the FBI had the scene covered with lots of agents and a few snipers. I'm up in the church bell tower with one of the snipers when the hearses arrive, and everybody is on maximum alert, looking for somebody with a weapon.

"The coffins are taken out of the hearses and set by the graveside, and my witness walks over, puts a rose on the first coffin and kisses it, then steps over to the other coffin, and, as she kisses it, both coffins explode."

"Holy shit," Dino said quietly.

"My sentiments exactly," Holly replied. "It's carnage, everywhere you look. More than a dozen people are dead and several dozen injured, some critically. Like I said, I'm in the church tower, and the shock wave from the explosions starts the bell ringing and nearly deafens the sniper and me."

"So he murders a dozen people, and still the FBI puts him in the Program?"

"Harry Crisp puts him in the Program, and once *anybody* in the FBI makes a move, they never want to reverse it; makes them look bad, they think."

"And I'll bet Crisp still has his job," Stone said.

"No, thanks to a little work of mine, but he still has *a* job: He's the AIC in American Samoa."

"*Samoa?*"

"It was the most remote place they could find to send him. The AIC in Miami is now one Grant Early Harrison, who was the FBI guy I was trying to save when I stuck Trini Rodriguez. He was undercover at the time."

"Well, Grant Early Harrison must be very grateful to you," Stone said.

"Grateful, but not very. He's how I know Trini Rodriguez is in the Program and in New York, but he stopped talking to me the moment he realized that I planned to take Trini."

"So there's no more help forthcoming from Agent Harrison?"

"None at all, the bastard, and after I got him his job, too."

"And how did you do that?" Stone asked.

"After this business was over, and Ed Shine and a lot of other people had been arrested, a deputy director of the FBI paid me a visit and asked me for my account of events. I managed to toss a couple of hand grenades into Harry Crisp's lap, resulting in his getting shipped to the farthest reaches of the Pacific Rim, and I said some very nice things about Grant, which, ultimately, got him the AIC's job in Miami."

"I don't ever want you for an enemy," Dino said. "You're not Italian, are you?"

"No, but I'm an army brat, and I put twenty years in, myself, commanding MPs. In the army, you learn how to work the system."

"Do you learn how to stick a knife in somebody's throat, too?"

Holly put a hand on Dino's arm. "Oh, Dino, that's the first thing they teach you in the army, didn't you know?"

"Are you armed?" Dino asked.

"No, I didn't want to deal with the hassle at the airport."

"You got your badge and your ID with you?"

"Sure."

Dino reached under the table and fiddled with an ankle, then he put his napkin over something and slid it across the table. "I think you're going to need this," he said.

Holly lifted the edge of the napkin and

peeped under it. "Oh, Dino," she said, "a Walther PPK. How sweet of you!"

Stone peeped under the napkin, too. "I've got one just like it," he said.

"That's yours," Dino said. "You didn't think I'd give her *my* piece, did you?"

"What are you doing with my Walther?" Stone demanded.

"You loaned it to me that time when we did that thing."

"And you never returned it?"

"Holly will give it back to you after she's shot Trini Rodriguez a few times," Dino explained.

Holly slipped the weapon into her handbag and returned Dino's napkin.

"Swell," Stone said.

"Holly," Dino said, "I've got a couple of friends on the organized crime task force. I'll mention Rodriguez's name and see if anybody has heard about him. Do you know what name he's using in the Program?"

"No, Grant wouldn't tell me."

"It would be a big help if you could find out."

"I don't know how to do that," Holly said.

"Let me work on it," Dino replied.

Their main course arrived, and there was no more talk of Trini Rodriguez.

On the way back to Stone's house, in a cab, he turned to Holly. "Are you and your friend comfortably situated upstairs?"

"Oh, yes, thank you. The room is very nice."

"I'm not sure how I feel about sleeping in the same house with somebody who could stab somebody else in the neck."

Holly patted his knee. "I promise not to stab you in the neck," she said. "At least not the first night."

The cab pulled up in front of Stone's house, and they got out. Stone went to the front door and unlocked it.

"Hang on!" Holly yelled. "I left my purse in the cab!" She ran toward the moving taxi, screaming at it.

Stone watched her catch up and stop the cab, then he turned back and stepped inside his front door. As he did, he heard a sound that made the hair stand up on the back of his neck. He froze.

Holly came up the steps behind him. "That was close," she said.

"Don't move," Stone replied.

"What? Oh, God. Daisy! Stand down!" She brushed past Stone and took the dog's collar. "Sit."

Daisy sat down and looked at Stone warily.

"This is Stone," she said. "Stone is good. Good."

Daisy walked over and nuzzled Stone's hand.

"How do you do, Daisy?" Stone said.

She licked his hand.

"Sorry about that," Holly said. "You okay?"

"My heart rate is returning to normal. So this is your friend?"

"Yep. Isn't she beautiful?"

"You didn't mention that your friend is a Doberman pinscher."

"Didn't I?"

"No."

"I hope it's okay if Daisy stays, too. We can always go to a hotel."

"Holly, in hotels, chambermaids enter your room several times a day when you aren't there. You don't want a dead chambermaid on your conscience, do you?"

"Daisy's not like that."

"I'm relieved to hear it."

"She only kills on command."

Stone looked at her askance.

"Just kidding."

"Go to bed," Stone said. He watched as she walked ahead of him to the elevator. It was a pleasant sight.

Stone was nearly asleep when he felt Holly sit on his bed. He wasn't all that sleepy after all, he thought. He reached for her, and his hand found a warm, furry body.

"Go to sleep, Daisy," he groaned.

Daisy sighed, snuggled against Stone, and settled in for the night.

Stone was sleeping soundly when he was disturbed by a *chink, chink* sound. He opened an eye and found Holly sitting on his bed in one of his terrycloth bathrobes, eating cereal from a bowl.

"Good morning," she said. "I made myself some breakfast. Can I get you some?"

Stone pressed the button that made his bed sit up, then rubbed his eyes. "What time is it?"

"Six-fifteen," she replied.

Daisy, who had been snuggled close to Stone, sat up and yawned.

"Six-fifteen," Stone repeated tonelessly.

"Too early for you? What time do you normally get up?"

"I wake up around seven, then have some breakfast in bed and read the *Times* and do the crossword. I usually get out of bed around nine."

"Lazy guy, huh?"

"I'm not running a police force in a Florida town," Stone said, "and I don't have people pounding on my door at the crack of dawn, demanding to see me. It's one of the advantages of being self-employed."

Holly nodded. "Guess so. I see Daisy slept with you last night," she said.

Stone nodded. "Apparently so. You'll need to avert your eyes while I dash to the bathroom. And doesn't Daisy have to go out in the mornings, or does she use a flush toilet?"

"She has to go out. And why do I have to avert my eyes?"

"Suit yourself," Stone said, getting out of bed and walking to the bathroom. When he came back, Holly was still there.

"And don't forget the plastic bag," he said, climbing back into bed.

"Plastic bag?"

"For Daisy."

"You want me to put Daisy in a plastic bag?"

Stone shook his head. "It's the law in New York that when the dog poops, the owner picks it up and puts it into the near-est trash can. It's a hundred-dollar fine if you fail to do so. And don't bring it back into the house."

"Well, I never," Holly said. "What'll they think of next in the big city?" She stood up. "Where do I find a plastic bag?"

"Kitchenette," Stone said, pointing. "Next to my dressing room; saves an elevator ride at breakfast time."

Holly went and found a plastic bag. "Guess I'd better shower and get dressed, if we're going out," she said to the dog. "Come on, Daisy."

"Doesn't she have to go out *right now*?" Stone asked.

"She can hold it, don't worry. You want to take her out?"

Stone rolled over and pulled the covers over his head.

At mid-morning Stone had finished break-fast and was dressing when Holly came up-stairs, looking good in a sweater and wool slacks, Daisy at her side.

"Nice neighborhood," she said. "Why is it called Turtle Bay?"

"There used to be a bay called Turtle Bay here, a long time ago. It got filled in."

She went and looked out a rear window. "Beautiful garden. Do all the houses get to use it?"

"Yep, it's a common garden. All the houses open onto it."

"Nice feature."

"So what are you going to do today?"

"Start looking for Trini Rodriguez, I guess."

"Oh? Where?"

"Where do mafiosi hang out?"

Stone slipped his feet into a pair of loafers. "Hang on a minute. Trini is in the Federal Witness Protection Program, right?"

"Right."

"Well, the Feds usually put people in there when they're going to testify against the Mafia, when they're *running* from the mob, you know?"

"Oh, I don't think Trini would ever testify against his people."

"Then who are the Feds protecting him from?"

"Probably me."

"Holly, that just doesn't make any sense. Why would they protect him from you?"

"Because he's theirs, and they don't want me getting him tried in Indian River County. And they think if he's theirs, nobody else has a right to him. Well, *I* have a right to him."

"You're a very determined gir . . . woman, aren't you?"

"Yes, and I don't mind being called a girl, except at work. So where do the Mafia guys hang out?"

"Well, they used to hang out in Little Italy, but these days they seem to be more scattered. I guess there are some in each borough."

"Borough?"

"There are five in New York: Brooklyn, Queens, Staten Island, The Bronx, and Manhattan. Until the turn of the century, they were separate cities."

"So where's Little Italy?"

"Downtown."

"Will a cabdriver know it?"

"That's problematical these days," Stone said. "Tell you what: I've got a light day; I'll drive you down there, maybe buy you some lunch."

"Hey, that sounds great, but I'm buying. You get the gas."

"Don't worry about it."

She put a hand under Daisy's chin and gazed into her eyes. "You stay here and be a good girl," she said, then she turned to Stone. "Do you want her to kill anybody who comes into the house?"

"No, thanks," Stone replied. "I wouldn't want to come home and find my secretary dead."

Stone slipped into a tweed jacket. "Okay, let's go." He led her downstairs to the garage, opened the door, and backed out, closing the garage door with a remote control.

"Your car makes a nice noise," she said, as he accelerated toward Second Avenue. It's an E55, isn't it?"

"Very good. Most people can't distinguish it from the ordinary E-class Mercedes."

"I drove one, once; pretended that I was a prospective customer. I liked it."

"Did you train Daisy yourself?"

"No, she was trained by an old army buddy of my father's who got murdered. I bought her from his daughter. Daisy is what's called in dog-breeding circles an 'Excellent Working Bitch.'"

Stone laughed. "I like that."

"Applies to me, too," Holly said, grinning.

Soon they were creeping through traffic through the little streets of Little Italy. "That's Umberto's Clam House," Stone said, pointing at a little restaurant. "Joey Gallo got shot there. Down the street is a coffeehouse, where some other don got it while playing bocce in the back garden. You may have seen that photograph of the corpse, with a cigar still clamped in his teeth."

"I think I saw that on the History Channel," Holly said.

"I guess you have a lot of time for things like the History Channel in Orchid Beach."

"Oh, we get out of the house once in a while." She pointed at a little restaurant. "Let's have lunch there."

"Okay. Let me find a parking space."

"I'll go ahead and get a table." She opened the door and got out. It took Stone another ten minutes before somebody freed up a parking space, and when he got back to the restaurant, she was sitting at a table in the window, looking at the menu. He stopped and just looked for a moment. He was finding her more and more attractive. He went in and took a seat.

"What looks good?"

"Pasta," she said. "I was thinking about the white clam sauce."

A waiter came over.

"I'll have the same," Stone said, after she'd ordered. "And let's have a bottle of the Frascati."

"I hope that's a dry white wine," she said.

"It is."

The waiter brought the bottle and poured them each a glass.

Stone raised his glass. "To . . ." But, to his astonishment, Holly had kicked over her chair and run out of the restaurant. He ran to the front door and looked down the street in time to see her sprinting through the crowds on the sidewalk, her handbag in one hand and his Walther in the other.

4

Stone ran a few steps in the direction Holly had taken, but she had disappeared into the crowd. He ran back to the restaurant, left some money on the table, and ran to his car. He executed a lucky U-turn and started down the street, checking both sides for Holly. A couple of blocks down, he found a parking place and got out of the car, searching the street for signs of her. Then he saw her half a block away, walking toward him. He leaned on the car and waited.

"I can't believe I let the son of a bitch out-run me," Holly said, though she wasn't even breathing hard.

"You saw Trini?"

"He walked right past the restaurant. Didn't you see him?"

"I don't have the slightest idea what he

looks like," Stone said. "You want to give me a description?"

"Six-two or -three, two hundred pounds, looks more Hispanic than Italian. He has black hair with a ponytail; evil face."

"Evil face? I don't recall ever having seen that description on a wanted poster."

"Trust me. What are we doing about lunch?"

Stone looked around. "I'm not giving up this parking spot. Follow me." He led her a few blocks into Chinatown, to a restaurant called Hong Fat, and soon they were eating noodles.

"So, are you a native New Yorker?" Holly asked.

"Born and bred in Greenwich Village; father was a cabinet and furniture maker, mother, a painter. Went to NYU and NYU law school. My last year I joined a program to ride with the NYPD, became enamored of law enforcement, and, on graduation, joined the department, became a detective three years later, partnered up with Dino, and had a hell of a good time. Put in fourteen years. That's the nutshell bio."

She shook her head. "Incomplete. Why'd you leave the force?"

"The force left me. We disagreed on an investigation I was ostensibly running, and they used a knee wound as an excuse to ship me out. I did a cram course on the bar exam, took it, passed, and joined the law firm of Woodman and Weld, courtesy of an old law school buddy. That complete enough?"

"For the moment," she said.

"How about you?"

"Born in the army, grew up in the army, mother died when I was twelve, joined the army after high school, got a degree in the service, went to OCS, got a commission, and commanded MPs for the rest of my twenty years."

"Why didn't you go for thirty?"

"Another female officer and I accused a bird colonel of sexual harassment—rape, in the other girl's case. We got him court-martialed, but he was acquitted. After that, there was no place to go in the army. He had too many friends in high and low places. Got an offer of the deputy chief's job in Orchid Beach; the chief got himself killed, and I was bumped up a rung. Met Jackson Oxenhandler, moved in with him, made plans to marry him. You know the rest."

"How are you living with that?"

"Better than can be expected. I'm pretty good at compartmentalizing things, so I tucked it away in the back of my mind. It comes out once in a while, but less and less often. Jackson, fortunately, had made a will, and he left me well fixed."

"Seen any men since then?"

"Just one—Grant Early Harrison. We had . . . well, I guess you'd describe it as a fling, and after he got the AIC's job in Miami, we cooled down. Before, he'd been an undercover agent, and that was interesting. Now he's a bureaucrat, and that's not."

"Ever thought of getting out of that little town?"

"Listen, so much happens in that little town you wouldn't believe it. I've busted up two major organized crime operations in three years, with all the attendant homicides and other felonies. You're looking funny—skeptical, maybe. What are you thinking?"

"I was just thinking, the idea of you waltzing into town, looking for some guy in the Witness Protection Program, then going down to Little Italy your first day and spotting him on the street is ludicrous; couldn't happen."

"That sort of thing happens to me all the time," Holly said, laughing. "Either there's some sort of angel watching over me, or I'm the world's best cop."

"Another thing: It's okay for you to pack my Walther while you're in town—the NYPD would overlook that, since you're a serving officer—but if you start shooting at Trini on the street and clip a civilian—well, that's big trouble. You might keep that in mind."

"I certainly will," Holly replied. "I'd take a dim view of something like that happening in my jurisdiction."

"Good. And if you remember that you're not in your jurisdiction, that would be a big help. Even if you hit Trini between the eyes with your first shot—that's a *lot* of paperwork for the locals, and the New York news media would fall on you from a great height."

"Okay, okay," Holly said, raising her hands in surrender. "Lecture heard and understood. You want the Walther back?"

"Keep it," Stone said, "but make sure the circumstances are dire before you use it."

"Dire," she replied. "I promise. So how's *your* love life, Stone? Now that we've covered mine."

"Varied," Stone said.

"I'll bet that's a New York City term, meaning 'nonexistent.' "

"You sound like Dino."

"And I've seen you looking at me. You look pretty horny."

Stone tried to repress a blush. "You're an attractive girl," he said, "but don't get cocky; it's unbecoming."

"Oh, I wouldn't want to do anything unbecoming."

"If I put my hand on your knee, is Daisy going to bite it off?"

"She will if I tell her to."

"Would you tell her to?"

"Oh, I wouldn't need her help to handle you."

Stone choked on a noodle.

5

After lunch, Stone drove them back to his house, and Holly and Daisy headed for Central Park and a long walk. Stone called down to his office.

"Good afternoon," Joan said dryly.

"Sorry I didn't check in this morning," he said. "I took my houseguest downtown for lunch."

"You didn't tell me you bought a killer dog," she said. "I went upstairs to find you, and, luckily, I slammed the door before he could tear my arm off."

"She," Stone said. "It's Holly's dog. Didn't you meet her when Holly arrived?"

"No, I was on my way out. I just gave her the key and the alarm code and pointed her upstairs. I guess the dog was still in the cab."

"Anything up this morning?"

"Well, a guy who says he's an old friend of yours has been waiting for you for more than an hour."

"Who is he?"

"He won't say, and he won't leave. Could you get down here and deal with him, please?"

"I'll be right there," Stone said. He got up and went downstairs to his office. As he came down the stairs he could see down the hall to the waiting area, and saw two long legs extended from a chair, with a very fine pair of shoes at the end of them.

"Good afternoon," Stone said. He couldn't see the face, but when the man stood up, it was familiar enough.

"Lance Cabot," he said.

"So *that's* his name," Joan's voice called from her office.

Lance offered his hand. "I'm sorry, perhaps I was being too cautious. I thought that if you called in and she gave you my name, you might not want to see me."

"Come into my office," Stone said, pointing the way. He was still trying to get his breath back. A little more than a year before, a man had walked into his office and offered Stone a lot of money to go to London to rescue his niece from the clutches of her bad, bad boyfriend, whose name had been Lance Cabot.

Stone had taken the job, only to learn that his client had used a false name and was trying to track down Cabot to kill him. The client, whose name turned out to be Stanford Hedger, was CIA, and Cabot was ex-Agency, then operating as a rogue. Stone had asked for help from a friend and had been contacted by British intelligence, who asked him to enter into a business arrangement with Cabot, who was trying to steal some important equipment from a military arms lab. With the help of an inside man, Cabot had stolen the item, presumably sold it to bad people, and had disappeared with Stone's money. A couple of weeks later, to Stone's astonishment, his money had been returned, along with the healthy profit Cabot had promised him.

Lance took a seat and crossed his legs. He was casually dressed in a tweed jacket and tan trousers, looking for all the world like a resident of New York, out for a walk and a cup of coffee.

"Can I get you some coffee?" Stone asked.

"Thanks, but your secretary provided that, in spite of her suspicions."

"What brings you to New York, Lance?"

"I live here now, a few blocks uptown."

Stone's jaw dropped. "Aren't you a fugitive? Is that why you're here, looking for a lawyer?"

Lance shook his head. "I'm not a fugitive, and I don't need a lawyer, at least for myself."

"For someone else?"

"Maybe, but not just yet."

"I'm sorry, but I'm baffled by all this. I thought you were being sought by every intelligence agency and police department in Europe, not to mention your own former people."

"They're not former," Lance said. He fished a wallet out of his pocket and handed it to Stone.

Stone found himself staring at a CIA ID card, complete with photograph. "How long have you had this back?"

"I always had it," Lance said. "Let me explain. When Hedger hired you—"

"Hedger was CIA, wasn't he?"

"Yes, he was, but he was led to believe that I had gone rogue. That's why he was looking for me."

"I don't understand."

"It's complicated. I was sent over there to . . . well, ostensibly to acquire a British invention, a piece of military hardware, you will recall, and sell it to a Middle Eastern country—Iraq, as it happens."

"The CIA wanted you to steal British military hardware and sell it to Saddam Hussein?"

"Yes. Well, not really. You see, Hedger wanted the hardware, too, ostensibly for our nuclear weapons program. He really wanted it to help him regain the Agency's high regard, in which he had formerly been held."

"This is very confusing: The Agency had two agents trying to steal the hardware, working at cross-purposes?"

"Now you've got it."

"And you were supposed to sell it to Saddam Hussein?"

"Yes, and I did, but not before it had been modified to make it useless. It needed the right software, too, and he didn't have that, but by that time, I had his money and was gone. You got a very nice slice of those funds, too. What did you do with the money?"

"I paid the taxes on it and invested the rest, as my accountant recommended."

"Good," Lance said. "Just what I would have done."

"Lance, it worries me to think I did what you would have done."

Lance laughed. "You have nothing to worry about, Stone. You're clean as a whistle."

"Does your agency know that I was paid the money?"

"Of course. I had a little trouble convincing them, but after I had repeatedly pointed out how valuable you had been to us, they agreed."

"But I was supposed to be helping the British."

"Well, yes, but you were really helping us all the time."

"Did the British know this?"

Lance pursed his lips. "Not exactly, but they do now. After all, I helped rid them of a man in their midst who was willing to sell their technology to anybody. Why do you care?"

"As it happens, I've spent a good deal of time in the company of one of their people, a woman called Carpenter."

"Felicity Devonshire?" Lance laughed aloud.

"I didn't even know that was her name until a few months ago."

"She's a piece of work, that girl. Did you know that, at this very moment, she's being considered to replace Sir Edward Fieldstone as head of her service? If she gets the job, she'll be the first woman to do so. She was prominently mentioned in the last Birthday Honours List, too. She's now Dame Felicity."

"I didn't know any of that," Stone said. "We parted on less than the best terms."

"Pity," Lance said. "She's a remarkable woman. My people are rooting for her to get the job."

"Good for her. Now, why did you come to see me, Lance?"

Lance chuckled. "I thought I might send some more business your way."

6

Stone's first reaction was to send Lance on his way, but, as it happened, things had been a little slow in the way of work, and a fresh injection of business could help his cash flow. "What are we talking about?" he asked.

"Just a little legal work," Lance replied, studying his well-manicured nails.

"Look at me when you lie to me, Lance."

Lance looked up. "Why do you think I'm lying?"

"Because you've never said anything to me that was the truth. Ever."

Lance shrugged. "Surely you understand that that was business. I was carrying out an assignment important to the national interest, and you were helping."

"Yes, but I didn't know that."

"I wasn't allowed to tell you, and it was important that you didn't know. In fact, you never would have been involved at all, if I hadn't been in a situation of, shall we say, temporarily interrupted cash flow. I needed your quarter of a million, which you very kindly supplied, and you made a very tidy profit from the arrangement. Where else could you have gotten a return of four hundred percent in less than thirty days?"

"*Everybody* was lying to me, especially Hedger."

"Hedger is dead. Did I mention that?"

Stone took a quick breath. "No, you didn't. Do I want to know how and why? I assume he didn't keel over of a coronary."

"No, he was expertly stabbed by somebody who worked for you."

"What on earth are you talking about?" Stone demanded.

"Remember those two retired British cops you hired to follow me around London and bug my house?"

Stone hadn't known that Lance knew about that, so he said nothing.

"You'll remember that Hedger's people beat up one of them very badly, so badly that he later expired."

"Go on."

"Well, his mate took exception to that and held Hedger accountable. He knifed him in a mews a short walk from the Connaught, while you were still in London."

"I didn't know," Stone said.

"Scotland Yard hushed it up, the knifer having been one of their own. Had an exemplary military record, too, killing people in the Special Air Services. That detective inspector, Throckmorton—unlikely name, isn't it?—didn't think a shady American spook's life was worth a blip in the happy retirement of one of their former officers."

"And what did the Agency have to say about that?"

"Almost nothing. Somebody gave Throckmorton a good lunch and received the details. They shook hands and went their separate ways. Hedger is now a star on the memorial in the lobby of the headquarters building at Langley."

"The more I learn about your business, the less I want to learn about it."

"You shouldn't feel badly about Hedger. He was a bad apple; been using his position for years to enrich himself in various underhanded ways, and the Agency was sick of him. Good riddance and no trial or publicity. His death didn't even make the tabloids, let alone the *Times*. His alumni newsletter ran a nice obit, though, most of it lies."

"An ignominious end," Stone mused.

"In Hedger's case, deservedly so."

"What is this legal work you want done? It isn't illegal work, is it?"

"Oh, no, no, nothing like that. It's pretty simple, really: A fellow we hired for some contract work got himself into a scrape with the local law, and—"

"The local law where?"

"Right here in Gotham, actually."

"Go on."

"There's a DUI and some other minor stuff involved. He needs a lawyer, and we feel honor-bound to provide him with one. We'll pay five hundred an hour."

Stone's normal fee for that sort of thing was three hundred an hour. "That is not ungenerous."

"We don't want it to go to trial, you see; could be embarrassing and might even reveal information detrimental to national security."

"You mean, detrimental to the Central Intelligence Agency."

"Same thing. Do we have a deal?" Lance held out his hand to shake.

"Oh, all right," Stone said, shaking the hand. He picked up a pen and pad. "What's your client's name?"

"Herbert Fisher, a professional photographer by trade."

Stone nearly choked. "Oh, no, no, no, no," he said, holding out his hands as if to ward off evil.

"You know Mr. Fisher?" Lance asked, looking surprised.

"I know him far better than I want to," Stone said.

"Well, come to think of it, he did ask for you. I'm glad you've agreed."

"Wait a minute, Lance. I'm not doing this. The guy is trouble from beginning to end—he won't take legal advice, won't do anything he's told."

"Stone, Stone, it's a simple matter, really. We just want you to negotiate something for him—get him off, if possible, sure, but we can't let it go to trial."

"Lance, sometimes these things go to

trial, and there's nothing you can do about it."

"Stone, we can do something about it, if necessary, but we'd rather let you handle it in the normal way."

"I don't like the sound of that, Lance."

Lance held up a placating hand. "Now don't go reading a subtext into my words."

"Do you know Herbie Fisher?" Stone asked.

"We've met."

"Well, let me tell you about him. Last year, I hired him—on the recommendation of a guy who does a lot of good work for me—to take some photographs. A domestic matter. Herbie fell through the skylight while taking the pictures, got himself arrested, then, when I got him out, jumped bail and ran for the Virgin Islands. I had to go down there and get him back to make his court appearance and get my bail money back."

"Well, he does sound lively, doesn't he? He did come well recommended."

"Lance, you don't want anything to do with this guy, and neither do I."

"Fine with me, Stone. See him through this, and we'll both kiss him off."

"You're not listening, Lance. I won't represent him."

"But you've already agreed, old sport, and you're a man of your word."

"But I didn't know who we were talking about."

"Then you should have asked before we shook hands on it, not afterward."

"Lance . . ."

"Tell you what: We'll make it seven-fifty an hour, in cash, and I'll send you over a retainer of twenty-five thousand. You can bank the unused portion, or stuff it into your mattress."

That stopped Stone in his tracks just long enough for Lance to place a card on his desk, get up, and walk out of his office.

"Thanks, Stone," Lance called over his shoulder. "Herbert will be in touch. Let's have dinner." He closed the door behind him.

"Oh, God," Stone moaned.

7

Stone was dressing when Holly and Daisy returned from their walk.

"Hi there," she said.

Stone looked at his watch. "That was a long walk."

"We went all the way to the north end of the park and back; really had a workout."

"You'd better grab a shower, then. Dino called and said he has some information for you. We're meeting him at Elaine's in an hour."

"I'll feed Daisy and change my socks," Holly said, and headed upstairs.

They settled into their table, and Elaine came over and sat down. "What's up?"

"This is my friend Holly Barker, who's visiting from Florida," Stone said.

The two women shook hands.

"Are you the lady cop?" Elaine asked.

"That's right. How did you know?"

"I read the papers. Not that Stone would have ever mentioned you."

"There wasn't a lot to mention," Stone said. "We met only once, before this week."

"Once has always been enough for you," Elaine said, rising to hop to the next table.

"What was *that* supposed to mean?" Holly asked.

"Pay no attention to Elaine," Stone replied. "She likes to needle me."

"About women?"

"About whatever she can think of."

Dino came in, hung up his coat, sat down, and ordered a Scotch.

"What would you like, Holly?"

"A three-to-one vodka gimlet, straight up, shaken, very cold," she said to the waiter.

"Make it two," Stone said.

"Sounds good. Cancel my Scotch and make it three," Dino echoed.

"I'm glad to be able to influence opinion," Holly said. "What information do you have for me, Dino?"

"You're right. Your guy, Rodriguez, is in town. He's been hanging out at the La Boheme coffeehouse in Little Italy."

"Holly's a little ahead of you, Dino. We had lunch down there, and she spotted Trini and gave chase."

"No shit? What do you need me for?"

"Well," Holly said, "I didn't know about the La Boheme coffeehouse."

"It's a mob joint. There's at least two bookies and a loan shark working out of there."

"Maybe tomorrow I'll stop in for a cup of coffee."

"Not without a SWAT team to back you up," Dino said. "They don't cotton to the company of women in that place."

"Maybe it's time I brought them up to date."

"Not unless you enjoy the sound of your bones breaking. They're not friendly to outsiders of any kind, but especially women."

"I'm sure there's a New York City ordinance that prohibits such behavior. Why don't you come down there with me and enforce it?"

"Because no law enforcement agency, local or federal, wants to disturb the action in the joint. Just between you and me, there's probably more audio and video equipment installed in the walls there than at the Wiz."

"What's the Wiz?"

"A great big audio and video store."

"I get the picture. Maybe I should just go down there and park outside until Trini shows up, then take him."

"Holly, you're not listening. You try to take somebody in that coffee shop, and a shooting war will break out. I wasn't kidding about the SWAT team."

"Can you arrange a SWAT team for me, Dino?"

"You got an extradition warrant?"

"It's in my handbag, right next to Stone's Walther."

"Tell you what: If you can get the governor of Florida to call the governor of New York, and the governor to call the mayor of the city, and the mayor to call the police commissioner, and the commissioner to call the chief of detectives, and the chief to call me and order me to do it, then I'll do it."

"Dino, you sound reluctant."

"What gave you that idea? Was it something I said?"

Stone spoke up. "Holly, the best you're going to get out of the NYPD, except in the circumstances Dino described, is for them to look the other way until you're on an airplane south with Trini trussed up like a turkey."

"Dino, did you hear anything about what name Trini is using in the Witness Protection Program?"

"He's using Trini at the La Boheme. Outside, who knows?"

"I've got an idea," Holly said, digging her cell phone out of her purse.

"That's it," Dino said. "Call the director of the FBI. I'm sure he'll be helpful."

Holly dialed two zeros, then another digit. "Hello, may I please have the number, under the United States Government, Department of Justice, for the Federal Bureau of Investigation field office in American Samoa? S-A-M-O-A. It's a bunch of tiny islands in the South Pacific. I'll hold." She turned to Stone. "Got a pen?"

Stone handed her his.

"Yes, that's right." She grabbed a cocktail napkin and jotted down a long number. "And everything but the last seven digits is

the dialing code? Thank you very much."
She punched off.

"What time is it in Samoa?" Dino asked.

"I don't even know what day it is," Holly
said, dialing the long number. "It's ringing.
Hello, may I speak with Harry Crisp,
please? Tell him it's Holly Barker calling."
She nodded at Stone and waited.

"Hello, Harry? Can you hear me
okay? . . . Why, Harry, that's not a very nice
thing to say. And I was trying to be helpful. . . . How? Well, I've been feeling badly
about your getting transferred to the Pacific
Rim, and I thought I might be helpful in getting you back to the States. . . . Well, I don't
know for sure if I can do that, but I can certainly put in a word with Deputy Director
Barron, the guy who shipped you out
there. . . . Well, of course there's a tit for tat,
Harry. Did you think you'd get my help for
free? Actually, it's a very easy one for you.
All I want is the name the Bureau gave Trini
Rodriguez in the Witness Protection Program. . . . Yes, Harry, I'm aware that that's
highly confidential," Holly continued, "but
when you weigh a slight breach of confi-
dentiality against a ticket home, well . . .

Look, Harry, you're the guy who put him into the Program. You don't even have to tap a few computer keys; the name is right there, lodged in your frontal lobe. They haven't lobotomized you, have they, Harry? . . . Now, how could this possibly get you in trouble? Nobody will know except me. I just want to look up Trini and say hello. He's of no further use to you, not that he ever was. You were just trying to keep me from arresting and trying him in my jurisdiction.

"Come on, Harry, cough it up. Look, I can't specify a new assignment for you, but honestly, wouldn't anywhere be better? . . . I didn't even know you had an office in Alaska. Would you like me to request Nome for you? Only joking, Harry. Now give me the name and you won't hear from me again. And if you *don't* give me the name, you might never hear from *anybody* again." Holly listened and jotted something on her napkin. "Thank you so much, Harry. I'll give Deputy Director Barron a call tomorrow, first thing. No, it's dinnertime here, Harry. Bye-bye."

She hung up and held up the napkin for Stone and Dino to see.

"Robert Marshall," Stone read aloud.

Dino took Holly's hand. "Holly, would you like to come work for the NYPD as liaison with the Feds?"

8

Holly got up and went to the ladies' room, leaving Stone and Dino alone.

"So, how's it going?" Dino asked.

"Well, I stepped in a steaming pile of shit today."

"What else is new? What is it this time?"

"Remember Lance Cabot?"

"The rogue ex-CIA guy in London?"

"Yes, but it turns out he's not a rogue, just CIA. The rogue was Hedger, the guy who hired me. Lance is in New York and he turned up at my office today and asked me to represent a guy who's been doing some contract work for them. Apparently, he's had a DUI and a couple of other things, and the Agency wants his mess cleaned up. I didn't want to do it, but he offered me seven-fifty an hour, and he sent around a brown envelope stuffed with twenty-five thousand in crisp, new hundred-dollar bills."

"That doesn't sound so shitty. What's the problem?"

"The guy I'm representing is Herbie Fisher."

"That schmuck that we had to hunt down in the Virgin Islands?"

"One and the same."

"Are you out of your fucking mind? There isn't enough money to make dealing with that guy worth it."

"Well, yes, but I agreed to represent him before he told me the name. We shook hands on it."

"Well, unshake his fucking hand."

"I gave him my word."

"Stone, Lance Cabot and the people he works for would screw you in the blink of an eye, if it was worth their while, and maybe just for the fun of it."

"Actually, my dealings with Lance have been, if not exactly straightforward, then conducted in an honorable manner."

"Stone, this is the guy who hustled you into putting up a quarter of a million dollars to finance a theft from the British government, then disappeared into thin air."

"I got my money back, remember?"

"Yeah, but he promised you a million-dollar profit, too. Whatever happened to that?"

"It's in my brokerage account, less taxes."

Dino stared at him, stupefied.

"No kidding."

"You never told me that."

"Where is it written that I have to tell you everything?"

"Where is it written that I can't put a gun to your head and pull the trigger? You'd fucking well *better* tell me everything. I was involved, remember?"

"As I recall, your involvement was pretty much confined to lying around the Connaught Hotel, watching cricket matches on TV and gaining weight on room service."

"Not all that much weight," Dino said defensively.

"Have you lost it?"

"Most of it."

"That's what I thought."

"Well, it was a pretty good hotel, and your friend Hedger was paying."

"By the way, Hedger is dead. He was

knifed near the Connaught by an ex-cop that I had hired to follow Lance."

"You had him snuffed?"

"Of course not; it was nothing to do with me. Well, not much to do with me."

Dino shook his head. "Wherever you go, people drop dead, and women take off their underwear. I don't know how you do either of those things."

Holly returned to the table. "So, have you been talking about me in my absence?"

"No," Dino and Stone said as one man.

"Well, that's insulting. I thought you might have said something nice about my ass as I walked away."

"It's a very nice ass," Dino said. "I mentioned that to Stone."

"You did not."

Stone turned to Holly. "He did not. I noticed, though. I just didn't say anything."

"Yeah, sure," Holly replied. "What's for dinner?"

"I'm having a spinach salad, chopped, and the spaghetti alla carbonara," Stone said.

"Me, too."

"All right," Dino said, "I'll join you. Why

confuse the waiter by ordering something different?"

Frank appeared, and they ordered.

"I'm confused," Frank said. "You all had the same drinks, and now you're having the same dinner?"

"What's confusing about that?" Dino asked.

Frank shook his head and walked away.

Stone's cell phone vibrated, and he dug it out and flipped it open. "Hello?"

"Stone?"

"Yes, who's this?"

"It's Herbie Fisher! How are you?"

Stone groaned. "I'm in the middle of dinner, Herbie. Call me in the morning."

"Isn't this great? You're representing me again!"

"No, it's not great, Herbie, and my food is getting cold. Call me in the morning."

"Do I take two aspirin?"

"What?"

"You know, take two aspirin and call me in the morning. Isn't that what lawyers say?"

"That's what doctors say, Herbie."

"Whatever. So you're going to make these charges go away?"

"I'm going to do the best I can for you, Herbie."

"Lance said you were going to make them go away."

"What did you do? What are the charges?"

"Wait a minute. I've got the ticket here somewhere." There was the sound of papers rustling.

"That your new client?" Dino asked, smirking.

"Oh, shut up."

"Why do I have to shut up?" Herbie asked.

"Not you, Herbie. Did you find the ticket?"

"Well, yeah, but you wanted me to shut up."

"Herbie, I was talking to somebody else. I'm in a restaurant, having dinner with friends. Or, at least, I was, until you called."

"Yeah, I got the ticket right here."

"What does it say the charges are?"

"Let's see: DUI, driving with a suspended license, and—you're not going to believe this, Stone—resisting arrest with violence."

"And why wouldn't I believe that, Herbie?"

"You know me, Stone. I'm not a violent person."

"What did you do to the cop, Herbie?"

"It's kind of hazy. I'd had a couple beers."

"Did the cop Breathalyze you?"

"Yeah."

"What was the reading?"

"Two-point-oh."

"Jesus, Herbie, that's more than double the legal limit! Could you even walk?"

"Not good. Like I said, it's all pretty hazy."

"Why was your license suspended, Herbie?"

"Oh, I guess that was that other DUI."

"You had a *previous* DUI? When?"

"I don't know, two, three weeks ago."

"So you've had two DUIs in less than a month?"

"I guess."

"What did the judge give you for the first one?"

"Community service and DUI school."

"Have you performed any community service?"

"Not yet. I been pretty busy."

"Did you attend DUI school?"

"Not all of it."

"How many times did you go?"

"Uh, once."

"It's three classes, right?"

"Uh, yeah."

"And you went to just one?"

"Stone, you have no idea how boring those classes are."

"Herbie, you have no idea how boring it is in a cell on Rikers Island."

"Well, you're not going to let that happen, are you? Lance said you'd make it all go away."

"Herbie, back to the resisting arrest with violence: What did you do to the cop?"

"Well, we argued a little."

"That's not violence. What did you do to him?"

"It's all pretty hazy. I might have kicked him."

"Oh, Jesus. Kicked him where?"

"Maybe in the balls."

Stone made a whimpering noise. "I have to finish dinner, Herbie. Call me in the morning."

"I have to be in court in the morning."

"You mean there's another charge?"

"No, it's the same one."

"And your court appearance is *tomorrow morning*?"

"Yeah."

"At what time?"

"Ten o'clock."

"That's just great, Herbie. I'll meet you in the hallway outside the courtrooms at nine-thirty, and you'd better be there, sober and neatly dressed."

"All right, I'll be there," Herbie said, sounding chastened.

Stone hung up.

"Where did Herbie kick the cop?" Dino asked.

"In the balls."

Dino and Holly collapsed in laughter.

9

Stone got to the courthouse at eight A.M. and went upstairs to the warren of cubicles and offices that housed the assistant district attorneys.

"Hey, Maria," he said to the middle-aged Italian-American woman who ruled the front desk. "You're looking beautiful today."

"You're so full of shit, Stone," the woman replied sweetly. "What brings you downtown? Haven't seen you since the Christmas party." She waggled her eyebrows meaningfully.

Stone ignored the reference to the Christmas party. "A client has an appearance this morning. Can you tell me who caught his case?"

"What's his name?"

"Herbert Fisher."

Maria giggled. "Oh, him."

"What's that supposed to mean?"

"He's the one who kicked the cop in the crotch, isn't he?"

"It is so alleged," Stone said. "Who's the ADA?"

"Oh, that would be Dierdre Monahan."

Stone winced.

"Yeah." Maria giggled again.

"What's that supposed to mean?"

"Well, there have been rumors."

"Don't ever believe rumors," Stone said. "Is Dierdre in the same stall?"

"Are you saying she's horsey?"

"Cubicle."

"No, she's moved up a little. She has an office now, but no window." She waggled a thumb. "Down at the end, there."

"Thanks, Maria." Stone walked around the desk and started down the hallway, feeling nervous. He and Dierdre had gotten drunk and had a little thing after last year's Christmas office party at the courthouse. The thing had occurred on a conference table next to the chief deputy DA's office, and the door hadn't been locked. He hadn't seen her since. He rapped on the glass door.

"Come in, but it had better be good!" she shouted.

Stone opened the door and stuck his head in. "Morning, Dierdre. Got a minute?"

Dierdre was a striking woman of thirty-something who came from a long line of Irish cops and had four brothers currently wearing the uniform. "Faith and begorra," she said sardonically. "And I was thinkin' you was dead in your grave." She dropped the Irish accent. "Come in and sit down, Stone."

Stone went in and sat down. "So, how have you been?"

"Since last Christmas, you mean? You could have called and asked."

Stone felt his ears redden. "It's been a crazy year," he said weakly.

"You're blushing, Stone. Don't tell me the memory of our little time together embarrasses you."

"Well . . ."

"Just because the chief deputy walked in on us? Now, why should you let a little thing like that bother you?"

"Well . . ."

"I've had to take the brunt of it around here. The razzing got so bad I managed to parlay it into a sexual harassment complaint that got me, among other things, this office."

"I'm glad you were able to turn the situation to your advantage," Stone said, trying hard to sound sincere.

"I'm glad you're glad, Stone. What can I do for you?"

"I've got a client at bat this morning at ten," Stone said, grateful for the change of subject. "Maria says you caught the case."

"Name?"

"Fisher."

Dierdre emitted a deep chuckle. "Oh, Mr. Fisher! What a perfect pairing of client and attorney! And I suppose you've come to propose a deal?"

"Well, this sort of thing is really a waste of the court's time—not to mention yours—and since Mr. Fisher is contrite and unlikely to repeat—"

"Mr. Fisher has already repeated," Dierdre said. "That's why I caught the case instead of one of the rookies."

"Yes, I'm aware of that, but—"

"And the cop in question—Mr. Fisher's victim—missed two days of duty because of his injury."

"Mr. Fisher is *very* sorry about that. He was *very* drunk at the time, and—"

"Which is why he was stopped in the first place," Dierdre replied. She consulted a sheet of paper. "A two-point-oh reading on the Richter scale," she said. "Judge Goldstein is going to just love that."

"Judge Goldstein is hearing the case?" Stone's heart sank. Goldstein's wife had been injured in a collision with a drunk driver a couple of years back, and he was known as a hanging judge where DUIs were concerned.

"Isn't that lucky?" Dierdre said. "What sort of deal did you have in mind, Stone?"

"I was thinking a written apology to the officer and community service," Stone said hopefully. It was only an opening gambit.

"Tell you what: If he pleads out, I won't ask for the death penalty."

"Heh, heh," Stone said.

"I'm glad you find this amusing. So do I."

"Come on, Dierdre, give me a break here, will you?"

"The poor cop didn't get much of a break, did he? There he was, just doing his duty, protecting the public from a driver too drunk to stand up straight—"

"All right, spare me," Stone said, throwing up his hands in surrender. "What can you do for me, Dierdre?"

"How about three to five in Attica?" she proposed.

"Dierdre, please. Let's be realistic; nobody died."

"Have you ever been kicked in the balls, Stone?"

"Once, a long time ago."

"I'm glad you had the experience. I was going to do it myself, just so you'd know the pain involved. Was it fun?"

"No, it hurt a lot."

"Funny, that's what the cop said. He'll be using a cane to make his court appearance today."

"Why don't we spare him the court appearance, Dierdre? Make me an offer I can take to my client."

"Six months and no license for five years."

"Dierdre . . ."

"He's lucky I don't want his license for life."

"Dierdre . . ."

"Propose what you feel is an appropriate punishment, Stone, all things considered."

"He doesn't deserve to go to jail, Dierdre."

"Doesn't he?"

"Let me explain something else: I've been retained by a branch of the federal government that I cannot name. He was doing their bidding at the time he was arrested."

Dierdre clapped a hand to her breast. "Oh, God, he was drunk and violent for the CIA, is that what you're telling me? I gotta admit, I've never heard that one before, though it's right up there with the dog ate his driver's license."

"Shhhh," Stone said, making tamping motions with his hands. "I didn't say that, and you mustn't repeat it."

"Is that your way of saying he *actually was* working for the CIA?"

"I can't go there," Stone said, pleading in his voice. "Please believe me when I tell you."

"All right, Stone," she said. "Since it's you, and you're a pretty good lay when no one is watching, here's my best offer: thirty days at Rikers, a thousand-dollar fine, and his license in my desk drawer for three years."

Stone slumped. Herbie wasn't going to like this. "I'll take it to my client," he said.

"Don't sound so down, Stone. You did pretty well for the guy, considering."

Stone didn't ask, Considering what? He said his goodbyes and left.

"Don't be a stranger!" Dierdre called after him down the hallway.

"Thanks, Maria," Stone said as he passed the front desk.

"Did I mention that the cop was Dierdre's baby brother, Colin?" Maria asked.

"No, Maria, you didn't mention that." Stone got out the door as quickly as he could.

10

Stone went down to the hallway outside the courtroom and was mildly surprised to find Herbie Fisher, dressed in a sober blue suit and tie, waiting for him, and on time, too.

"Hey, Stone," Herbie said. "How's it hanging?"

"You're the one who's hanging," Stone said. "You're in a lot of trouble."

"Stone, it was only a DUI, that's all."

"It was your *second* DUI, and you haven't bothered to do your penance for the first one, which was less than a month ago."

"Well, hell . . ."

"Let me tell you a few other things that you ought to know," Stone said. "The cop who received your kick in the crotch was the younger brother of the lady DA who's prosecuting your case, and the judge who's hearing it has a wife who was hurt in an accident caused by a DUI. He loves stringing them up by their thumbs."

Herbie seemed to pale a little. "Can't we get the DA and the judge, whatchacallit, excused? I mean, they're both prejudiced against me."

"Recused. It's not going to happen because I've already gotten you the best possible deal."

Herbie blew out a sigh of relief. "I knew you'd come through for me, Stone. Lance said you'd make it go away."

"I didn't say it was going away. I said I got you the best possible deal."

Herbie looked worried. "What kind of a deal?"

"You do thirty days, pay a thousand-dollar fine, and lose your license for three years."

"*WHAT?*" Herbie yelled. "I'm not doing time for this, and I'm sure as hell not going to give up driving. I just bought a new car!"

"You're lucky they're not taking the new car," Stone said. "When Giuliani was mayor, that's what they did—first DUI, they towed it away."

"Stone, Lance promised me . . ."

"Then talk to Lance about it."

"I can't do that."

"Why not?"

"Well, Lance is sort of hard to get hold of, you know? He always called me."

"That's tough, Herbie. You've fucked yourself, so you may as well lie back and enjoy it."

Herbie was shaking his head vigorously. "I'll go to trial," he said. "I'll get a better deal than that from a jury."

"Are you insane?"

"I know how to talk to a jury," Herbie said. "They'll believe me."

"So your idea of dealing with this is to perjure yourself?"

"Absolutely not. I'll tell the truth."

"You'll tell a jury you were on your second DUI in a month, with a blood alcohol level of more than double the legal limit, and that you kicked a cop in the balls? Do you want to end up in Sing-Sing?"

Herbie was still shaking his head. "Lance said you'd make it go away."

"What do you want me to do, bribe the judge?"

Herbie brightened. "How much would that cost?"

Stone dragged Herbie over to a bench and sat him down. "Now you listen to me," he said. "You've behaved stupidly by driving drunk twice in a row. You've injured a young policeman who is the brother of the ADA prosecuting you, and the judge has a thing about DUIs. What do you think that adds up to?"

"Okay, I'll do the fine and the license thing, but no jail time. I'm too pretty to go to jail. I'll get raped the first day."

"First of all, you're not all that pretty. Second of all, you're extraordinarily lucky to have to do only thirty days. The DA's first offer was six months, and if you went to trial, you'd probably get a year. Can't you understand that you've fucked up royally, and that now you're going to have to take responsibility for your actions?"

Herbie brought himself up to his full five-feet-six. "I have no problem taking responsibility. I just won't do time, that's all."

"Herbie, that's *how* you *take* responsibility."

"Stone, do you know how to get hold of Lance?"

"Lance can't help you here, Herbie; only I can help you. You can help yourself by be-

ing a stand-up guy and taking your punishment."

"I *am* a stand-up guy," Herbie protested,
his voice taking on a whine.

"Herbie, do you know who Lance is? Do
you know who he works for?"

Herbie looked around furtively. "Well, I do
have my suspicions. He's mobbed up, isn't
he?"

"Worse than that, Herbie."

"What's worse than mobbed up? Russian
mob?"

"Worse."

"I can't think of anything worse than the
Russian mob."

"Herbie, think about the work that Lance
hired you to do."

"You mean photographing that ambassador guy with his boyfriend?"

"I don't want to know that, Herbie," Stone
said, throwing up his hands defensively.
"But think for a minute: Who would want
that kind of work done?"

Herbie thought about it. "You don't
mean . . ."

"Go ahead, Herbie, say it."

Herbie licked his lips and gulped. "*The
National Enquirer?*"

Stone buried his face in his hands. "Herbie, Lance works for a branch of the federal government, a branch that does dirty little things like photographing ambassadors with their boyfriends. Can't you think of who that might be?"

"You're not talking about the CIA, are you?"

"Congratulations, Herbie, you're coming out of the fog."

Oddly, Herbie seemed pleased. "You mean I'm working for the CIA?"

"Not anymore."

"Man, that should get me laid." Herbie chuckled.

"Herbie, it could get you a lot worse than laid," Stone said.

"What do you mean?"

"Lance intimated to me that, if your case came to trial, his people might use other means to stop it."

"You mean like bribing the judge?"

"No, Herbie."

"Well, anybody who'd want an ambassador photographed with his head buried in another guy's crotch wouldn't have a problem with bribing a judge, would they?"

"Herbie, you're not thinking this out to its

logical conclusion. These are people who own weapons with silencers, if you get my drift."

"You mean, they might shoot the judge?" He didn't seem displeased at the thought.

Stone shook his head. "No, Herbie. It would be a lot simpler just to shoot you, wouldn't it?"

Herbie froze.

Stone thought he'd finally reached Herbie. "Of course, they'd probably make it look like an accident; a suicide, maybe."

Herbie seemed speechless now.

"You see where this is headed, Herbie? Look, I'll see what I can do to make life a little easier for you inside."

"How can you do that?" Herbie asked.

"You can buy nearly anything in jail, Herbie. Do you have any money?"

Herbie shook his head. "My credit cards are pretty much maxed out."

"Herbie, they don't take MasterCard at Rikers."

"Well, I sure don't have any cash."

"Maybe I can get some money out of Lance," Stone said. He saw his retainer getting smaller.

"You really think this is the right thing to

do, Stone? I mean, as my lawyer and my friend, you think this is right?"

"Herbie, it's the *only* thing to do, trust me."

"I trust you, Stone."

"Thanks, Herbie."

"I just don't want to go to jail."

"The best you can do now is to try not to do anything ever again that will get you sent to jail. Now come on, it's time for court." Stone grabbed Herbie's wrist, hauled him off the bench, and towed him toward the courtroom.

"You're *sure* we can't bribe the judge?" Herbie asked.

"Shut up, Herbie," Stone said.

11

Stone led Herbie into the courtroom, tightly holding his wrist so that he couldn't run. His client came along only reluctantly. Stone shoved Herbie into a seat and sat down beside him.

Herbie stood up. "I gotta go to the men's room."

Stone grabbed his coattail and jerked him back into his seat. "Sit on it, Herbie," he said. "You're not going anywhere until we're done here."

"But I gotta go."

"You should have gone when you had the chance. Am I going to have to handcuff you?"

Herbie stared at his feet. "I didn't bring nothing that I need for jail, no toothbrush or anything. I thought you were going to make this go away."

"They have a little store at Rikers where you can buy what you need. They'll let you keep twenty dollars."

"And I wore my good suit."

"They'll keep it for you, Herbie, and they'll supply all the clothes you need. It's a free service to guests."

"All rise!" the bailiff yelled, and the courtroom crowd got to its feet.

Stone looked to his left and saw four uniforms sitting in the front row directly behind the table where Dierdre Monahan sat. He nudged Herbie. "Those are the four brothers of the ADA," he said.

"Which?"

"The ones in police uniforms. The youngest is carrying a cane. You knocked him off duty for two days."

"They're big guys," Herbie whispered.

"Very big."

The judge came out of his chambers and headed for the bench. To Stone's astonishment, Lance Cabot came out the same door immediately afterward and took a seat on the other side of the courtroom. He

didn't look at Stone. What the hell was going on here?

The judge rapped sharply. "Order! Court
is in session!" He turned toward Dierdre.
"Ms. Monahan, approach."

Dierdre got up and approached the
bench. There was a brief conversation, and
the judge did nearly all the talking.

Dierdre went back to her seat, taking time
to glare at Stone on the way.

"Why is she pissed off at you?" Herbie
asked.

"I don't know, but I think we're about to
find out."

"If she's pissed off at you, does that
mean more jail time?"

"Herbie, she couldn't be more pissed off
at me now than she was an hour ago, believe me. Listen, this is going to take a
while. Our case is pretty far down the
docket, and I don't want to hear any more
whining about the men's room."

The bailiff looked at his clipboard. "People versus Herbert J. Fisher!" he yelled.

"Oh, shit," Stone said under his breath.

"What's the matter? This means we get
out of here sooner, doesn't it?" Herbie
asked.

"Herbie, try and get this through your head," Stone said, dragging Herbie toward the gate in the rail that separated the lawyers from the courtroom. "You're not getting out of here, except in a police van. Got it?"

The judge watched Stone drag Herbie through the gate, and his gaze could have melted ice. He looked down at his papers. "Mr. Fisher, you're charged with driving with a suspended license, DUI, and resisting arrest with violence. How do you plead?"

"Well, Your Honor . . ." Herbie began.

Stone leaned toward him. "Say guilty and nothing else."

"Guilty and nothing else," Herbie called out to the judge.

Stone winced.

"Mr. Barrington, do you have any objection to sentence being imposed at this time?"

"No, Judge," Stone replied.

"Ms. Monahan," the judge said, "do you have a sentence recommendation?"

Dierdre stood up. "Yes, Judge. The people recommend suspension of Mr. Fisher's driver's license for five years, twelve months' imprisonment, and a ten-thousand-dollar fine."

"*WHAT*?" Herbie yelled.

"Shut your mouth," Stone said. Something had gone terribly wrong here.

"That sounds good to me," the judge said. "Mr. Fisher, you are sentenced to suspension of your driver's license for five years, a ten-thousand-dollar fine, and twelve months' imprisonment."

Herbie began to cry.

The judge looked down at his desk and said, quietly enough so the full courtroom could not hear him, "Imprisonment suspended on condition of good behavior."

The four policemen sitting behind Dierdre were on their feet, protesting loudly, while Dierdre tried to calm them.

"Pay the clerk," the judge said, rapping his gavel. "Next case?"

Stone took Herbie's arm and dragged him out of the well of the courtroom, hoping to get him out before the Monahan brothers regrouped and came after Herbie.

Lance moved out of a row of seats and met them at the rear of the courtroom. "Let's step outside," he said, and they went into the hallway.

"You said you'd make it go away!" Herbie wailed.

Stone grabbed him by a lapel and shook him. "It did go away. Didn't you hear the judge?"

"He said a year!"

"He also said suspended."

Herbie wiped away a tear. "He did?"

"He did," Lance said. He took an envelope from an inside pocket and handed it to Stone. "Pay his fine, and let's get him out of here. Go ahead, we'll wait here."

Stone went back into the courtroom, found the clerk, and paid Herbie's fine with the ten thousand dollars in cash in Lance's envelope. He got a receipt, then rejoined Herbie and Lance in the hallway.

Lance led them out of the courthouse, and they paused at the bottom of the steps.

"Herbie," Stone said, "do you know what 'suspended' means?"

"It means I'm a free man, doesn't it?"

"No, it means you're a free man until the second you fuck up again—until you get a ticket for jaywalking or for playing your car radio too loud—for anything at all. That happens, you're doing a year at Rikers. You understand that?"

"Yes," Herbie said.

"Herbie's not going to fuck up again,"

Lance said, staring at Herbie. "You remember your little sojourn in the Virgin Islands last year, Herbie?"

"Yeah, sure," Herbie said.

"Did you like it there?"

"Yeah, it was great. I had this great deal going where I took pictures at the hotels."

Lance took an envelope out of his coat pocket and handed it to Herbie. "I'm glad you liked it, Herbie, because you're going back. Here's your ticket."

"I am?"

"Your flight leaves at six-twenty this evening. A man will pick you up at your home at four o'clock. You have until then to sell your car and pack."

"I have to sell my car?" Herbie wailed. "But I just bought it!" He pointed at a new Mustang parked at the curb ten yards from where they stood. There were three parking tickets on the windshield.

"I'm afraid there's no car ferry service to the Virgin Islands," Lance said. "And since you can't drive that or any other car for five years, you'll have no need of it. By the way, there's a voucher in the envelope for two weeks in a small hotel in Charlotte Amalie and transportation from the airport. There's also two thousand dollars in cash, to help you get on your feet."

"Herbie," Stone said, "if you get into the slightest trouble in Charlotte Amalie, your previous and current convictions will pop up on the police computer, and you'll find yourself back here, in Rikers, in a heartbeat. Do you understand?"

But Herbie wasn't listening. "Hey!" he yelled, pointing at his car. A tow truck had pulled to the curb ahead of it. Herbie sprinted to the car, dove inside, got it started, and roared away from the curb, scattering parking tickets in the wind.

"I can't believe he's driving home," Lance said.

"I wouldn't have expected anything else," Stone replied. "Lance, what did you say to Judge Goldstein?"

Lance shrugged. "Let's just say the judge is a patriot. Nice doing business with you again, Stone."

"Please, Lance, no more."

"We'll see," Lance replied and strolled toward a black Lincoln parked at the curb with its motor running. Lance opened the door and paused. "Dinner tonight?" He didn't wait for an answer. "Elaine's, eight-thirty." He got into the car and it pulled away.

Stone noted that the car had a diplomatic license plate. He wanted one of those.

12

Stone got home around noon and went to his office. "Where's Holly?" he asked Joan.

"Oh, she borrowed your car and went somewhere."

Stone blinked. "She borrowed my car?"

"She said you said it would be okay, so I gave her the extra set of keys."

"Any idea where she went?"

"Not a clue."

Stone went into his office and signed some letters, then picked up the phone and dialed his car phone number. It rang four times before she figured it out.

"Hello?"

"Holly, it's Stone. Where are you?"

"Sitting outside the La Boheme coffee-house, in Little Italy."

"You're not going to get my car full of bullet holes, are you?"

"A brochure in the glove compartment says it's armored."

"Well, it is, sort of, but I've never actually tested the armor. I'd prefer it if you returned it in the same shape as when you drove it away."

"Well, sure, I'll try."

"When, exactly, did I say you could borrow my car?"

"At dinner. Don't you remember?"

He did not. "I guess. When are you coming home?"

"A couple of hours, if Trini doesn't show up. If he doesn't come for lunch, I'll leave it until later. Can I buy you dinner tonight?"

"No, but a guy from the CIA will buy us both dinner at Elaine's."

"The CIA? No kidding?"

"I'm afraid not."

"I've never met anybody from the CIA. This ought to be interesting."

"I hope not. I've just spent an all-too-interesting morning in court because of him. I've learned that you don't want interesting, where the CIA is concerned."

"Holy shit!" Holly yelled.

Stone heard his car start. "What's going on, Holly?"

"It's Trini! He's leaving the La Boheme right now and getting into a Cadillac!"

"Holly, please don't try a car chase in downtown Manhattan. It's not like at home in Orchid Beach." He heard the car's engine rev.

"I don't think he saw me," she said.

"Holly, don't hang up the phone."

She hung up the phone.

Stone was left holding a dead receiver. He hung it up and buzzed Joan.

"Yes?"

"Joan, call my insurance agent and confirm that my car is insured for any driver. If it's not, add Holly Barker as an insured driver, and hurry."

"Will do."

Stone tried to think what he could do about this, and he came up with a quick answer: absolutely nothing. This hick-town cop was loose in Manhattan with his seventy-thousand-dollar car, and involved in a chase with an FBI-protected murderer at the front end of things. He buzzed Joan again.

"Yes, Stone?"

"Did you get that insurance thing done?"

"I have them on the other line now."

"Make sure it's effective immediately."

It was after five when Holly returned to Stone's house.

"Hello?" she called up the stairs.

"Come on up," Stone called back.

Holly came into his bedroom, shucking off her coat. Daisy padded along beside her, then hopped up onto the bed with Stone, who had been reading the *Times*.

"Hello, Daisy," Stone said, half expecting her to reply. She gave him a big kiss, then lay down and snuggled against him.

"She likes you," Holly said.

"I'm relieved to hear it." To his surprise, she started undoing buttons.

"Mind if I use your shower?" she asked, continuing to undress. "The water pressure isn't too great upstairs."

"Sure, go ahead," Stone replied. "In New York, we have these water tanks on the roof, and sometimes the upper floors don't get the best pressure." As she continued to undress he reminded himself not to get the water pressure problem fixed.

"Water tanks? No kidding?"

"You can go up and take a look," he said, "but I wouldn't go like that." She was down to a bra and panties, or more accurately, some sort of semi-thong thing. "You'd have the neighbors climbing out windows."

"Aren't you sweet," she said, flashing him a big smile. She turned and went into the bathroom, reaching behind her for the bra hook while displaying the backside of the semi-thong thing and a fine pair of buns. She left the door open, but he couldn't see her. He heard the shower turn on, though.

"How was your day?" she called from the bathroom.

"Hairy," he replied. "A very strange morning in court."

"You can tell me about it later," she said.

He heard the shower door open and close.

Five minutes later, she came out, loosely dressed in his terry robe, toweling her hair. She hopped onto the bed and turned toward him, close. Daisy was between them. "So, tell me about your morning in court."

"I had this extremely annoying client, Herbie Fisher, with whom I've dealt before. He was charged with—"

"The one who kicked the cop in the balls?"

"Yes, and the cop was there with his three big brothers. Their sister was prosecuting."

"Stacked deck, huh?"

"You might say that."

"How many years did he get?"

"Twelve months, suspended, a ten-thousand-dollar fine, and loss of his license for five years, which is a godsend to the community."

"Suspended? Wasn't this his second DUI?"

"Right."

"We're tougher in Florida. You must be some kind of lawyer."

"I employed no lawyering skills this morning. The CIA guy fixed the judge."

Holly lifted her head off the pillow. "You're kidding."

"I kid you not. Now Herbie is on a plane to Saint Thomas, and the world is a better place, except in Saint Thomas."

"How did he fix the judge? Pay him off?"

Stone shook his head. "I don't think Judge Goldstein is the sort who would take a payoff. Lance said the judge was a patriot."

"Lance is the CIA guy?"

"Right."

"So he said something to bring out the judge's patriotic instincts?"

"Apparently."

"What did he say?"

"I don't want to know. By the way, did I mention that we're having dinner with Lance?"

"Yes. Why?"

"I don't know," Stone admitted. "I'd just as soon not see him again."

Holly planted a kiss on his cheek. "Don't worry, I'll protect you from the bad CIA guy."

"I don't know that he's bad. I used to think so, but now I'm not sure." He liked the kiss. He wanted to put his arm around her, but Daisy was staring right at him.

"Daisy," Holly said, "get off the bed and lie down."

Daisy immediately hopped off the bed and lay down beside the bed.

"Go to sleep," Holly said.

Daisy laid her head on her paws and closed her eyes.

"Is she really asleep?" Stone asked.

"Close enough," Holly said. She turned his head toward her and kissed him on the lips.

13

Stone woke with a crick in his neck, the result of napping most of the afternoon with Holly's head on his shoulder. That was all they had done, nap, and he wasn't too happy about that, but somehow, he hadn't felt it was the right time to go further.

The sound of his hairdryer was coming from the bathroom, then it stopped, and Holly emerged, stark naked, her underwear in her hands. "I'm going to take Daisy for a nice long walk," she said. "I'll be back in time for dinner."

"Wear something," he called after her, while appreciating the sight of her departure. "I wouldn't want you to get arrested."

She laughed and disappeared upstairs.

Stone got up, still groggy, and got into a

shower. He emerged feeling brighter. The phone rang.

"Hello?"

"It's Dino. Dinner?"

"Sure, meet me at Elaine's. Lance Cabot will be there."

"No shit? The CIA guy?"

"One and the same."

"How'd Herbie's courtroom appearance go?"

"You wouldn't believe me if I told you."

"Tell me anyway."

Stone told him.

"I don't believe it."

"See?"

"Goldstein did that? I thought he was Mr. Ironass."

"Lance says he's a patriot."

"He's lucky Goldstein didn't have him arrested on the spot. I wouldn't mess with that guy on a bet, especially about a DUI."

"A DUI that included violence upon the crotch of a police officer. Turns out the cop was Dierdre Monahan's little brother, and she caught the case."

"You're lucky Lance showed up."

"Herbie was lucky. I had negotiated thirty days in Rikers for him, and he got off with a suspended sentence because of whatever Lance said to Goldstein."

"Go figure."

"Yeah. Eight-thirty?"

"See ya." Dino hung up.

Holly came back into the room, this time, to Stone's disappointment, fully dressed. "Is there some sort of park that's closer to your house than Central Park?" she asked.

"Not so's you'd notice it," Stone said. "In Manhattan, a park is often the space where a building used to be. By the way, did I mention the leash law?"

"No, but I figured. Not in the park, of course."

"Especially in the park. It's a hundred-buck fine."

"That's cruel to dogs."

"And to dog owners."

"You're perfectly serious about this?"

"You didn't believe me about picking up the dog poop, either, did you? We do things differently in New York."

"This is taking some getting used to."

"Daisy seems to be managing."

"She's very adaptable, like me."

"*You're* adaptable?"

"Of course. Have you heard any complaints from me? I mean, any *at all*?"

"Only about having to pick up dog poop."

"That's about Daisy, not about me."

"You're the one picking it up. Daisy is just doing what comes naturally."

"All right. Have you heard any complaints from me, except about Daisy?"

"Not so far."

"That sounds as though you're expecting some."

"I hope not."

She came over, grabbed him by the front of his robe, and kissed him. "Don't worry about it." She turned and walked down the stairs, followed closely by Daisy.

They got a cab to Elaine's. As they approached the restaurant, Stone noticed a man standing out front, just uptown from the yellow awning, holding a briefcase. He looked out of place somehow. Stone wasn't sure how. "Driver, stop here," he said. The cab halted a couple of doors uptown, and Stone looked hard at the man. He shifted his weight from one foot to the other and switched hands with the briefcase. Stone noted a Cadillac double-parked just down-town from the entrance.

"That's seven-fifty," the cabbie said.

"Drive around the block," Stone said.

"Huh?"

"Start the meter again and drive around the block to your right, slowly."

"Whatever you say, mister." He pulled away from the curb.

Stone got out his cell phone.

"Are we early?" Holly asked. "Do you have a thing about being early?"

"Shhh," Stone said. "Dino?"

"Yeah, I'm on my way."

"Listen, do you remember a few years back we had that weapons guy come into the precinct and show us a lot of stuff?"

"Vaguely," Dino said. "What about it?"

"Do you remember that Heckler & Koch thing he showed us with the H&K machine gun in the briefcase? There was a hole in one end that took the barrel, and the shell casings were routed to the bottom of the case when the thing was fired?"

"Yeah, I think I do."

"Well, there's a suspicious character standing outside Elaine's holding a briefcase that looks just like the H&K one, and it has a hole in it."

"Where are you?" Dino asked.

"Driving around the block, slowly," Stone replied.

"Keep doing that until you hear from me," Dino said. "I'm on it."

Stone closed his cell phone.

"What's going on?" Holly asked.

"This afternoon, you said you were following Trini in a Cadillac?"

"Yes." She put a hand to her mouth. "And there was a Cadillac double-parked outside Elaine's. It was black, too, just like the one I followed."

"Yeah. I didn't ask you what happened with your pursuit."

"I lost him in Brooklyn. I think it was Brooklyn, anyway. I followed him across a bridge."

"Any chance the Cadillac could have followed you back to my house?"

Holly sank down in her seat. "Oh, my God. You were right. New York is not like Orchid Beach."

14

The cab went around the block again, and when they turned downtown on Second again, Stone told the driver to stop at the corner before the restaurant. He opened the door and got out so he could see better. Holly did the same on the other side.

Dino's car was double-parked a few yards ahead of them, and Stone could make out a commotion on the sidewalk in front of Elaine's. A man Stone recognized as Dino's cop driver was pointing a gun into the Cadillac and barking orders.

"Holly, do you have my Walther with you?" Stone asked.

"In my purse," Holly said.

"Get back in the cab and hand me the gun." He leaned down, reached across the backseat, and accepted the pistol.

"There's one in the chamber and six in the magazine," she said.

"Please stay in the cab until I wave you in." Stone gave the cabbie a twenty, then closed the door and went to the sidewalk and started down the street toward Elaine's with the Walther in his hand. He could see now that Dino was on the sidewalk, cuffing the man with the briefcase.

Then, as he approached and Dino was dragging the man to his feet, the rear door of the Cadillac opened, and Lance Cabot got out, his hands in the air.

"Stone!" he yelled. "That guy is mine!" He nodded toward the handcuffed man.

Stone walked up to Dino. "Hang on," he said. "That's Lance Cabot over there at the car, and he says this guy belongs to him."

Dino looked back and forth from his captive to the Cadillac. "All right, Mike," he yelled to his driver, "we're clear, no problem." He unlocked the handcuffs and handed the man his briefcase. "Is there a machine gun in here, pal?" he asked him.

"Talk to Cabot," the man said.

Lance walked up and offered his hand to Dino. "I'm Lance Cabot," he said. "I'm sorry about the misunderstanding."

Dino shook his hand. "Don't worry about it. It was all Stone's fault."

"That's right," Holly said from behind Stone. "I'm a witness."

"Thanks so much, everybody," Stone said. "How did I call this wrong?"

"Well, you weren't *entirely* wrong," Dino replied. "You just didn't know who you were dealing with."

"It's dinnertime," Stone said, and they went into Elaine's.

Elaine was at a front table, and she waved them over. "Are you guys having street fights outside my place again?"

"Just a misunderstanding," Stone said. "Elaine, this is Lance Cabot, and, Lance, you haven't met Holly Barker, either." Everybody shook hands, and Stone didn't like the way Holly was looking at Lance.

They settled in at a table.

Lance turned to Holly. "Are you the police chief in Orchid Beach, Florida?"

"That's right," Holly replied, looking stunned. "How could you know that?"

"Anybody who pays attention knows that," Lance said.

Holly seemed to melt a little in her seat, annoying Stone. "So, Lance," he said, "do you normally travel with bodyguards who have machine guns in briefcases?"

"No, not normally," Lance replied smoothly, as if he had been asked if he wore pleated pants. "Just today."

"What's so dangerous about today?" Stone asked.

"Well, around lunchtime today I picked up a tail."

Stone felt a penny drop. "Yes? Where?"

"I was in Little Italy doing some business, and I picked up on an evil-looking black Mercedes following me. We lost it in Brooklyn, but policy is, when you pick up a tail, you increase security."

Holly hid behind her menu.

"A wise policy," Stone agreed. "Holly, can we get you a drink?"

Holly lowered the menu to eye level. "Knob Creek on the rocks," she said, then raised the menu again.

"Make it two," Lance said.

"Three Knob Creeks on the rocks and whatever poison Lieutenant Bacchetti is having this evening," Stone told the waiter.

"Dino," Lance said, "your reputation precedes you."

"Oh, yeah?" Dino asked.

"We have a list of reliable police officers in various cities who we sometimes deal with. You're on it."

"That's news to me," Dino said.

Lance turned to Holly. "I'll see that your name is placed on it, too."

Holly put down the menu. "How nice," she said, noncommittally.

"He's turning us all into spies," Dino whispered loudly.

"Oh, nothing as sinister as that. Sometimes, during the course of our work, we stumble across criminal activity that, technically, is outside our purview. When that happens, it's nice to know some people in local law enforcement."

"Tell me," Stone said, "in the course of your work have you run across somebody named Trini Rodriguez?"

Lance furrowed his brow. "I don't believe so."

"How about a Robert Marshall?"

Lance shook his head. "Nope."

"I think I'd better come clean," Holly said. "It was Stone's car that was following you today."

Lance turned to Stone and looked at him askance.

"Don't point that thing at me," Stone said. "Go on, Holly."

"And I was driving it."

The drinks arrived, and Lance raised his glass. "To coincidence," he said. "You put enough coincidences together, and what you get is . . ." He gazed at Holly. ". . . fate."

Holly blushed. "Let me explain. I'm in New York looking for a man named Trini Rodriguez, who may be using the name Robert Marshall."

"Why?" Lance asked.

"Multiple homicides," Holly replied. "Today, he came out of the La Boheme coffeehouse and got into your car."

"*That* was Trini Rodriguez?" Lance asked.

"Yep. What was he doing with you?"

"Well, I can't tell you that, but I can tell you it was nothing to do with multiple homicides."

"What name did he give you?" Holly asked.

"I was told he was called Bobo. He was to assist me in some enquiries, as the British would put it."

"Did he?"

"I'm afraid I can't answer that."

"Swell," Holly said. "First, the FBI protects this bastard, and now the CIA."

Lance looked around and made a tamping motion with his hand. "Please. I wish I could help you, Holly, but until today I'd never clapped eyes on Mr. Rodriguez, and I never expect to again. However, if he should cross my line of vision again, I'll be glad to call you. May I have your number?"

Holly gave him her card while Stone rolled his eyes.

"Anything else you can tell me about him or about the people who sent you to him?"

"Alas, no," Lance said sadly. "The nature of the work, I'm afraid." He turned to Stone. "By the way," he said, "have you, by any chance, heard from Herbert J. Fisher?"

"No, I haven't," Stone said. "Should I have?"

"Just a thought. Herbie didn't make his flight to Saint Thomas this evening."

"I thought you had a man on him," Stone said.

"I thought so, too, but Herbie, the little shit, eluded him. Herbie is out there in the land, somewhere, in his red Mustang, moving about with reckless abandon."

"That's just terrific," Stone said. "If I hear from him, what shall I tell him?"

"Tell him to go and stand on the corner of Forty-second Street and Broadway, then call me," Lance replied. "I'll have someone go there and shoot him."

Stone wasn't at all sure he was kidding.

15

They had finished dinner and were standing on the sidewalk in front of Elaine's, saying their goodbyes. Dino got into his waiting car and was driven away.

"May I give you a lift?" Lance said to Holly and Stone.

They spoke at the same time. "No," Stone replied. "Yes," Holly said.

Lance opened a rear door and motioned them in. "Stone, I know where you live. Holly, where can I take you?"

"You can take us both to my house," Stone said.

"Ah," Lance mused. He gave the driver an address, then pressed a button and a thick glass partition rolled up, separating them from the two men in the front seat.

"Actually," Lance said, "there's something I'd like to talk to the two of you about."

"Shoot," Holly said. She was sitting between Lance and Stone.

"You may have read in the papers that the Agency is working very hard on terrorism since nine/eleven."

"I believe I've seen reports to that effect," Stone said.

"As a result, we're stretched a little thin these days, and we've had to neglect some other matters, particularly those which require attention on our own soil."

Stone snorted. "And I thought you folks were proscribed from dealing with home matters."

"Formerly, yes. Since nine/eleven, things have changed a bit."

"I'll bet," Stone said.

"Stone," Holly said, "could you just shut up so we can hear what Lance has to say?"

"Thank you, Holly," Lance said. "I couldn't have put it better myself."

Stone smoldered in silence.

"As I was saying," Lance continued, "we're stretched a little thin these days, and, as a result, I have been authorized to add a few . . . consultants, shall we say, to our roster."

"Consultants?" Holly said. "What do you mean?"

"People who are sometimes in a position to render services to us, but who are not permanent employees."

Stone couldn't stand it anymore. "You mean people to whom you don't have to pay pensions or offer medical plans?"

"You misunderstand," Lance said. "I'm referring to people who have built lives outside our service, and who have independently acquired information or contacts that might be of use to us in the future. Let me give you a couple of examples. Stone, you were recently involved, quite inadvertently, of course, in a British intelligence operation dealing with an assassin who was causing problems in Europe and New York." He paused.

"If you say so," Stone said, surprised that Lance knew about this.

"We would have liked to know about this during the fact, instead of afterward," Lance said. He didn't wait for Stone to respond. "Holly, you were recently involved in a major federal investigation in Florida, and, as I understand it, you had a great deal to do with its successful conclusion. We would have been very pleased to know about that at a much earlier date. Is this making any sense at all to the two of you?"

"Sure," Stone said, "you want us to become CIA snitches."

"No, no," Lance said placatingly. "We would like for you both, from time to time, to perhaps participate more actively in certain situations that might arise. Of course, we're always receptive to pertinent information."

"What sort of situations?" Holly asked.

"For instance, Stone has been of help to us in dealing with the Herbie Fisher problem, and, although that problem has not yet been entirely solved, that certainly isn't Stone's fault. Holly, you might similarly be of help in some other situation, on your own home turf. One never knows when."

"I see, I think," Holly said. "We'd just be on call, sort of."

"Yes, sort of. And we'd never wish to interfere with your own duties in your main work."

"And this is work for which we'd be paid?" Holly asked.

"Of course, and generously. Ask Stone."

Stone spoke up. "There isn't enough money in the CIA's coffers to make it worthwhile dealing with Herbie Fisher and his problems."

"Still, you didn't come off all that badly, did you?" Lance asked. "What did you spend—a couple of hours?"

"Well, yes, it didn't occupy a great deal of time," Stone admitted, "and I was well paid."

"You see?" Lance said, spreading his hands. "We're starting to be of one mind."

"And," Holly said, "if we were consulting, so to speak, and we had some little problem, then the CIA might be helpful to us."

"What sort of problem did you have in mind?" Lance asked, sounding slightly suspicious.

"Oh, nothing at present," Holly said, "but you can never tell what might come up in the future, can you?"

"I suppose there might occur, at some point, circumstances in which we might be informally helpful," Lance said, "but of course, I can't make you any promises about that, it being so vague."

"Of course not," Stone said. "Tell me, is there a contract for this sort of service?"

"I suppose there could be," Lance said, "if it were deemed necessary."

They had pulled up in front of Stone's house. "Tell you what, why don't you send the contracts to me, and I'll take a look at them," Stone said.

"You'd be representing Holly, then?"

"Yes," Holly said, "he would be."

"All right, I'll see what I can put together."

"Good night, Lance," Stone said, opening the door, "and thanks for the lift."

"Same here," Holly said.

Stone closed the car door and they walked up the front steps.

"Did you think that was really, really weird?" Holly asked as they entered the house.

"I think that anything to do with Lance is really, really weird," Stone replied. They got on the elevator and headed upstairs. When Stone got off, Holly followed him to his bedroom.

She took him by the lapels and kissed him.

Stone kissed her back. "That was very nice," he said.

"Just what do I have to do to get you into bed?" Holly asked, kissing him again.

"Well, I . . ." He was stopped by a tongue in his mouth.

"I mean, I've been parading around here half naked—no, entirely naked, and that usually gets results, but you actually fell asleep."

"I'm sorry, I . . ."

She pushed off his jacket and began untying his tie. "A girl could feel hurt by such treatment, you know." She was working on his buttons.

"Doesn't Daisy have to go out?" Stone asked weakly.

"Daisy is half bladder; don't worry about it." She was working on her own buttons now. "You think I could have a little help here?"

"Anything at all I can do," Stone said, feeling for her buttons, zippers, and snaps. "I certainly don't want you to feel neglected."

"I feel neglected," she said. "Make it better."

Stone did what he could.

16

Stone felt a gentle kiss near his ear. He turned toward Holly and, for his trouble, received a much bigger, wetter kiss, full on the mouth. It was accompanied by more tongue than he was accustomed to.

He opened his eyes to find Daisy's head between his and Holly's. This was made possible because he and Holly were lying crossways on his bed. He gave Daisy a scratch behind the ears and pushed her head gently away.

Holly turned toward him and opened her eyes. "Wow," she said.

"Wow, indeed."

"Why don't we have any covers?" she asked.

"I don't know," Stone replied. "Why are we sideways in the bed?"

"I think we boxed the compass," she replied.

Daisy made a tiny grunting noise.

"Uh-oh," Holly said, "I think I forgot something last night." She sat up. "I'm coming, Daisy." She looked down at Stone's naked body. "Although there are things I'd rather do." She hopped out of bed.

When Stone woke up again she was sitting on the edge of the bed in his terry robe, toweling her hair dry.

"Good morning," she said.

"I must have dozed off."

"Why? You couldn't possibly be tired; it's after nine. We must have gotten, oh, two or three hours of sleep."

Stone rolled over on his stomach and put his head in her lap. "Scratch my back," he said. "That's all I have energy for."

She began scratching his back. "You have sheet marks on your back. That's what comes from sleeping on wrinkled sheets."

"It's the price you have to pay," Stone muttered, burrowing his head farther into her lap.

"Now *that's* a nice place for your head," she said.

He pulled the robe back and burrowed into her, feeling with his tongue.

"Nicer still." She lay back on the bed and turned toward him, giving him more access, then she took him in her mouth. They both were becoming excited now. Two minutes later, they shared an orgasm.

"I didn't know I had that left in me," Stone said.

"I'm glad you did. Want to do it again?"

"You want me to die right here and now?"

"Poor baby. You take a nap."

Stone woke from his nap to find a tray next to his head bearing a sandwich and a glass of iced tea.

"See what you get when you're nice?" Holly asked.

Stone struggled into a sitting position and found the remote control for the bed, raising it to support his back. "What about you?" he said.

"I had lunch in the kitchen, so as not to disturb you. Daisy and I have already been for another, longer walk, too."

"Such energy!" he said, biting into the sandwich.

"Such a long time since I watched a naked man eat a sandwich," she replied, smiling at him.

"So what's your plan for the day?"

"I don't suppose it would do any good to keep watch at the La Boheme again," she said. "I must have scared Trini out of Little Italy by now. You think Lance knows more than he's telling about Trini?"

"I think Lance always knows more than he's telling. He surprised me last night, with this consultant thing."

"I think I might do it," she said, arranging herself next to him. "This is a very nice bed. Does it vibrate?"

"Yep."

"I'm getting tired of my job," she said.

"Which job? Me?"

"No, my chief's job in Orchid Beach."

"I thought you loved it."

"I did for a long time, but it's becoming more and more routine. I mean, I've improved the department, trained people better and all that, but it's not as though I have to do it for a living."

"That's right, you're retired army; you have a pension."

"Yes, and Jackson left me very nicely fixed, too."

"That was very nice of Jackson. Why don't you travel, see some of the world?"

"I'm an army brat," she said. "I've seen the world twice."

"What do you want to do, then?"

She shrugged. "I don't know. I'm enjoying myself in New York, but I'm not sure I'd want to live here."

"New York is a better place to live than to visit," Stone said.

"If you say so."

"You've hardly started to see it. We haven't eaten anywhere except Elaine's."

"Do you ever eat anywhere but Elaine's?"

"On occasion," Stone said dryly. "Why don't I take you somewhere else tonight?"

"I'm yours."

After lunch Stone showered and went down to his office.

"Good afternoon," Joan said pointedly.

"Don't start. I'm still tired."

"I won't ask why."

"I just didn't get much sleep, that's all."

"I won't ask why."

"Anything happening?"

She handed him a large brown envelope. "This was hand-delivered half an hour ago."

Stone took the envelope to his desk and opened it. Inside were two contracts, for Holly and himself. Lance hadn't wasted much time. The employer was listed as the Woodsmoke Corporation; its address was in the Seagram building. He read Holly's first.

It was surprisingly brief and straightforward. It guaranteed her a thousand dollars a day, or any part of a day, and deluxe travel, should she need to.

His was much the same, but he crossed out the daily fee and inserted the words "his usual hourly or daily rate." That should keep Lance from calling on him too often.

He called Holly, and she came downstairs. "Lance has been busy," he said, handing her the contract. "This seems all right to me. If you want to sign it, I'll messenger it back to Lance."

She read it and signed it. "By the way," she said, "could you please stop being jealous of Lance?"

Stone looked shocked. "Me, jealous? Of Lance?"

"There were a couple of times last night when I thought you were going to slug him."

Stone blushed a little. "I'm sorry if I seemed that way. I'll work on it."

"I should think that, after last night, you wouldn't have anything to feel jealous about."

Stone got up and closed the door.

"What, on the desk?" Holly asked. "There's a bed upstairs, as I recall."

"I just don't want Joan to overhear this. She's giving me a hard enough time already."

"Oh, I was looking forward to doing it on the desk."

"I'm already a shell of my former self," Stone said, sitting down.

"Yeah, sure," she said. "You've got a lot more mileage left in you."

"If I have a month to rest."

She got up and opened the door. "You've got until after dinner," she said, then she went back upstairs.

Stone hoped he could recover in time. He gave the signed contracts to Joan and told her to copy and return them to Lance.

17

Stone took Holly to the Four Seasons, because it was the most elegant New York
restaurant he could think of, and because it
was within walking distance.

Holly had spent the afternoon shopping
and had come home with bags from Armani
and Ralph Lauren, the result of which was a
black Armani dress that made Stone forget
he had had too much sex the night before.
They settled into a good table in the Pool
Room.

"What would you like to drink?" Stone
asked.

"A vodka gimlet, three-to-one, straight
up, shaken so cold the bartender's fingers
stick to the shaker."

"Two," Stone said to the waiter.

"Would you like a particular kind of vodka?" the waiter asked.

"Anything will do," she replied. When the waiter had gone she said, "Vodka is nothing but grain alcohol that has been cut in half with water. I don't know what the big deal is about brands. It's not as if it's eighteen-year-old Scotch."

"I agree," Stone said. "Do you always give such explicit directions when you order a drink?"

"Just with vodka gimlets," she replied. "Bartenders never measure, and they always put too much vodka in them."

"You're a control freak, aren't you?"

"Just with vodka gimlets."

"The dress is . . . You make that dress look gorgeous."

"Well put, and just in time. I thought you were going to tell me the dress makes me look gorgeous."

"Certainly not," said Stone, who had been about to do just that. "You don't look like a cop at all this evening."

"Even higher praise! You know, there just isn't any way to look feminine in a police uniform, unless you're wearing shorts."

"You wear shorts?"

"We're in Florida, remember? Actually, I don't, but I encourage some of my female officers to."

"Which female officers?"

"The ones who look good in shorts. It encourages tourism."

Their drinks arrived, and they sipped them appreciatively.

"Now *that's* a vodka gimlet," Holly said. "You can tell if it's right by the color. It should have a pretty, green tinge."

"And it does."

"Stone, I need your advice about something."

"Shoot."

"This is legal advice and must remain confidential."

"Shoot."

"I have five million seven hundred and sixty thousand dollars I don't know what to do with."

"Buy a jet airplane."

"I don't think so."

"You want me to introduce you to my broker?"

"No."

"What do you *want* to do with the money?"

"I haven't the faintest idea."

"You could give it to your favorite charity."

"That would involve a paper trail."

"Uh-oh," he said.

"What's the matter?"

"This is illegal, isn't it?"

"That's what I wanted to ask you about."

"Okay, where'd you get the money?"

"Well, last year I was investigating this thing where the proceeds of various crimes were being put into a vault back home. I was watching some of these guys unloading a van filled with suitcases and boxes. And, wanting to know what was in them, I snatched one of them, a large briefcase, which turned out to be filled with five million seven hundred and sixty thousand dollars."

"And where is the money now?"

"In a tree."

"What do you mean?"

"I mean, I climbed a tree and wedged the briefcase into the branches."

"This is in Florida?"

"Yes."

"They have hurricanes in Florida. What if there's a hurricane?"

"Then there will be hundred-dollar bills all

over Indian River County, and my problem will be solved."

"All right, let's go to basics: This is illegal; you've committed a crime."

"I figured."

"Why did you do this?"

"Well, I took the briefcase to find out if they were transporting cash, so I could hardly hand it back to them. I hid it, and I didn't even think about it until a couple of weeks after we had arrested the whole bunch."

"Why didn't you give it back then?"

"Give it back to whom? The criminals? They were all in jail."

"Did you tell anybody about this?"

"Yes. I told Grant Harrison, my FBI friend. Well, former friend. This was before he became such a bureaucratic ass."

"And he didn't arrest you?"

"I told you, we were, ah, friendly at the time."

"How friendly?"

"Very friendly."

"And he didn't do anything about this?"

"About the money? No."

"Well, that makes him an accessory."

"Funny, that's what I told him the last time he mentioned it to me."

"What did he say?"

"He didn't say anything. In fact, he stopped talking altogether for quite a while."

"Why don't you just give it to the FBI?"

"I suggested that to Grant, but he turned pale. He wanted to know how I could explain the long delay in turning it in. I told him *we* would have to explain."

"And what was his reaction?"

"He told me to shut up and never mention it to him again."

"Were there any witnesses to this conversation?"

"No, we were in bed at the time."

"Then I guess you weren't wearing a wire."

"Good guess."

"I don't think I've ever run into a problem quite like this," Stone said.

"Me, either."

"I suppose you've thought about spending it."

"Well, yes, but I have everything I need, and I can afford a lot more, so what would I do with it?"

"You could put a big ribbon on it, leave it on the doorstep of your favorite orphanage, ring the bell, and run like hell."

"I've thought of that, but I'm sure somebody would see me, and I'd get caught. Anyway, I don't have a favorite orphanage."

"You could just leave it in the tree until some lucky lumberjack chops it down and finds the money."

"I'd worry about it. I'm tired of worrying about it."

"How about this: You give the money to your lawyer . . ."

"Yeah, sure."

"Wait a minute, I'm not finished. Then your lawyer calls the local chief of police and says he has a client who has come upon some money that he suspects is illegal, and the client wants to turn it in, if he can do so anonymously."

"*I'm* the local chief of police. Aren't we talking about a conspiracy?"

"A conspiracy to do the right thing?"

"I think you're beginning to see the size of my problem."

"Yes, I am."

"Stone, you have an airplane, right?"

"Yes."

"There's an airstrip on the property. Why don't you and I fly down there tonight, get the money, and bring it back up here. I'll split it with you, fifty-fifty."

Stone held up his hands as if to ward her off. "Oh, no, you're not sucking me into this. Anyway, I've had a vodka gimlet. I can't legally fly for eight hours. By the time we got down there it would be broad daylight."

"So, we'll do it tomorrow night."

"Holly, I need some time to think about this."

"I'll bet you know how to get this into an offshore account, don't you?"

"Sure, that's easy. We just fly my airplane down to the Cayman Islands, find a bank, deposit it, and fly back. Customs doesn't search you on the way out."

"I like the sound of that," Holly said.

"Of course, we'd have to sign a form saying that we haven't taken more than five thousand dollars in cash or negotiable instruments out of the country. If we lied about it, that would be a felony."

"It seems like such a little felony, doesn't it?"

"That's it. I'm not having any more to drink."

"So you can fly?"

"So I'll stop thinking like this. You're making me crazy."

She leered at him. "It's about time."

Later, in bed, they forgot about the money.

18

Stone was at his desk the following morning when Joan buzzed him.

"Yes?"

"Lance Cabot is here to see you."

"Send him in."

Lance came into Stone's office carrying an envelope. "Good morning," he said, his usual affable self.

"Good morning, Lance. What can I do for you?"

"I wanted to talk to you about your contract."

"All right."

"Holly's is fine. I've sent it on to Langley, where it will be countersigned, dated, and a copy returned to her. Your contract, however, has a problem: I can't include words like 'his usual hourly or daily rate.' We must be specific."

"All right, five hundred dollars an hour."

"I think it would be to your advantage if we kept it at a daily rate, like Holly's contract."

"All right, four thousand dollars a day."

"I was thinking two thousand."

"Thirty-five hundred."

"Three."

"Done."

Lance removed the contract from the envelope. "Do you think your secretary could retype this page?"

"Of course." He buzzed for Joan.

Lance made the changes and handed the page to Joan, who disappeared.

"So, we have a deal?" Lance said.

"Yes, we do."

"Good. I'd like you to go to London today."

Stone managed not to look amazed. "Today?"

"Yes."

"What for?"

"That will be explained to you when you arrive at the Connaught, which is where we're putting you up."

"How long will I be gone?"

"One, possibly two nights."

"I'm afraid that won't be possible."

"Why not?"

"I have a houseguest."

Lance sighed. "Holly can't go with you."

"It's only a Concorde ticket."

"Not even if you pay for it yourself, and I was thinking business class."

"My contract calls for deluxe travel."

"Oh, all right." Lance raised his hands in surrender.

"When and how will my expenses be paid?"

"Our travel agent will make your travel arrangements. You can bill us for anything other than your plane tickets, hotel, and airport transfers. My people will send you an expense form. It's a pain in the ass, but your secretary can do it."

"Do what?" Joan asked, entering the room. She handed a sheet of paper to Lance.

"My expenses," Stone said.

"What expenses?"

"From my London trip."

"What London trip?"

"The one that starts today."

"Is this for the Woodsmoke Corporation?"

Lance spoke up. "Exactly."

"What, exactly, is the Woodsmoke Corporation?"

"Thanks, Joan," Lance said. "That'll be all for the moment." Lance spread the contract on Stone's desk, and they both signed it.

"There," Lance said. "All done. I'll have your tickets and hotel confirmation sent over in an hour or so. You'd better start packing." He turned to go.

"Wait a minute. What am I supposed to do when I get there?"

"Get a good night's sleep, if that's possible, then expect a phone call in the morning. Somebody will mention Woodsmoke. Have a good trip." Lance walked out.

Stone went upstairs and found Holly. "I'm afraid I'm going to have to disappear for a couple of days," he said.

"Why?"

"I have to go to London."

"What for?"

"I don't know."

"Sounds like Lance."

"It is. You'll have a signed copy of your contract soon, he says."

"Why don't I go with you?"

"I asked. He says no, and it's his party."

"Party?"

"So to speak. Make yourself at home in the house."

"Can I sleep in your bed?"

"By all means. I'd like to think of you sleeping in my bed."

"And in London, whose bed will you be sleeping in?" she asked archly.

"The Connaught Hotel's bed. I don't believe they supply sleeping partners."

"Good. You won't tell me what you're going to be doing there?"

"I told you, I don't know what I'm going to be doing there, and I may not be able to tell you, even after I find out."

"I love all this cloak-and-dagger stuff," she said.

"No, you don't. You'd rather know what's happening."

"Well, that's true, I guess."

"I have to pack," he said, going to his closet and taking down a carry-on suitcase.

"Can I watch?"

"Watch?"

"I want to see what you take."

"Whatever turns you on." He packed three changes of underwear, socks, and shirts, a couple of nightshirts, and folded a suit on top of it.

"No toiletries?"

Stone took down a small duffel from a shelf. "Already packed."

"That was pretty simple."

"I can go just about anywhere with a blazer and a blue suit."

"What if you get a black-tie invitation?"

"If I think that might happen, I'll take a dinner jacket, but that's for a longer trip. Worse comes to worst, I can wear a black bow tie with the blue suit, or I can rent."

"What are you taking for shoes?"

"A pair of black alligator loafers. They'll work with anything."

"Everything is so simple for men."

"Yeah? Try shaving every day."

"Stubble is in."

"Along with bad haircuts and three-button suits, which are as ridiculous as stubble and bad haircuts."

"Why?"

"They're boxy and unflattering."

"Have a good trip. Daisy and I are off to

the park. Call me when you get there, just to let me know you're still alive."

"If I don't call, I'm dead."

"You'd better be." She kissed him good-bye and left with Daisy.

19

As Concorde began its takeoff roll, Stone started to think about Carpenter, whose real name was Felicity Devonshire. They had parted on not very good terms a few months before, and he wasn't sure if she'd want to see him. Come to that, he wasn't sure he wanted to see her.

He took a nap and woke up as a flight attendant announced their descent into Heathrow. He made short work of Immigration, and he had no checked luggage. He walked through customs without being stopped and began looking for his name among the drivers gathered outside customs, waving cards with their passengers' names on them. His was not among them. So much for deluxe travel.

A man wearing a dark suit stepped up to him. "Mr. Barrington?"

"Yes."

The man relieved him of his case. "Please follow me." His accent was American.

Stone followed the man outside, where a black Mercedes waited at the curb, a driver at the wheel. Stone got into the back, while the man stowed his luggage in the trunk, then got into the front seat beside the driver. The car moved swiftly away.

"I had expected an American car," Stone said.

"Too much of a tip-off to the opposition," the man said. "The Mercedes is more anonymous in London."

"What opposition?"

"Whoever."

"Any news on what I'm doing here?"

"Somebody will call you in the morning. I'm told you may be finished in time for an afternoon flight tomorrow. If so, we'll pick you up at the Connaught."

Nothing was said for the remainder of the drive into London.

Stone checked into the Connaught and was given a handsome suite on the top floor. He booked a dinner table downstairs, had a nap, showered and changed, and went down to dinner.

Something was wrong. He looked around the handsome, paneled room as he was shown to his table. The big chandelier was gone; there was an odd, contemporary carpet on the floor; there were strange new sconces on the walls; the waiters were not dressed in their usual tailcoats; Mr. Chevalier, the restaurant manager, was nowhere to be seen; the elaborate menu had been replaced by a much shorter one.

"Where is Mr. Chevalier?" he asked the captain.

"He has left the Connaught. I understand he's at Harry's Bar now."

"What about the chef?"

"Gone, too. We have a new chef."

Stone's dinner was good but different. It wasn't the Connaught dining room anymore. He felt as if he'd lost an old friend.

Stone was wakened at 7:00 A.M. by the telephone.

"Hello?"

"It's Carpenter."

"Hello. How'd you know I was here?"

"Well, it certainly wasn't because you called me, was it? You needn't have spent the evening alone."

Stone didn't know what to say.

"A car will pick you up at eight-thirty this morning," she said. "Please be out front. And think carefully before you speak."

"Speak about what?" But she had hung up.

Stone had a full English breakfast, then dressed and went downstairs at the appointed hour. The doorman opened the door to an anonymous black sedan, a Ford, Stone thought, and he got inside.

"Good morning, Mr. Barrington," one of the two men in the front seat said. His accent was Cockney.

"Good morning. Where are we going?"

"We have a twelve- or fifteen-minute drive, depending on traffic," the man said.

"But where?"

"Please make yourself comfortable."

Stone looked out the window as the car drove down to Berkeley Square, up Conduit Street to Regent Street, down to Piccadilly Circus, then Shaftsbury Avenue to Cambridge Circus. They turned off into a side street, then into an alley, and the car stopped.

The man got out, looked carefully up and down the alley, then opened Stone's door. "Just here, Mr. Barrington," he said, indicating an unmarked door.

Stone got out, and the door was opened for him just before he reached it.

"Please follow me," a young man in a pin-striped suit said. His accent was upper-class. Stone followed the young man to an elevator with unmarked buttons, and they rode up a few stories and got out. He was shown into a small room containing a leather sofa and some chairs.

"Please be seated, Mr. Barrington. You'll be called in a few minutes."

"Called for what and by whom?" Stone asked, but the door had already been closed. He felt as if he were in the waiting room of a psychiatrist's office.

Stone rummaged through a stack of old *Country Life* magazines and chose the most recent, which was more than a year old. He sat down and leafed through it, reading about country houses for sale in Kent and the Cotswolds. Perhaps twenty minutes passed and then a door at one side of the room opened.

A middle-aged man in a good suit stood in the doorway, holding a file folder under one arm. The shrink? "Mr. Barrington, will you come in, please?" He stood back to let Stone pass.

Stone walked into a conference room. Four men, ranging in age from their early fifties to their early seventies, sat at the opposite end of a table that seated twelve. A chair was pulled out at Stone's end, and he sat down.

"Good morning," said a gray-haired man seated down the table from Stone.

"Good morning," Stone said. He had the feeling that either he was present for a job interview or he had done something terribly wrong and was being called to account. Then the man who had shown him into the room handed him a Bible and a sheet of cardboard.

"Please take the Bible and read aloud from the card," he said.

Stone took the Bible and read, "I swear by Almighty God that the evidence I am about to give in this proceeding is the truth."

The man took back the Bible and the card.

Was this a court? A grand jury? He noticed for the first time that a woman sat in a corner before a stenographic machine.

The man at the other end of the table answered Stone's unasked questions. "This is an inquiry," he said, "into the events which occurred at the Waldorf Astoria Hotel in New York City earlier this year in your presence, Mr. Barrington. Also present were a Lieutenant Dino Bacchetti and a person you know as Carpenter. Do you recall the occasion?"

"Yes," Stone said, "I believe so."

"The three of you were in pursuit of a young woman named Marie-Thérèse du Bois?"

"Yes, we were."

"We have heard testimony that Mademoiselle du Bois took refuge in a hotel room."

"That is correct."

"Please tell us what transpired after you and Lieutenant Bacchetti and Carpenter arrived at the room."

"*Think carefully before you speak,*" Carpenter had said.

Stone took a breath; he would keep his account to a minimum. "Marie-Thérèse du Bois emerged from the room, riding on the back of a large man, using him as cover."

"Was she armed?"

"Yes, she was pointing a semiautomatic pistol at the man's head."

"Were the three of you armed?" the man asked.

"Yes."

"What happened next?"

"The large man surprised us by slamming Mademoiselle du Bois against a wall, stunning her."

"Go on."

"She raised her pistol as if to fire at us, but Carpenter fired first." This statement obscured the truth somewhat.

"Did Mademoiselle du Bois fire her weapon?"

"No, there was something wrong with it, I think."

"Do you know what?"

"I suppose it jammed or misfired."

"We have heard testimony that her weapon contained no ammunition. Do you know if that was the case?"

"I did not examine her weapon," Stone said, avoiding a direct answer.

"Mr. Barrington, did you feel that your life was in danger during these events?"

"Yes," Stone said.

"How many times did Carpenter fire?"

"Twice, I believe. I'm not entirely sure."

"Did Lieutenant Bacchetti fire?"

"No."

"Did you fire?"

"No."

"If you felt your life was in danger, why did you not fire your weapon?"

"Carpenter was quicker than we were, and it was obvious that further firing was unnecessary. Mademoiselle du Bois had been shot in the head."

"Do you feel that Carpenter was justified in shooting Mademoiselle du Bois?" the man asked.

Stone hesitated only a moment. "Yes," he lied.

"Have you anything to add to this statement?" the man asked.

Stone looked down at the table for a moment, then at the man again. "No," he said.

"Thank you, Mr. Barrington," the man

said, "that will be all. We are grateful for your testimony."

Before Stone knew it, he was back in the alley, in the car. Fifteen minutes later, he was back at the Connaught. As he walked into the room, the phone was ringing. He picked it up.

"Hello?"

"Thank you," Carpenter said.

"Did you get the job?"

"I've been acting in the job since returning to London," she said. "This morning's proceeding was part of an investigation to determine whether I shall keep it."

"I lied," Stone said. "You didn't have to kill her."

"Yes, I did," Carpenter replied. "But thank you. I hope I'll see you again before long."

"Good luck."

"Thank you. Goodbye." She hung up.

Stone was back at home in Turtle Bay by late afternoon, New York time.

Holly greeted him warmly. "That was quick," she said. "What was it about?"

"I have a feeling I'm not supposed to tell

you," he said. "You want to go to Elaine's for dinner?"

"Dino called and suggested we meet there; so did Lance. I said yes to both of them."

20

Lance's Cadillac with the diplomatic plates was double-parked outside Elaine's, and the man with the briefcase with a hole in it was back in his old spot by the awning. Lance got out of the car almost as soon as Stone and Holly got out of the cab. They all shook hands, and, as they entered the restaurant, Lance whispered something to Holly.

Before they could sit down at their table, Holly said, "Excuse me, I have to go to the powder room."

Stone and Lance sat down. "Did you send her to the powder room?" Stone asked.

"Yes. How'd it go in London this morning?"

"You mean you don't already know?"

"I'd like to hear it from you."

"I lied for her. You knew I would, didn't you?"

"You might recall that not only did I not ask you to lie, I didn't even tell you why you were going. Should anyone in an official position ever inquire about the hearing, you might remember to mention that."

"Is anyone in an official position likely to inquire?"

"In the words of the immortal Fats Waller, 'One never knows, do one?'"

"Will she get the job?"

"There will have to be a cabinet meeting on the subject, but I'm reliably informed that she is being favorably considered. Your testimony this morning was the final piece of evidence taken. She will be the first woman to hold the job, but her credentials are as top-notch as those of any man they could have considered, including the fact that both her father and grandfather were in the service, going back to the Second World War."

"She mentioned that once."

"The father mostly fought his battles with the IRA. It was the grandfather who was the swashbuckler. Did she tell you about him?"

"Not much."

"He spent half his childhood in France—his father was a diplomat assigned to the Paris embassy—so he had the language. He was parachuted in not long after France fell, with instructions to organize and arm resistance units. He was captured twice by the Gestapo, with all that that entailed, and escaped twice. On both occasions he killed several of his captors with his hands. On D-Day, units he organized blew up roads and railways that the Germans could have used to bring in reinforcements and armor. I met him once; he was the perfect English gentleman: erudite, courteous to a fault, and, it was said, the most cold-blooded killer anybody could remember from the war."

"I guess that's where Carpenter gets it," Stone said.

"She won't be Carpenter anymore; she'll be Architect, if all goes well, and it should. I'd like you to make it your business to keep in as close touch with her as you can manage. Consider it an assignment."

"At my contract daily rate?"

"I won't be charged for phone calls; you're not being used as a lawyer. But I'll consider dinner with her a day's work. Anything beyond that you can think of as a bonus."

Holly came back from the ladies' room. "Was I gone long enough?" she asked Lance.

"Quite," Lance said, offering her a wide grin. "Stone has been debriefed."

"So happy to have been of service," she said. "By the way, when will I actually be of service?"

"Be patient," Lance said. "Your time will come."

"Is patience the most important attribute of an agent?" Holly asked.

"No. Suspicion is. One must doubt everybody."

"That sounds like a corrosive way to live."

"If you say so."

They were ordering drinks when Dino arrived, looking tired. He sat down and loosened his tie. "A double Johnnie Walker Black," he said to the waiter.

"What's happened?" Stone asked.

"A cop got killed today, in Little Italy."

Holly spoke up. "Not at the La Boheme coffeehouse, I hope?"

"No, but not far away."

"Somebody undercover?" Stone asked.

"Nope, a beat patrolman. He'd parked his squad car and was ordering coffee at a deli, when somebody walked in and put one in the back of his head. An assassination, pure and simple."

"Of a beat cop?" Stone asked. "That doesn't sound right."

"No, it doesn't. We're looking at, maybe, a gang initiation, or maybe just somebody who hates cops."

"How are you involved with something so far downtown?" Stone asked.

"I'm not, really. I was at a meeting with the chief of detectives when the call came in, so we both went to the scene. I loaned them a couple of detectives. How was London?"

"Quick. In and out."

"Did you see Carpenter?"

"I spoke to her, briefly."

"What were you doing there?"

"You'll have to ask Lance."

Dino looked at Lance.

"None of your business," Lance said. "Why don't we order dinner?"

Holly spoke up. "Did you get a description of the shooter?"

"White male, six feet, maybe more; well built. Black ponytail."

"It's Trini Rodriguez," she said.

"Why the hell would your perp kill a New York City cop?" Dino asked.

"For the fun of it," she replied.

"Excuse me." Dino got up and walked away, his cell phone clamped to his ear.

Stone looked at Holly. "Your chances of nailing Trini have just gone up," he said.

"No," she replied, "Dino's chances have. I'll never take him home now."

21

Stone was having breakfast the following morning when Holly and Daisy returned from the park.

"I had a call on my cell phone this morning," she said. "My FBI ex-friend, Grant Harrison, is in town, and he wants to see me; says it's business."

"So, see him," Stone said. "You want to ask him over here?"

"I said I'd meet him for lunch, but I didn't know a good place."

"Tell him La Goulue, Madison at Sixty-fifth. I'll book a table for you."

"Will you come along?"

"Why?"

"I don't know, I'm just not comfortable with this. He's less likely to shout at me if you're along."

"Oh, all right."

Grant Early Harrison was standing in front of La Goulue when their cab stopped.

"That's him," Holly said, pointing.

He was better-looking than Stone had imagined.

They got out of the cab and approached him.

"Hello, Grant," Holly said, "this is my friend Stone Barrington."

Grant managed a perfunctory handshake. "I thought I was seeing you alone."

"Why did you think that?" Holly asked. "Anyway, anything you have to say, you can say in front of Stone. He's also my lawyer."

Grant cut Stone a sharp glance. "Do you need a lawyer?"

"Oh, no, nothing like that," Holly said.

Stone kept a straight face. "Shall we go in?"

They were greeted by Suzanne, and Stone gave her a kiss. "Something in the back, I think," he said.

"Right this way." She led them to a table.

"Does this place get crowded?" Grant asked.

"It'll be jammed in fifteen minutes," Stone replied.

They ordered a glass of wine and looked at menus. When they had ordered lunch, Grant started in. "I got a call from our New York office last night," he said. "The NYPD is all over them about Trini Rodriguez. What did you have to do with that?"

"Last night, Trini apparently shot a New York City cop, in a deli in Little Italy," she said. "I had nothing at all to do with that."

"Why do they think it was Trini?" Grant asked.

"Oh, I had something to do with *that*. The perp's description matched Trini's, and I mentioned that to an NYPD detective."

"Great, thanks a lot."

"What, you wanted nobody to bother Trini? Gee, I'm awfully sorry about that."

"He's working something very important to us."

"So, he killed a cop on his coffee break?"

"You don't know it was Trini."

"You don't know it wasn't."

"He denies it."

"So you've talked? What did you expect him to say?"

Grant turned to Stone. "How do you come into this?"

"Holly is staying at my house," Stone said, "and I sometimes give her legal advice. Otherwise, I'm not in it."

"Then that's where you should stay," Grant said, "not in it."

"Leave Stone out of this, Grant," Holly said.

"That's what I'm hoping to do."

"Tell me, exactly why is the FBI so interested in keeping a cop killer on the streets?"

"I can't tell you that," Grant said.

"Is what he's doing more important than the lives of cops on the street?"

"Of course not."

"Then why haven't you turned him in to the NYPD?"

"We only need another day or two to wrap up this whole thing, then they can have him, as far as I'm concerned."

"You'd better hope to God the newspapers don't get wind of this," Holly said.

"Oh? Are you going to tell them?"

"I hadn't planned to, but . . ."

"That's what I thought. If you blow this case, Holly, I'll . . ."

"You'll what?"

"Hey, hey," Stone said. "Let's hold it down, all right? People are staring at us."

Grant threw his napkin on the table and stood up. "If you screw up this case, I'll have you for obstruction of justice, and I may throw in that money thing, too."

"Oh? What money thing is that?"

"Your five million dollars."

"What five million dollars?"

"Just remember what I said," Grant said, and stalked out of the restaurant.

Stone thought the other customers looked relieved. "Now why did you want to go and piss him off?" he asked.

"I enjoy pissing him off," Holly said.

A waiter brought three lunches and went away.

"Holly, speaking as your sometime lawyer, he has a point about interfering with a federal investigation."

"Oh, sure. You think he's going to arrest me and let it get out that the FBI has been harboring a cop killer?"

"Well, probably not."

"That was just a lot of bluster. Grant blusters a lot."

"Especially where you're concerned, I'll bet. And he knows about the money?"

"He's known about it almost from the day I put it in the tree."

"Does he know which tree?"

"He has no idea where it is. He can't even prove that it exists, and even if he could, he'd have a hard time explaining why he's known about it for months and didn't report it. Don't worry, Grant isn't going to cause any trouble for himself."

"Holly, I've been thinking about this, and I think you should leave the money in that tree."

"And wait for the putative lumberjack to discover it?"

"If somebody finds it, then you can confiscate it as the fruit of a crime."

"Anybody who found it would be a fool to tell anybody."

"And you'd be a fool to go back to the tree. Right now, you're clean. Only Grant knows about it, and, as you've pointed out, he's unlikely to mention it to his superiors. But if you go back to the tree and get it, there's always the chance that someone will see you do it or that something else might go wrong. You just can't take the chance."

"Okay, I've had your full views on this subject. Can we change it now, please?"

"Sure, what would you like to talk about?"

"How can I take Trini before the NYPD does?"

"Holly, you'd better forget about Trini. Let them take him, then you can get in line to prosecute him."

"Which means never."

"Lots of people could match that description, surely you know that."

"It's Trini. I know it in my bones."

"If it is, wouldn't you just as soon see him get the death penalty in New York as in Florida?"

"No, I wouldn't. I want to sit in a Florida prison and watch him take the needle."

"Dino can arrange for you to sit in a New York prison and watch. Wouldn't that do?"

"No. I want to arrest him."

"You want to kill him, don't you?"

"If he gave me an excuse, I would."

"Don't you realize that he'd have as good a chance of killing you, maybe better?"

"I'll take that chance."

"So you're going to pursue Trini with reckless abandon."

"Right up until the moment somebody takes him off the street, and I hope it's me." Holly set her empty plate aside and started eating Grant's lunch.

22

Stone was about to ask for a check when Lance strolled up to their table.

"Mind if I join you?" he asked, sliding into the banquette seat next to Holly.

"We've just finished lunch," Stone said.

"I won't keep you long. Let me buy you coffee." He was sitting too close to Holly for Stone's comfort.

A waiter appeared, and Lance looked at Holly.

"Decaf cappuccino," Holly said.

"Stone?"

"Double espresso, please. The real thing."

"Same for me," Lance said.

"How did you know we were here?" Holly asked.

"The CIA knows all," Stone said wryly.

"Oh, not all, perhaps," Lance said. "Truth said, one of my people followed Agent Harrison and called me."

"And why is the CIA following the FBI?" Stone asked.

"We have come to expect a certain . . . how shall I say? . . . lack of candor from our colleagues at the Bureau," Lance said.

"Even after nine/eleven?" Holly asked.

"They've become more candid about certain things since nine/eleven," Lance said, "and less candid about others."

"Why?" she asked.

"Because they're the Bureau," Lance said.

"Oh. I knew that."

"Frankly, in part because of this behavior, I don't expect them to survive as a discrete entity much longer."

"Oh, come on," Stone said. "Congress would never allow the Bureau to expire as an agency."

"Mark my words, Congress will insist on it," Lance replied. "They have become too devious for their own good. When senior officials start lying to congressional committees, the Bureau does not enhance its longevity."

Stone snorted. "Whereas Congress expects the Agency to tell the truth?"

Lance nodded gravely. "Certainly not. They simply expect a certain lack of frankness, given the work we do."

"So why are you here, Lance?" Stone asked. "Certainly not for the coffee."

Lance sipped the cup that had been set before him. "A plentiful reason for being here," he said, looking around. "I've always liked this place. It's like Paris without the French."

Holly laughed, but Stone restrained himself. "Come on, cough it up."

"I merely came to suggest that you watch the six o'clock news this evening."

"Why?"

"You don't want me to take all the fun out of it by telling you in advance, do you?"

"Yes," Stone replied. "Besides, wouldn't you enjoy watching the expressions on our faces?"

"Well, there is that," Lance said, smiling. "Oh, all right: On tonight's local news you'll learn that the killing of the policeman in Little Italy was the result of a random gunshot from the street, not an execution."

Stone and Holly gaped at him.

"You're right, Stone, the expression on your faces was worth it," Lance said.

"Tell me," Holly said, "how do you get a witness's description of the shooter from a random incident?"

"An excellent question," Lance said.

"So who is manipulating the media, and why?" Stone asked.

"An even better question. Look at it this way: Who benefits from the altered perception of the incident?"

"Trini Rodriguez," Holly said quickly.

"Of course, but not just Trini."

"I think I'm picking up the thread," Stone said.

"Enlighten us."

"If the cop was killed as a result of a stray bullet, then the NYPD is no longer investigating an execution, but an accident—manslaughter, not murder."

"Very good!"

"So what?" Holly said.

"Detectives loaned from other precincts will be sent home, and the investigation will become much less intense," Stone explained. "And that takes some of the pressure off Trini, at least for the moment."

"But why would the NYPD want to take pressure off a cop killer?" Holly asked.

"Not the NYPD," Lance offered. "The FBI."

"Excuse me," Holly said, "but this is way too sophisticated for my simple mind."

"You have an excellent mind, Holly," Lance said, "but not as devious as that of the collective guile of the Bureau."

"Holly," Stone said, "Grant has just told us that Trini's use to the Bureau is important for only another couple of days."

"Bingo!" Lance said.

"So they want Trini on the street long enough to complete whatever the FBI wants him to?"

"Bingo again!" Lance said. "And would you like to know what Trini is doing for the Bureau?"

"Yes, please," Holly replied.

"Now I must remind you that you two are, each in your way, arms of the Agency, and as such, you may not reveal to anyone what I am about to tell you."

Stone sighed.

"Specifically, you may not reveal it to Dino," Lance said.

"Why not?" Holly asked.

Stone spoke up. "Because Dino is NYPD, and he would be outraged to learn that the Bureau is messing with the investigation into a cop killing for its own purposes, and he might intervene."

"Exactly," Lance said. "Are we all in the tent now?"

Stone and Holly nodded.

"Well," Lance, said, looking around to make sure he was not being overheard in the crowded restaurant, "it seems that our Trini has somehow convinced the Bureau that there is a financial connection between his mob friends and a certain Middle Eastern terrorist fraternity, the name of which shall not escape my lips."

Stone shook his head. "The Mafia financing a terrorist organization? Not possible."

"Stone, you forget that the Mafia *is* a terrorist organization, in its small way, and that their sympathies become altered when there is money to be made."

"No, Lance, the mob is—in its small way, as you put it—a bunch of patriotic guys who are very grateful for the opportunities the United States has given them to become rich—stealing, extorting, and killing."

"You have a point, Stone. Perhaps it is

the case that the mob has been let in on the little secret—given an opportunity to do something patriotic."

"And what would that be?" Holly asked.

"The boys have a great many money-laundering connections that our Middle Eastern foes covet. Since the Treasury Department has cracked down on wire transfers to suspect locales, and since the National Security Agency has greatly in-creased their surveillance of Middle Eastern cell and satellite phones, not to mention penetration of their websites, it has become much more difficult for them to move money around the world. On the other hand, the increased scrutiny of terrorists has had the happy effect, for the mob, of di-verting attention from their own financial transactions."

"I suppose it makes a kind of weird sense," Stone said.

"Not to me," Holly replied.

"Look at it this way, Holly," Lance said. "Would you be willing to put your pursuit of Trini Rodriguez on hold for a couple of days, if the payoff were to destroy a terrorist money-management cell and confiscate a lot of their available cash?"

Holly looked into her cappuccino. "If I had to, I suppose."

"Voilà!" Lance exclaimed. "A patriot!"

"And what happens after this little operation is over?" Holly asked.

"Then," Lance said, "I might be able to help you achieve your objective."

"You swear?" Holly demanded.

"I swear to try," Lance said. "I'm afraid you'll have to be content with that."

"Oh, all right," Holly said.

23

Stone let them into the house and closed the door behind him. "Pack some things," he said. "Casual—jeans, et cetera, something you can wear to a good restaurant, but still casual."

"Where are we going?" Holly asked.

"Away for the weekend. Daisy will love it."

"That's good enough for me," Holly said.

Daisy looked pleased, too, when she heard the news.

Stone had previously backed the car into the garage. Now he pressed the remote, and by the time the door had opened, he had started the car and had it in gear. He pulled across the sidewalk gingerly, then turned toward Third Avenue, driving as quickly as he could and frequently checking the rearview mirror. A touch of the remote closed the door behind him.

"Why are we leaving town?" Holly asked.

"One, it's a weekend; New Yorkers leave town on weekends. Two, it's good for Daisy. Three, I need some country air. And four, to keep you out of trouble for the next couple of days."

"And why do you think I need to be kept out of trouble?"

"I know damned well that if we stay in the city this weekend, you'll be looking for Trini. You won't be able to help yourself."

"I said I wouldn't interfere for a couple of days. Why do you keep looking in the rearview mirror?"

"For safety reasons," Stone replied. "New Yorkers are very careful drivers."

"Not from what I've seen. Who do you think might be following us?"

"Maybe the two men who were watching the house."

"*What*?"

"There were two men in the block: one across the street, wearing a black leather jacket, and one a few buildings up, wearing blue coveralls, looking in a shop window."

"What's so odd about a man looking in a shop window?"

"It's a knitting and sewing shop," Stone explained.

"Maybe he knits?"

"Maybe he's FBI, if we're lucky. Maybe he's a friend of Trini, if we're not."

"How would Trini know where to find us?"

"You do recall chasing him all over Little Italy?"

"Yes."

"Maybe that annoyed him. Maybe a friend of his got the license plate number of my car when you were camped outside La Boheme."

"Oh."

Stone turned left on Sixty-fifth Street and, eventually, crossed Central Park. Daisy looked longingly at the trees and grass.

"Don't worry, baby," Holly cooed. "We're going to find you a place to play." She looked at Stone. "We are, aren't we?"

"Yes," Stone said. "Lots of grass and trees."

"How long a drive?"

"An hour and forty-five minutes, if we beat the worst of the traffic. If we don't, who knows?" He tapped a number into the car phone.

"Mayflower Inn," a woman's voice said.

"Hi, this is Stone Barrington. May I have a table for two at eight?"

"Of course, Mr. Barrington. We'll see you then."

"We're going to a country inn?" Holly asked.

"Only for dinner." He left the park, turned right on Central Park West, then left onto Seventy-second Street.

"Why won't you tell me where we're going?" Holly asked.

"What's the matter, don't you like surprises?"

"I like them if they're pleasant ones, and when they happen suddenly," Holly said. "But not when I have to ponder them for an hour and forty-five minutes."

"Daisy isn't worried."

"Yes, she is. She's just being polite."

"You be polite."

"All right, I'll shut up." She laid her head against the headrest.

Stone switched on the radio and pushed a button, tuning it to 96.3 FM. Classical music filled the car. "Mozart," he said.

"I know."

He turned onto the Henry Hudson Parkway, then reached under the dash and fiddled with something. A loud beeping ensued, accompanied by flashing red lights. Then everything was quiet.

"What was that?"

"That was my super-duper radar detector and laser diffuser."

She leaned over and looked at the speedometer as he changed lanes and accelerated. "I'd arrest you in Florida," she said.

"I'll get arrested in New York, if my detector doesn't work. Would that make you happy?"

"Very. I like to see justice done."

"Thanks."

"Don't mention it."

Soon they were taking the curves of the Saw Mill River Parkway.

"Aren't radar detectors illegal in New York State?" she asked.

"I'm not going to answer that without a lawyer present."

"There is a lawyer present."

"Oh, yeah. My lawyer just advised me not

to answer. Anyway, we're just passing through."

"You mean, we're going to another *state*?"

"Other states are not very far away, when you live in New York City."

"You ever heard of the Mann Act?"

He laughed. "You think I'm transporting you across a state line for immoral purposes?"

"I certainly hope so," she replied.

They turned onto an interstate, then, after a few minutes, another. Twenty minutes after that, they were driving along country roads with forest on both sides.

"We're in Connecticut," she said.

"You recognize the trees?"

"No, I was tipped off by the sign a few miles back that said, 'Welcome to Connecticut.'"

"No wonder you're such a good cop."

"I don't miss much," she said.

Holly dozed and woke up as they came to a stop sign. "Where are we?"

"Still in Connecticut; a town called Washington." He turned left, went up a steep hill, then turned left at a white church. "This is the village green," he said. A moment later, he turned into a drive and parked before a shingled cottage with a turret.

"Who lives here?" Holly asked.

"I do, when I can."

They got out of the car, and Daisy immediately bounded into some bushes. Stone got the bags out and unlocked the front door. "Welcome to Washington," he said.

"It's lovely," Holly replied, walking in and looking around. Daisy joined them and seemed to approve. "Who decorated it?"

"I sought various counsel," Stone said.

"You mean various women."

"Now I'm going to fix us a drink, then we'll take Daisy for a walk on the property next door."

"Will the owner mind?"

"He is not in residence. A writer used to live there, but he sold it to a producer, who never moved in. It's back on the market."

"How much?"

"You couldn't afford it."

"You forget: I have five million seven hundred and sixty thousand dollars stashed in a tree."

"That might do it, but then you couldn't afford the taxes. This place used to be the gatehouse, but the properties got separated fifty years ago. Bourbon?"

"Good."

He made her the drink and handed it to her. "Now I want you to take three deep breaths."

She did.

"Now drink your drink and stop thinking about what's in New York."

"Did those guys follow us?"

"I don't think so. My guess is, they didn't expect us to drive away."

"Neither did I," she said, sipping her bourbon.

24

Stone led Holly and Daisy through an opening in a hedge, and they emerged onto a broad lawn decorated with magnificent old trees before a large, comfortable-looking, American shingle-style house.

Daisy ran here and there, sniffing the ground and poking her nose into bushes.

"I could live here," Holly said.

"So could I, but I'll never be that rich."

"No hope at all?"

"I'm afraid not."

"Can we break a window and see the inside of the house?"

"You're suggesting breaking and entering? And you a law enforcement officer? As your attorney, I advise against it."

"Oh, all right."

Daisy had discovered the large swimming pool and was sniffing the surrounding bushes when a deer rocketed out of the brush and ran across the lawn, sending Daisy fleeing back to Holly.

"She's never seen a deer before," Holly laughed. "Don't worry, sweetie," she said, patting the dog, "I won't let the bad deer get you."

After half an hour's walk they left Daisy in the house with her dinner and drove to the Mayflower Inn.

"Don't you lock the door?" Holly asked.

"No need, it's a peaceable sort of place."

They drove past a pond and up a steep driveway, emerging from the trees to find a large, shingled building with broad porches on two sides.

"It's beautiful," Holly said. "It reminds me of the house we just saw—what was it called?"

"The Rocks. It belonged to an architect named Ehrick Rossiter, who designed twenty-seven houses and public buildings in this little village, twenty-two of which still stand. The Mayflower is one of them, and it's been gorgeously renovated."

Stone and Holly sat at a table overlooking the back lawn and garden, which were surrounded by old trees.

"So, is a country house a big part of living in New York?" Holly asked.

"A very big part of it. A lot of people have houses out on the eastern end of Long Island, in the Hamptons, but that's too expensive and too crowded for me. Washington is just perfect—nice village, maybe the most beautiful in Connecticut, lovely countryside, and interesting people."

"Nobody in Florida has a country house," Holly said. "I wonder why?"

"Not enough contrast between first and second houses."

"Maybe you're right."

They dined on salads, veal chops, and a bottle of California Cabernet. The waiter had just brought coffee when Holly suddenly sat up straight. "Something's wrong," she said.

"Didn't you like the food?"

"No, not that. Something's wrong back at the house."

"Are you telepathic?"

"No, but Daisy may be. We have to go."

Stone signed the bill, and they hurried

back to the car. "Does this sort of thing happen to you often?"

"No, never before, but it's a very strong feeling. Drive faster."

Stone did the best he could, and five minutes later they turned into his drive and got out of the car. The door to the cottage stood wide open. "I didn't leave the door open. Did you?"

"No. Where's Daisy?"

They arrived at the front door to find Daisy sitting in the front hall, staring at the door. She ran to Holly.

"Hey, baby," Holly cooed. "What's wrong?"

Stone reached down and picked up a piece of blue cloth dotted with blood. "Somebody's missing part of his pants," he said. "Is my Walther in your purse?"

She dug it out and handed it to him. "I don't think anybody could still be here, not with Daisy sitting calmly in the hall. Not unless our intruder is dead."

"He did some bleeding," Stone said, handing her the spattered piece of cloth. "I just want to be sure." He left her in the hall with Daisy, looked around, and came back, handing Holly the gun. "All clear."

"Who do you think belongs to this?" Holly asked, holding up the fabric.

"One of the men outside my house in New York was wearing blue coveralls," Stone said, fingering the cloth. "This is the same sort of utilitarian fabric."

"I don't like this," Holly said.

"Neither do I," Stone replied.

Later, in the middle of the night, Stone came awake. He had heard something downstairs. He eased himself out of bed, so as not to wake Holly, rummaged quietly in her handbag until he found the Walther, then tiptoed down the stairs and looked around the rooms. Nothing.

He went back to the entrance hall and bent over to pick up the scrap of blue cloth that Holly had apparently left there. As he did, something icy and wet made contact with his bare buttocks. Emitting an involuntary cry, he spun around to find Daisy standing there, looking at him as if he were crazy.

"You have a very cold nose," he said, rubbing her head.

"What's going on?" Holly asked from the stairs. She came down to join him, as naked as he in the moonlight filtering through the windows.

"I heard something down here," Stone said, "and I came to investigate."

"That would have been Daisy. She tends to patrol during the night."

"She has a cold nose," Stone said, rubbing his ass.

Holly laughed. "She certainly does, and she loves sticking it where it shouldn't be. Don't worry, there's no one in the house. Daisy would have let us know."

Stone looked her up and down. "You look very nice in the moonlight."

She placed a hand on his chest. "You look pretty good yourself," she said. "Daisy, guard."

Daisy went and sat by the door, and Holly took Stone by the hand and led him back upstairs. She took the gun from him and dropped it in her purse, then she went to the bed and pulled Stone on top of her. "As long as we're awake," she said, wrapping her long legs around him.

"Funny," he replied, "I'm not in the least sleepy."

She reached down and put him inside her. "I'm glad to hear it," she said, thrusting.

25

Stone woke to find Holly sprawled across his chest. Gently, he rolled her over until she was beside him, on her back.

"Am I awake?" Holly asked, her eyes still closed.

"Probably not."

"I think I am. You must be, too."

"I think we should go back to the city this morning," he said.

"Why?"

"I don't like the idea of somebody following us up here, especially since I don't know who or why."

"Neither do I, come to think of it."

"I'd feel better in the city. I'm not sure why."

"I'll trust your judgment."

Stone showered, got dressed, and

scrambled them some eggs, while Holly took Daisy for her morning walk around the Rocks, next door.

When they had finished breakfast, they put their things and Daisy into the Mercedes and drove away from the house.

"Why are you driving so fast?" Holly asked.

"Because I like driving fast; because for once, nobody is in front of me on these roads; and because if these people are still keeping tabs on us, I don't want to make it easy for them."

"All good reasons," she said. "Anyway, you drive well, and I don't see how anyone could drive this car slowly. Do you ever get tickets?"

"Not as long as I carry a badge," Stone replied.

"You do? Let me see it."

Stone reached into an inside pocket and fished out the wallet that held his ID card and badge. "It's not the real thing," he said, handing it to her. "It's something like a seven-eighths reproduction. Most retirees carry one."

"It says 'retired' down at the bottom of

your ID card," she said, "but in very small letters."

"You learn to cover that with a finger, when you're flashing it," Stone said.

"Does this allow you to carry a weapon?"

"No, but the department gives you a carry license when you retire. It's in the wallet, behind the ID, along with a Connecticut carry license."

Holly looked at them. "Do you carry a lot?"

"Not a lot, just when I feel nervous about the situation."

"I can't imagine you being nervous."

"All right, wary."

"Wary is more like you."

They turned onto the interstate just north of Danbury, and Stone caught sight of a black SUV a quarter of a mile behind them. "There they are," he said.

Holly didn't look back. "What are they driving?"

"Black SUV, probably an Explorer."

"That sounds like government, not something Trini's friends would drive."

"You could be right. After all, your boyfriend is pissed off; he could be keeping tabs."

"He's probably jealous," she said, putting her hand on his thigh.

"Good."

"You enjoy annoying the Feds?"

"Always."

"What do you have against them?" she asked.

"I find them untrustworthy. When I had to work with them as a cop, they always wanted the collar and the press, and they usually got it. They were lousy at sharing information, and you couldn't trust it when they did."

"That pretty much sums up my experience, too," she said. "Why do you suppose they're that way?"

"It's the federal culture, I think. They think they're the pinnacle of law enforcement, and they tend to look down on anybody at the local level as backward children."

She laughed.

"I don't find them all that good at solving crimes, either."

"Stone, you're driving nearly a hundred miles an hour."

"It's Sunday morning, and the traffic is light."

"Doesn't this car attract cops like flies?"

"If they're around, and if they feel like a pursuit."

"Is the Explorer keeping pace?"

Stone glanced in his mirror. "So far." He turned off I-84 and accelerated through a long curve and onto I-684. "There's a place a few miles down the road where the New York State cops like to lie in wait with their radar gun." He accelerated some more.

"You just passed a hundred and twenty," she said.

"Don't worry. Our speed is electronically limited to a hundred and fifty-five."

"Oh, good," she said. "I feel better now."

A beep sounded and a tiny red light on the steering column began to flash.

"Radar detector?"

"Yep."

"Why aren't you slowing down?"

"I want to try something." He pointed ahead. "There they are."

A state police vehicle was parked in the meridian, a radar gun hanging out a window.

Stone took out his wallet, rolled down the window a bit, and held his badge in the slipstream, creating wind noise. They flew past the police car, and Stone rolled up the window and checked his mirror. "They're not budging," he said. "Not yet, anyway. Hang on, there go the cops."

Holly looked back. "They're after the Explorer," she said.

"I guess they're not flashing a badge," he said, checking the mirror again. "Yep, light's on, they've got him." He accelerated again.

"A hundred and forty," she said. "Do you always drive this fast on the interstate?"

"Well, we know the cops are all involved with the Explorer," he said, "so unless they radio ahead for a trap, we're home free. Something else: If the guys in the Explorer are Feds, they'll call ahead for somebody to pick up the tail at the other end. The goombahs wouldn't think of that." He pressed on through the light traffic, passing cars doing eighty as if they were standing still.

In what seemed an incredibly short time, they were turning into Stone's block.

"Two guys on my front steps," Stone said, slowing.

"It's Ham!" Holly said. "What's he doing here?"

"Who's Ham?"

"My father."

"Oh, God," Stone said.

"You don't want to meet my father?"

"The other guy on the steps is Herbie Fisher."

"Who?"

"The guy Lance had me represent in court. I told you about him."

"What does *he* want?"

"I dread to think."

26

Ham Barker was taller than Stone, and skinnier. Stone stuck out his hand. "Hello, Ham, I'm Stone Barrington."

"Good to meet you," Ham said gravely.

"Herbie," Stone said, "what the hell are you doing here? You're supposed to be in the Virgin Islands."

"I just thought I'd drop by," Herbie said, offering his hand.

Stone ignored it. "Don't do that," he said.

"Do what?"

"Drop by."

"Aw, Stone . . ."

Ham spoke up. "Stone, there are two men in your block, watching this house."

"Oh, my God!" Stone said. "Herbie, they're after you!" He stuck a hundred-dollar bill in Herbie's hand. "Get out of here, quick!"

"Where am I going to go?" Herbie wailed.

"Go to your mother's place, in Brooklyn. They'll never think of looking for you there. Get out of here!"

Herbie sprinted down the block and was gone.

"Sorry about that," Stone said to Ham. "Herbie's a pest, hard to get rid of."

"Quick thinking, there," Holly said. "Ham, what are you doing here?"

Stone picked up Ham's bag. "Let's talk inside. The Feds may be able to read lips."

"Is that who those two guys are?" Ham asked as Stone unlocked the front door and turned off the burglar alarm.

"Yep," Stone said. "Holly's boyfriend put them on us. Where are you staying, Ham?"

"Haven't figured that out."

"We've got room here." He punched the elevator button and set Ham's bag in the car. "Third floor, second door on your right."

"Why, thank you," Ham said.

"When you're settled, come down and we'll have some lunch."

Ham got onto the elevator and started upstairs.

"Is your stuff out of my bedroom?" Stone asked Holly.

"Mostly. There are some things drying in the bathroom. Why?"

"Because if your father spots them, I'm dead. He's a killer. You can see it in his eyes."

"Oh, stop it, Stone. Ham knows I'm a grown-up."

"He's a father, and you're his little girl; that's all he knows. You're sleeping in your own room while he's here. Why is he here?"

"I don't know. When he comes downstairs, I'll ask him."

"Why are you here, Ham?" Holly asked. They were eating pasta that Stone had prepared.

"Somebody messed up your place," Ham said.

"What?"

"I went by to check on the house, and the front door was off the hinges. The place had been ransacked."

"Anything missing?" Holly asked.

"How would I know? They had a go at your safe, but didn't get in."

"Not much in there—some papers and a couple of handguns."

"Oh," Ham said, reaching into an inside pocket. "I brought you a piece; thought you might need it." He handed her a small pistol.

"Sig-Sauer P232," she said, hefting it. "Nice. Thanks, Ham."

"The magazine's full, and there's one in the chamber. The rest of a box of cartridges is upstairs, when you need it."

"How'd you manage to get it here?"

"I showed the airlines my badge and declared the weapons. They were locked in a little case inside my bag."

"What badge?" Stone asked.

Ham put a wallet on the table

Stone opened it. "Lieutenant, Orchid Beach PD?"

"Ham's kind of a consultant," Holly said. "Dollar-a-year man."

"Good idea. Makes carrying firearms easier, doesn't it? What are you packing, Ham?"

Ham reached under his tweed jacket and put a Beretta 9mm on the table.

"Can you hit anything with that?" Stone asked.

"I fired expert in the army with the old automatic," Ham said.

"I couldn't hit a wall with that thing," Stone said.

"Ham fired expert with everything the army had," Holly said. "He's the best shot in the world."

Ham shook his head. "No, just the best shot you ever saw."

"I'll keep that in mind," Stone said, glancing at Holly, who made a face at him.

"Be nice to my little girl," Ham said.

Stone turned to Holly. "See?"

"Oh, Ham, shut up," Holly said. "Don't go scaring the men off."

"I'm just saying," Ham said.

"It's all right, Ham," Stone replied. "I understand."

"Good. Good spaghetti, too," he said.

"It's penne, actually."

"It's all spaghetti to me." He stuffed another forkful into his mouth and chewed thoughtfully.

"Did you do anything about my house?" Holly said.

"I got you a new door and installed it. Ginny was cleaning up the place when I left for the airport."

"So you came up here to rescue me?"

"I just thought you might need somebody to watch your back."

"The Feds seem to be doing that," Stone pointed out. "After all, she's the one who's dogging their witness."

"Any luck?" Ham asked.

"A couple of sightings, no collar."

"Want me to collar him for you?"

"It's a little more complicated than that, Ham. The Feds are involved, so is the Mafia. Grant's up here. That's why those guys are out in the street. They followed us to Connecticut, too."

"I guess that boy is taking a proprietary interest in you."

Stone laughed, and Holly shot him a glance.

"Don't worry, it's all business."

"I liked him, till he got to running the Miami office," Ham said. "After that, he was just another bureaucrat."

"That's what I hear," Stone said.

"So who the hell are you, Stone?" Ham asked.

"Lawyer," Stone replied.

"Oh."

"Don't take it so hard, Ham," Holly said. "He's also a retired cop."

"Little young to be retired, aren't you?"

"Bullet in the knee," Stone said, realizing that he was adopting Ham's mode of speech.

"Uh-huh," Ham said. "Must of hurt."

"Oh, yeah."

"You two are going to be comparing scars in a minute," Holly said.

"Who was that Herbie character?" Ham asked.

"Former client and current nuisance," Stone replied.

"He's dangerous."

"Why do you say that?"

"You can smell it on him. He'd sell you to save his own ass."

"You're a fine judge of character, Ham."

"I trained a lot of young men in the army. You get to know what to expect of them."

The doorbell rang. Stone picked up a phone, pressed a button, and listened for a moment. "Come on in," he said, pressing another button. He turned to Holly. "It's Lance."

"Who's Lance?" Ham asked.

"Tell you what, Ham," Stone said. "You meet him and tell me."

27

Lance ambled into the kitchen, dressed in a yellow cashmere turtleneck, a tweed jacket, cavalry twill trousers, and short alligator boots. He might have been a visiting movie star. Introductions were made, and he sat down. Daisy walked over and sniffed him. Lance scratched the top of her head, then ignored her.

"What's up?" Lance asked.

"The Feds are all over us," Stone said. "Followed us up to Connecticut yesterday. They're camped outside right now."

"Well," Lance drawled, "I guess they take exception to Holly's trying to arrest their man."

"Their murderer," Holly said.

"Or is there some other reason they'd be interested in the two of you?" Lance asked.

"You take that one, Holly," Stone said.

"Oh, a guy I went out with a few times works for them, followed me up here."

"You were living with him," Ham said.

Holly turned beet red. "Herbie was here when we got back," she said, looking for cover.

Lance permitted himself a small groan. "Stone, I wish you'd take charge of your client."

"He's not my client anymore, Lance. You shipped him off to Saint Thomas, remember?"

"Except he didn't ship."

"That's not my fault."

"Where did he go?"

"I gave him some money and told him to go to his mother's place, in Brooklyn."

Holly laughed. "Stone told him they'd never think of looking for him there. I think he bought it."

"If there's one thing I've learned about our Herbert," Lance said, "it's never to expect him to do as he's told."

Ham nodded. "I know the type."

"You're ex-army," Lance said.

"Yep."

Lance regarded him coolly for a long moment. "I read your service record," he said.

Ham evinced mild surprise. "Did you, now?"

"I did. You want to shoot somebody for me?"

"Who'd you have in mind?"

"Herbie."

Ham chuckled. "I can see why, but he doesn't seem to be a threat to national security just yet."

"Would you shoot him if I told you he was?"

"I wouldn't believe you if you told me he was."

"Why not?"

"Because I think I know who you work for, and folks in your line of work tell the truth on only the rarest occasions."

Lance laughed. "You judge us too harshly, Ham. But then, you've had some experience of us, in Vietnam."

"I have."

"I was too young for that godawful mess," Lance said, "and I'm glad of it. But you shouldn't judge us now for how we operated then. You might find some satisfaction in working with us again."

"Lance is recruiting," Stone said.

Ham shook his head. "No, thanks. You want somebody shot, you do it yourself."

"I was speaking metaphorically before," Lance said.

"No, you weren't," Ham replied.

Stone was proud of him.

For the slightest moment, Lance looked nettled, but then he relaxed. "Holly, I came to tell you that it's going to be another day or two before you can put your hands on Trini Rodriguez without an unduly large reaction from the federales."

"Shit," Holly said. "I'm getting impatient. Ham, you want to shoot Trini for me?"

"Him? It would be my pleasure. Just point him out."

Stone couldn't tell if they were kidding. "Hang on," he said. "We don't need a shoot-out on our city streets."

"Wouldn't be a shoot-out," Ham said. "Just a single *pop*." He made a little gun with his fingers and fired it.

"Why didn't I think of that?" Lance said.

"Because there's nothing in it for you," Stone replied.

"You have a point," Lance admitted. He got to his feet and stretched. "Well, if you'll excuse me, I have a lunch date up the street." He shook Ham's hand, waved goodbye, and was gone.

"Your assessment, Ham?" Stone asked.

"Now *that*," Ham said, "is your large-bore, fully automatic Agency spook. Where the hell did you come by him?"

"I came by him in London a while back," Stone said. "It's a long story. I'll tell it to you someday when I'm less sober."

"I'll look forward to it," Ham said. "He's more dangerous than Herbie."

"Why?" Holly asked.

Ham got to his feet and moved his shoulders around. "Because he thinks of himself as a patriot, and they're always the most dangerous. Well, I think I'll have a nap. It's an old man's prerogative, and I've been traveling since dawn. See ya." He headed upstairs, leaving Stone and Holly to ponder his assessment of Lance Cabot.

28

Holly got into some sweat clothes, stuffed the Sig-Sauer into her jacket pocket, clipped on Daisy's leash, and headed uptown.

She and Daisy walked briskly until they entered the park, then Holly started to jog, with Daisy easily keeping pace. They ran past the zoo, then the pond where people raced model boats, and the statue of Alice in Wonderland, then they cut cross-country. Somewhere north of Alice, Holly became aware of another jogger not far behind.

Everything was perfectly normal until Holly noticed that there was something red attached to Daisy's back. She stopped to pull it off and discovered that what was in her hand was a dart. Daisy sat down, panting, then collapsed, and then something struck Holly in the head.

Stone was napping in a big wing chair in his library, a book in his lap, when the phone woke him. "Hello?"

"Is this Stone Barrington?" A man's voice.

"Yes."

"This is the desk sergeant at the Twenty-second Precinct in Central Park. There's been a homicide in the park; I think you'd better get up here."

"Who's dead?"

"I don't have that information. Just get up here, okay, Mr. Barrington?"

"I'm on my way. Will you get hold of Lieutenant Bacchetti at the one-nine and ask him to meet me there?"

"Okay." The cop hung up.

Stone thought of waking Ham, but changed his mind. He ran outside and hailed a cab.

Stone walked into the precinct, and he was scared. He presented himself to the desk sergeant.

"Right," the sergeant said. "See Detective Briscoe back there." He nodded toward a door.

Stone walked into a small squad room and looked at the only detective there.

"Barrington?" the man asked.

"Yes. What's happened?"

"You were a detective over at the Nineteenth, weren't you?" the man asked.

"What the hell has happened?" Stone demanded.

"Are you acquainted with a cop from Florida named Holly Barker?"

"Yes, she's staying at my house."

"Come with me." He got up and walked down a corridor with Stone at his heels. He opened the door to an interrogation room. "In here."

Stone walked in and the door closed behind him. Holly was sitting at the table stroking Daisy, who was stretched out on the tabletop.

Holly looked up at him. "It's okay," she said. "She's coming around." She stroked Daisy's head. "It's okay, sweetheart. Just take your time. You'll be all right in a minute."

Stone sank into a chair and gave Daisy a pat. "I thought you were dead," he said.

"No."

"The desk sergeant who called me said there was a homicide."

"There was a shooting—self-defense."

"Who?"

"I don't know; a guy. There were two of them. The second one ran when I shot the first one."

"Why did you shoot him?"

"Because he was trying to kill me with a knife."

"Where did all this happen? Start at the beginning."

"Daisy and I were running, and she was shot with a dart, then somebody hit me upside the head, but not hard enough to put me out. I rolled over a couple of times and got hold of the gun Ham gave me. It was in my jacket pocket. The guy was walking toward me with the knife, as if he didn't expect any opposition. I shot him." She held up a corner of her jacket, where the bullet had gone through. "I didn't have time to draw."

Stone put a hand to her cheek. "You're cold," he said. "Are you feeling all right?"

"I am now," she replied. "I had a case of the shakes for a while. A cop on horseback found me. I guess he heard the shot."

"Can I leave you here for a couple of minutes?"

"Sure, we're all right. Daisy's going to have a hangover, but she's not hurt."

Stone got up, went back to the squad room, and found Briscoe. "She's told me what happened. It was a good shooting."

"Looks that way," Briscoe said, "but I don't have the final call on that."

Stone noticed for the first time that Holly's new Sig-Sauer was on Briscoe's desk in an evidence bag, and her badge lay beside it. "She's on duty," he said. "She's got a fugitive warrant."

"I got that," Briscoe replied. "That ought to cover it. We want to see the warrant, though."

"It's at my house. I'll get it to you. Will you release her to me?"

"Oh, we're not holding her. She can go. She can have her gun and badge back, too." He handed them to Stone. "We took a sample round for the file."

Dino burst into the room. "What happened?"

Stone told him.

"Are we all square here?" Dino asked Briscoe.

"Yes, Lieutenant. We need a phone number for her, and we want to see her fugitive warrant, but that's it. It's clearly self-defense."

"You got an ID on the guy with the knife?"

"He had nothing on him but the knife, but we'll run his prints."

"What happened to the second guy?"

"He beat it out of there. The gunshot must have scared him off."

"Thanks, Briscoe," Dino said. He pulled Stone aside. "How's Holly taking all this?"

"She's okay, I think. She's mostly worried about Daisy."

"Where are they?"

"In an interrogation room back there. Are you in a car?"

"Yeah. Let's get her back to your place, and I'll pick up the fugitive warrant." He gave Briscoe Stone's number.

By the time they were back at the house, Daisy was walking, but slowly.

As they walked in the front door, Ham came down the stairs. He pointed at Holly's jacket pocket. "Was the bullet going in or out?"

"Out," Holly said.

Ham put an arm around her. "Let's get you into bed."

"Ham . . ."

"Tell me about it later."

When Holly and Daisy were tucked in, Stone and Ham went down to the kitchen and had a beer.

"She can take care of herself," Ham said.

"Apparently so."

"What's going on here, Stone?"

"My best guess? Trini doesn't like being dogged, and he decided to do something about it. From what I've heard about him from Holly, he wasn't there today, because Holly's alive. I guess he put a couple of his pals on her."

"So the two guys outside your house weren't Feds?"

"Maybe, maybe not." Stone had an idea. He picked up the phone and got the number for the New York State Police in Albany. He called, identified himself, and asked about the traffic stop on I-684 earlier that day. He was transferred to the relevant field office and, good luck, managed to get one of the traffic officers who had made the stop.

Stone identified himself. "You stopped a black SUV on 684 this morning?"

"Yes, we did."

"I was the guy out front in the black Mercedes."

"How fast were you going?"

"I'll take the fifth on that, but I was transporting an officer on duty. Did you get an ID on the guys in the SUV?"

"Yeah. They were FBI, and they wouldn't tell us what they were doing. I wrote 'em a ticket for grossly excessive speed."

"Good for you. Thanks, that's all I needed to know." Stone hung up and turned to Ham. "Well, it looks like absolutely *everybody* is following us."

"What's your take on what happened in the park?" Ham asked.

"I think they wanted it to look like a mugging, and they didn't want to attract anybody with the noise of a gunshot. They used a dart on Daisy, then tried to knife Holly. They would have knifed Daisy, too, once she was out. So somebody would have stumbled on a jogger and her dog, both dead."

"Why not use a silencer on both?" Ham asked.

"Because it would then look like a profes- sional hit. The dart thing is funny, though. It's not the sort of thing mob guys would normally think of using."

"This Trini guy is not a normal mob hood," Ham said. "He's a lot smarter and a lot worse. He would think of the dart."

"Maybe so."

"Good thing I came up here," Ham said. "While I'm in New York, she doesn't leave this house without me watching her back."

"Sounds good to me," Stone said.

"Oh, and you may as well move her back into your room," Ham said. "I get the idea that's where she wants to be."

Stone gulped. "Up to her."

29

Holly and Daisy slept straight through until the following morning. When they came down for breakfast Stone was scrambling eggs, and Ham was having coffee.

"Daisy looks like she had a few too many beers last night," Ham said, rubbing her flanks.

"She's fine, just a little groggy," Holly replied.

Stone set three plates of eggs on the table and they all dug in.

"This is good, Stone," Ham said. "What's in it?"

"Smoked salmon and a little cream."

"You're going to make some girl a wonderful wife one of these days," Ham said.

Holly spoke up. "I guess that means Ham

approves of you, Stone. Otherwise he wouldn't be trying to marry me off to you."

"I never said—" Ham began.

"Oh, shut up, Ham. You're transparent." She turned to Stone. "Ham has suddenly decided it's time I got married. I think he wants grandchildren."

"Now, I—"

"Well, not much chance of that, Ham."

"I can live without grandchildren," Ham said. "You do what you want. That'll make me happy."

"I want Trini Rodriguez, and I don't want to wait another couple of days for the FBI to spirit him out of town. You know they're not going to hand him to me, don't you, Stone?"

"I wouldn't think so," Stone replied. "You got any ideas?"

"Well, I can canvas Little Italy for him again."

"I may have a better idea," Stone said.

It had been quite some time since Stone had visited the old man in the outer reaches of Brooklyn, and he wasn't sure how he felt about it. He finally decided that what had made him reluctant was not the father, but the daughter who was locked in an upstairs room of his house.

He parked his car and was met at the front door by Pete, the short, thick former hoodlum who served as Eduardo Bianchi's butler and bodyguard.

"Long time," Pete said.

"Yeah," Stone said, and followed the man through the house and out into the back garden, where Eduardo sat at a wrought-iron table, wearing a dark suit, as was his custom. He rose to meet Stone, and it took him a little longer than on Stone's last visit. "How are you, Stone?" Eduardo asked.

"I'm fine, Eduardo. Are you well?"

"I'm better than a person of my years can reasonably expect to be. Please sit down. Lunch will be here soon."

"You look wonderful." Stone paused. "And how is Dolce?" Dolce was Eduardo's younger daughter, to whom Stone had once been married for a few minutes before she had degenerated into a murderous psychotic.

"I wish I could tell you she was well," Eduardo replied, "but she's not. Her condition has worsened to the point where she has tried to kill everyone who has anything to do with her, including me. She has a degenerative brain disease, something like Alzheimer's, that has caused all her behavior. Now she doesn't even recognize her family. I've had to have her removed to a facility where she can be made comfortable and where she can be secured from harming herself or others."

"I'm very sorry to hear that," Stone said. "She was a beautiful and intelligent girl."

"My mother died the same way," Eduardo said, "and an aunt of hers, as well. Of course, they didn't understand the reason in those days. It seems to be passed down to one daughter in each generation, so Anna Maria will be all right." Anna Maria, who was married to Dino, preferred to be called Mary Ann.

"It's a tragic situation."

"Yes, and thankfully, rare. Anna Maria has told me that she plans to have no more children, for fear of having a daughter, so the disease will die out with Dolce."

"I didn't know about this."

"Neither does Dino," Eduardo said. "I would be grateful if you would not tell him. I don't want him to be worried."

"As you wish."

Lunch arrived, and Stone labored through three courses of old-fashioned Italian cooking, doing the best he could.

When the dishes had been cleared away, and Pete had brought them small glasses of Strega, Eduardo turned to Stone. "Now, why have you come to see me? I believe you must need my help."

"Yes, I do," Stone said, "for a friend. I want to locate someone who is hiding in the . . . Italian community in New York."

"For what purpose?"

"So that he can be tried and imprisoned."

Eduardo shrugged. "I appreciate your candor, but that is not the sort of reason that would engender cooperation in the community."

"I know that, but you must understand that this man is a multiple murderer, who kills without thought or feeling, and who does not limit his killing to reasons of business. He once put a bomb in a coffin and exploded it during a funeral."

"That is an outrage," Eduardo said.

"Do you know a man named Ed Shine?"

Eduardo permitted himself a small smile. "I've known him since the day he got off the boat from Italy. He was a valuable man to friends of mine. Of course, he is in prison now. Ed could not remain retired. He could have lived out his life in peace, but he got greedy."

"Yes. The man my friend wants to find is Shine's out-of-wedlock son with a Cuban woman in south Florida. He goes by the name of Trini Rodriguez."

Eduardo nodded. "I've heard of him, and I haven't liked what I've heard, but he was under Ed's protection."

Suddenly, Stone had a thought. He might end this whole business by simply imparting a small piece of information to Eduardo. "Have you ever wondered who else's protection he might be under?"

Eduardo looked at him. "What do you mean?"

"Hasn't it occurred to the people who are helping him that he would not be a free man without the protection of . . . well, those who would, normally, put him away?"

"And that would be the federal men, would it?"

Stone shrugged. "He would be far too important a fugitive to be allowed to roam

New York City without the protection of someone."

"You have a point," Eduardo said. "It makes you wonder."

"I wonder, too."

"Perhaps it is because he has convinced them that, while he may be protected by these federal people, he is not truly working for them."

"Perhaps. It's my understanding that he is helping them root out a Middle Eastern terrorist organization that wants to use his friends to help them launder large amounts of money."

"Certainly, no one I know would knowingly help such an organization," Eduardo said smoothly.

"I didn't think so."

"Perhaps this is complicated," Eduardo said.

"I've no doubt of that."

"I do very little business these days, but I will ask a few questions and see what this man means to the people who are helping him."

"I'm sure the answers would be interesting," Stone said. "I think there is one thing of which you may be sure: that Trini Rodriguez is acting in his own interests, and not those of either the federal people or those who are helping him."

Eduardo stood up. "Thank you for coming to see me, Stone. Perhaps you will come again soon, now that Dolce is not in the house. I know her presence made you uncomfortable."

"I hope you will forgive me that, Eduardo. I would like very much to come again soon."

"Someone will call you to arrange a meeting, when I have something to tell you," Eduardo said. "It should not be long."

The two men shook hands, and Stone followed Pete back through the house to the car.

30

Stone left the Bianchi house and drove back toward Manhattan, thinking about his conversation with Eduardo. The old man had seemed genuinely concerned about the situation with Trini Rodriguez, but that didn't mean he was going to help. Over the years he had distanced himself from his past criminal associations, concentrating on the work of his foundation and his membership on the boards of the museum, the opera, and others of the city's cultural institutions, and he seemed reluctant to revisit old acquaintances.

Dolce had helped him in these endeavors until she had begun to behave erratically, then violently. Eduardo was a lonely man now, Stone reflected, and he really should make an effort to see him at a time when he didn't want something from the old man.

Stone had made his way across Brooklyn in fairly light traffic, making good time. He paid little attention to other cars along the route, but now a motorcycle cop caught his eye in his rearview mirror. Instinctively, he slowed down, and as he did the bike drew alongside him.

Stone was reaching for his badge when an alarm bell went off in his mind. There were two men on the motorcycle, and cops didn't ride tandem. They were no more than three feet from his window. They wore black leather and white helmets with goggles, and one of them had something in his hand.

Simultaneously, there was a loud noise, and two splatters appeared in the window's glass. Stone braked sharply, and the motor-cycle shot past him, then slowed, as the man on the passenger seat twisted around for another shot. Two more splatters ap-peared, this time in the windshield, but the bullets did not penetrate the armored glass.

Stone, unarmed, fought back with the only weapon he had at his disposal: his car. He slammed the accelerator to the floor, and the tachometer needle shot up as he aimed at the rear of the motorcycle. The driver hadn't been expecting that, and he failed to react quickly enough. Stone's car struck the motorcycle hard, propelling the bike across the central divider of the bridge, directly into the path of an oncoming cement truck. The cycle and its two riders ricocheted off the grille of the truck, and Stone lost sight of them. Behind him he could hear the screech of brakes and the blowing of horns.

He braked to a halt and got out of the car, looking back. The driver of the car behind him had done the same thing, and traffic had come to a halt on the Brooklyn Bridge.

Stone watched the detective as he laboriously wrote the last of his notes. He had been in the police station for more than four hours.

"Anything else you can remember?" the man asked.

"No. Did somebody call Lieutenant Bacchetti?"

"Who knows? You think you need the help?"

"That depends on your attitude," Stone

said. His badge and ID card lay on the table between them.

"Not my call," the detective said, standing up and stretching. "That's my watch commander's, but just between you and me, I think you did the world a favor by what you did. There's a few greasy spots on the Brooklyn Bridge, but what the hell?"

The door opened, and Dino walked in. "First, Central Park, now Brooklyn," he said. "Is there a precinct left where you aren't up to your dick in homicides?"

"Dino, it was a hit. They tried to kill me. Twice."

"Yeah, I saw your car outside. Nice to know that armored glass helps."

The detective spoke up. "I forgot to ask: How come you drive an armored car?"

"It's not an armored car," Stone said. "It's *lightly* armored. It will repel small-arms fire. I was car shopping, and it was in the showroom, and I thought, what the hell, why not?"

"Well," the detective said, "it was a good idea, because if that had been regular glass between you and the shooter, it would be *your* brains spattered all over the Brooklyn

Bridge instead of the two guys on the motorcycle."

"You get an ID on them yet?" Dino asked.

"Nah. They weren't carrying anything. Maybe their prints will ring the bell."

"Don't count on it," Stone said to Dino. "The guy that Holly shot in the park still doesn't have a name, does he?"

Dino shook his head. "He ain't going to, either. C'mon, let's get out of here."

"I don't have to talk to anybody else?"

"Nah, I had a chat with the watch commander. They'll call you if there's anything else they want to know."

The two walked out of the precinct together, and Stone took another look at his car. "Follow me to the Mercedes garage?" he asked.

"Why not?" Dino replied. "It's not like I have to work for a living."

The car sat in the middle of the shop, surrounded by half a dozen Mercedes-Benz mechanics in blue coveralls.

"This is my first one of these," the service manager said. "We've sold a few of these cars, but it's the first time one of them ever came back with bullet holes in it."

"How about the bumper?" Stone said.

"We'll have one here tomorrow, but it's got to be painted. The armored glass is going to take longer, maybe two or three weeks. It has to come from Germany, and there's customs and all of that."

"Put regular glass in it," Stone said. "I'll bring it back when the armored stuff comes in."

"In that case, we'll have it together by the end of the week," the service manager said.

"Can we go now?" Dino asked.

Stone signed the service order and followed Dino back to his car.

"You thought about how you're going to explain this to your insurance company?" Dino asked as they drove away.

"I don't think I'll mention it to them," Stone said, "because I didn't mention to them in the first place that the car was armored. I thought it might upset them."

"Stone, maybe you ought to take Holly and get out of town for a while," Dino said.

"That's an attractive idea," Stone replied, "and I'll talk to Holly about it, but I don't think she's going to want to go. She's mad now, and she's going to get madder when I tell her what's happened."

"Better mad than dead," Dino said.

"Whoever's doing this has wasted three men trying, and you may have pissed him off by now."

"You think it's Trini?" Stone asked.

"You got somebody else in mind?"

"Maybe," Stone replied.

31

Dino slowed down as he turned into Stone's block, pointing ahead at a cluster of people outside Stone's house. "You must be dead, because you're attracting flies."

Stone groaned. "Stop here." Dino pulled over. Stone got out his cell phone and called his secretary.

"The Barrington Practice," Joan Robertson said.

"Joan, it's me."

"Are you all right?"

"Yes, I'm right outside. I want you to go to the garage, count to five, and open the garage door. As soon as we're inside, close it."

"Okay. Bye."

"Slowly," Stone said. Dino edged his unmarked car up the block and, when he saw the garage door start to move, accelerated. He turned into the drive, crossed the sidewalk, and braked before he could run into the rear wall. The door closed behind them.

Stone had seen at least two television cameras in the mob. "Come on in, I'll buy you a drink."

"I can't get out anyway, without running down a few members of the fourth estate."

"What happened on the Brooklyn Bridge?" Joan asked. "It's all over the TV."

"Come on upstairs, so I won't have to explain it more than once," Stone said.

Holly and Ham met them at the top of the stairs. "You okay?" she asked.

"I'm fine, except I just killed two men."

"That ain't good," Ham said.

Stone led them into his study and poured everyone but himself a drink, then he explained what had happened. "Holly, I think we've got to get out of town." He held up a hand. "I know you don't want to get any farther from Trini than you already have, but that crowd outside makes staying here impossible. We won't be able to move without them tagging along."

"Why don't you go up to Connecticut?" Dino asked.

"Can't do that. Some of the people who've been following us know about the house."

"Yeah," Holly said, "but they're FBI. You think they're trying to kill us?"

"I doubt it, but somebody on their team may be talking to somebody on Trini's team, or we may be dealing with another team entirely."

"And what team would that be?" Dino asked.

"I don't know, and I don't want to find out the hard way."

"Then let's go to Florida," Holly said. "I have a perfectly good house, and if we get rumbled there, we can go to Ham's place."

"Sounds good to me," Ham said. "You two can sleep in the hammock on the porch. Hasn't been anybody there to feed the mosquitoes."

"You make it sound irresistible, Ham," Stone said. "How quickly can you two get packed?"

"Ten minutes," Holly said.

"Dino, can you give us a ride to Teterboro?"

"Sure."

Stone picked up a phone and called Atlantic Aviation. "Please top off my inboard and outboard caps," he said. "Be there in half an hour." He hung up, then dug out a chart, called Flight Services and got a weather report, then filed a flight plan. He went upstairs, threw some things into a couple of duffels, and came back down to find everybody waiting for him. "Okay," he said, "let's run the gauntlet."

They trooped downstairs and got into Dino's car while Joan stood by the garage door switch.

"I'll be on my cell phone," Stone said. "Hit it."

Joan opened the door, and Dino started backing up. He switched on his flashing lights and hit the whooper for a minute, and the crowd scattered. As he pulled away from the house, reporters ran alongside the car, shouting questions, while photographers fired their strobes. They lucked their way through the traffic light at the corner and, with the help of the lights and whooper, were soon out of range.

At Teterboro, Dino faked his way through the security gate and pulled up to Stone's airplane, which had been pulled up front. The fuel truck was finishing the top-off.

Stone stowed everybody's luggage in the rear compartment, then did a preflight inspection of the airplane.

"Wish I was going with you," Dino said. "I could use some sun."

"I've got plenty of room for you and your wife," Holly said.

"I'll ask her." He shook Stone's hand. "Call me in a couple of days, and I'll let you know if things have cooled off."

"Will do."

"By the way, we were followed out here by a black Lincoln Town Car. I wasn't sure until we made the last turn."

Stone laughed. "Let them try to follow us now." He got onto the airplane, showed Holly and Ham how the door worked, then settled in the pilot's seat, with Holly beside him. "Everybody buckle up." He worked his way through the checklist, got a clearance from the tower, and taxied to runway 24. He did a runup, then called the tower and was cleared for takeoff. A moment later they were climbing through a thousand feet, with the setting sun to their right, bright orange through the New Jersey haze.

Stone climbed to flight level 250, switched on the CD player, and, having gone through his cruise checklist, relaxed. He noted that Holly and Ham were both already dozing.

With the autopilot flying the airplane, Stone began to think back over the events of the day, but the scene that kept flashing through his mind was the memory of the motorcycle propelled across the meridian of the Brooklyn Bridge into the path of the cement truck. He tried not to think of the aftermath.

Finally, he checked the airplane's Garmin AirCell phone to be sure he had a signal, then he called a New York cell phone number, pressing a button on the audio panel to isolate his headset from those of Holly and Ham.

"Yes?" a familiar voice said.

"Lance, it's Stone."

"Nice to hear from you," Lance said smoothly. "I've been hearing about you on the news. Are you okay?"

"Just fine, thanks."

"What's that noise in the background?" Lance asked.

"Just road noise," Stone replied. "I'm in the car."

"Where you headed?"

"Out of town."

"Where?"

"If I wanted to get Holly and myself killed, I'd tell you."

There was a long silence before Lance spoke again. "That's an odd thing to say," he said finally.

"I suppose it is," Stone replied, "but you're the only person in all this who has the resources to make what's been happening happen."

Another long silence. "That's not an outrageous conclusion to come to, but why do you think I would want you dead?"

"I'm still thinking about that," Stone said. He pressed the end button on the phone and put it back into its cradle. It was dark now, and the lights of the cities and towns of the Atlantic seaboard stretched out before them. He was glad to be leaving them behind.

32

Stone woke, disoriented, with the sun streaming through the windows. He was alone in bed, and he couldn't hear anyone downstairs.

He found a robe in a closet, put his cell phone in a pocket, and walked downstairs. Nice place, he thought, looking around the living room and the kitchen. He opened the sliding glass doors and stepped outside. Dunes stretched away to his left and right, and the Atlantic Ocean was only yards away. The air was warm and soft, and the small surf made a pleasant noise.

He looked up and down the beach and found himself alone, so he shucked off the robe and ran naked into the sea, running as far as he could, then diving in and swimming away from the shore. Fifty yards out, he turned and swam back in, found his robe, and went back into the house. He found juice, cereal, and milk in the kitchen and made himself some breakfast. He was having coffee when the telephone rang. He let the machine get it.

"Stone, it's Holly," she said. "If you're awake, pick up."

Stone picked up the phone on the kitchen counter. "Hi."

"What time did you get up?"

"Just a few minutes ago. I had a swim and some breakfast."

"Great. Make yourself at home. Daisy and I are at work, and I've got a lot of mail to clear up. Did you bring a gun with you?"

"Yep, I brought the Walther."

"Good. I don't like to think of you being unarmed, what with all that's happened."

"Neither do I. Can I carry in this state?"

"Not with the word 'retired' on your police ID. When you get dressed, come to the station and ask for my secretary. She'll fix you up with something." She gave him directions. "Use my car. The keys are in a bowl on the kitchen counter."

"Sounds good."

"I won't be here when you come, and I

won't be home until around seven. Can you amuse yourself?"

"I'll try."

"See you then." She hung up.

Stone took a shower and dressed in light clothes, then drove into town and, following Holly's directions, found the station and asked for her secretary.

A middle-aged woman came to the front desk to get him. "Morning, Mr. Barrington. Would you come this way, please? We're all ready for you."

He followed her through the squad room to the rear of the building, where she stood him before a wall and took a photograph of him with a Polaroid passport camera.

She handed him a form and a pen. "Please sign at the bottom."

Stone signed. She went away and came back with a laminated ID card and a badge in their own wallet.

"Congratulations, you are now a consultant lieutenant with the Orchid Beach Police Department, without pay."

"Thank you."

He went back to the car, opened the glove compartment, and took out the Walther in a Galco Executive shoulder holster. He got into the light harness and put his windbreaker on over it. "Now I'm armed and dangerous," he said aloud to himself.

That evening Stone, Holly, Ham, and his girlfriend, Ginny, a lovely redhead, were at a table at the Ocean Grill, in nearby Vero Beach, sipping vodka gimlets.

"Stone," Holly said, "do you think Lance could have had anything to do with the people who've been trying to kill you and me?"

"It crossed my mind," Stone said. "Certainly, he has the resources to do it."

"I can't think of a motive, can you?"

"Not so far. I can't think of anything we know that we shouldn't know. I think it's a better guess that somebody in the FBI is talking to Trini about us, but I can't see the FBI sanctioning the killing of two citizens. The whole thing is baffling."

Ham spoke up. "I think it's Trini, one way or another, and I don't think he needs the FBI to help him. From what Holly has told me, he could have followed her to your house, so he would know about you. And just because the Feds are following you, that doesn't mean that Trini's people can't follow you, as well. Lance doesn't have any reason to kill two people who are supposed to be working for him."

"Apart from that," Holly said, "Lance just doesn't strike me as the killer type."

"There are all sorts of killer types," Stone said.

"Too true," Ham echoed.

Their dinner arrived and they turned the conversation to other things.

They had just arrived back at Holly's house when Stone's cell phone vibrated in his pocket. "Hello?"

"Stone, it's Lance."

"Good evening."

"Our last conversation set me to thinking. I ordered a DNA check of our three anonymous assassins, and I just got a call from my people with the results."

"You have a database to check the results against?"

"Yes, but they're not in our database, or the FBI's."

"So the tests were useless?"

"As far as identification goes, yes; but the

tests turned up some other useful information."

"What kind of information?"

"It was possible to conclude that all three men were Arab—very likely Lebanese or Syrian."

"You can tell that from DNA?"

"Yes. Also, they were related—not brothers, but certainly cousins."

Stone looked at Holly. "So you're saying that the people who are trying to kill Holly and me are a family of Lebanese or Syrian assassins?"

"You make it sound like something out of *The Arabian Nights.* More likely, the three cousins are members of the same terrorist cell, that's all."

"What do you mean, that's all? That's more than enough. Why would a terrorist cell have an interest in Holly and me?"

"I think it's fairly obvious," Lance said.

"Well, you're going to have to make it even more obvious if I'm going to get it."

"Think about it: Trini Rodriguez is dealing with an Arab group on this money-laundering thing, right?"

"Right."

"So he tells his contacts that you and Holly are a threat to their transaction."

"Okay, now it's obvious."

"What is also obvious is that by killing three of them, you've probably annoyed the other members of the group, so I think you and Holly should stay in Orchid Beach until the FBI has thrown a net over these people."

"Wait a minute. Why do you think we're in Orchid Beach?"

"Because you filed a flight plan for Vero Beach, which is the airport serving Holly's hometown."

"You figured that out, huh?"

"Yes, but I doubt if your Lebanese friends did. Anyway, I thought you'd like to know that I'm not trying to kill you."

"And do I know that? You could be making all this up."

"Stone, use your head. The reason you should know I'm not trying to kill you is that you're still alive." He hung up.

Stone turned to Holly. "You'd better sit down," he said.

33

Holly listened to Stone's report of his conversation with Lance. When he had finished she shook her head. "I don't know whether to laugh or cry."

"Neither do I."

"I mean, the part about the Arab assassins would be funny if you and I hadn't already killed three of them. I wouldn't believe it, otherwise."

"Neither would I."

"And he said they wouldn't know we're in Orchid Beach?"

"He said that he figured it out, but they wouldn't."

"I hope to God he's right."

"So do I."

"Still, I'm sleeping with a gun."

"Good idea."

"Speaking of sleeping . . ."

"I'm right behind you." Holly let Daisy in from her nightly run in the dunes, then led Stone upstairs. "Daisy, get in your bed," she said, and the dog curled up where she had been told.

"Good," Stone said, stroking her hair, "I don't want anybody between us tonight, and I'm glad Ham's out of the house, too."

"I'm glad, if you're glad," she said, helping him shuck his shirt over his head.

Stone worked on her buttons and unhooked her bra. "Alone is good," he said, kissing her breasts.

She pulled him to her and pushed down on his shoulders until he was on his knees, pulling off her clothing. "Ooooh, that's the place," she said, running her fingers through his hair.

He pushed her onto the bed, and she opened her legs. For the next few minutes he concentrated on making her happy, and the noises she was making confirmed her feelings.

She came with a series of cries and little convulsions, then she pulled Stone on top of her. "I want everything tonight," she said.

Stone slipped inside her. "The works," he

said, kissing her ear as he moved slowly in and out.

"The works!" she cried and moved with him.

For the better part of an hour they explored each other with fingers and tongues. They changed positions and laughed at the intensity of their pleasure. Then they took turns coming and collapsed in each other's arms.

"It occurs to me," Stone panted, "that my heart must be in pretty good shape, because if it weren't, I'd be dead right now. That's the best stress test in the world."

Holly rested her head on his shoulder and threw a leg over his. "Okay, the Arab assassins can shoot me now."

"I hope not."

"If they showed up right now, I wouldn't be able to hold a gun. I can't make a fist."

"Then we're both helpless."

"We could rely on Daisy."

"We'd have to."

Stone suddenly thought of something. "I just had a troubling thought."

"Not now, please."

"If they don't know we're here, who ransacked your house a few days ago?"

"Don't make me think about it now." Her voice trailed off. "I'm going to sleep."

"Oh, no. You have to answer that question. You're not sleeping until I'm sleeping, and I can't sleep thinking about that."

"What was the question again?"

"Who broke into your house?"

"How the hell should I know?"

"Didn't your police force investigate?"

"Yes, but they didn't leave any prints."

"Who do you think it was?"

"Are you saying it was Arab assassins?"

"It would certainly seem to be Trini-connected, wouldn't it?"

"Trini's a Florida boy. If he wanted my house broken into, he wouldn't need Arab assassins, he'd just make a call to some of his homeboys."

"Well, I'm relieved that it wasn't Arab assassins."

"I'm so glad."

"Is the burglar alarm on?"

"No, but there's a keypad right here by the bed."

"Would you turn it on, please?"

With a groan, Holly rolled over and tapped in the code, then rolled back. "There you go."

"Good. I think I can sleep now."

"But I'm wide awake."

"I'm sleepy."

"Oh, no you don't," she said, taking his testicles in her hand and squeezing.

"Hey, I can't sleep with you doing that."

"That's the idea." She stopped squeezing and began lightly kneading instead.

"You don't really think I can . . ."

"Sure you can."

"It's impossible after what we've just done."

"Then why is this working?" she asked, continuing.

"Oh, God."

Holly rolled on top of him and put him inside her. "In fact, it's working very well indeed."

"I can't argue," Stone said, arching his back. "But I'll never be able to come again."

"Wanna bet?" she asked.

34

When Stone woke up he was lying on his side, and Holly was curled up with him, in the spoon position. Stone had a notion of starting something, but Daisy was staring at him intently from across the bed. She was difficult to ignore.

"You want to go out, girl?" he asked.

"No," Holly replied sleepily.

"I wasn't talking to you."

He got out of bed and walked downstairs naked with Daisy. He opened the sliding door to the beach and left it open so that she could come back in.

Holly came down the stairs, getting into a robe. "I like you naked in my house," she said.

"Why are you up?"

"It's after eight, and I really ought to at

least check in at the station before I come back and fuck your brains out." She pinched him on the ass as she passed.

"So I have to wait?"

She made coffee and switched on the TV to CNN.

"In New York City last night," a reporter was saying, "the FBI pulled off a major sting against a large terrorist organization. After setting up a bogus money-laundering apparatus, they lured the terrorists' financial people to an address in Little Italy and, posing as members of the Mafia, videotaped their transaction, then arrested everybody. No names have been announced yet, but sources say that seven members of the as yet unnamed terrorist organization were arrested and more than ten million dollars in Euros and Swiss francs was confiscated."

The scene switched to a group of smiling men at a microphone. "We're very pleased about this," a man was saying.

"Look, there's Grant Early Harrison in the back row," Holly said. "They've done it. I can go after Trini now."

"I guess so," Stone said. "Lance didn't mention this last night."

"I guess the FBI didn't let him in on the timing. You ready to go back to New York?"

Stone shrugged. "Sure. I don't know how much more of this sunshine and sea and clean air I can take, anyway. Can I have breakfast first?"

"Sure." She went to work in the kitchen.

An hour later, Holly left the house in uniform. "I've got a couple of hours' work at the station. You go ahead and file your flight plan. I'll bring sandwiches for lunch on the airplane."

"Are you going to call Ham?"

"I'm going to leave Daisy with him. I'll tell him then."

"Whatever you say."

She left, and Stone phoned for a weather forecast, which was favorable, and filed a flight plan, then he called the airport and asked for the airplane to be refueled. Holly dropped Daisy off with Ham, who didn't like her going back to New York without him.

"You call me if you need me," he said.

"I will," she replied, kissing him on the cheek.

With Holly in the copilot's seat they climbed out of Vero Beach airport and headed north, by way of Ormond Beach and Charleston, South Carolina. Stone noted a nice, thirty-knot tailwind, so they made good time along the route.

They had just passed Charleston when the AirCell phone rang, and Stone answered it. "Hello?"

"Stone?"

"Yes."

"It's Eduardo. I hope you don't mind my phoning you on the airplane. Your secretary gave me the number."

"Not at all. It's good to hear from you, Eduardo."

"Where are you?"

"I've been in Florida for a couple of days, and I'm headed home now. I should land at Teterboro in about two and a half hours."

"I have some information for you."

"Go ahead."

"The business you and I discussed apparently took place last night."

"Yes, I saw something about it on television this morning."

"Your Mr. Rodriguez took part in the process, and when the arrests had been made, he left the scene in an FBI car. My, ah, acquaintances do not now know where he is. They haven't heard from him at all."

"Do they expect to hear from him?"

"Apparently so, but they didn't expect him to leave with the FBI. They're assuming he has either been arrested or is being questioned about some other matter."

"I see. Thank you very much, Eduardo. I'm grateful for your assistance."

"I'm glad I could be of service, and I hope the information I gave you is of some use."

"I hope so, too."

"Please come and have lunch again soon."

"I will, and thank you again. Goodbye." Stone punched off. "You heard that on your headset?" he asked Holly.

"Yes," she said. "Maybe they're holding him for me."

"You think?"

"Can I use the phone?"

"Sure." He handed it to her.

"How do I get information?"

"Dial four-one-one, just like on the ground."

She did that and got the number of the FBI office in New York and was connected.

"Special Agent Grant Harrison," she said to the operator.

"Just a moment. I'll see if he is in the office. Who's calling, please?"

"Chief Holly Barker of the Orchid Beach, Florida, Police Department."

Half a minute later, Grant came on the line. "Holly?"

"Yes, it's me."

"Where are you? What's that noise?"

"I'm in an airplane between New York and Florida."

"There's good news: We made our bust last night."

"I saw it on television this morning. Where's Trini Rodriguez now?"

"I'm afraid I can't tell you that."

"Why not?"

"Trini has been given immunity from prosecution for his cooperation, and he's back in the Witness Protection Program."

Holly turned red. "Grant, you can't give somebody immunity from multiple state murder charges."

"He has immunity from all federal charges."

"I have a warrant for his arrest on twelve

counts of murder one, resulting from the bombing at the church."

"I understand that, but I can't tell you where he is."

"So, by hiding him, you're effectively giving him immunity from state charges?"

"I wouldn't put it that way, but you can characterize it as you wish."

"This really stinks, Grant."

"I'm sorry you feel that way, Holly. This operation was vital to national security, and we couldn't have pulled it off without Trini's help. Listen, I'm headed back to Miami later today. You want to get together this weekend?"

"No, I don't. Not this weekend or ever again."

"I'm sorry to hear that. I was hoping we could . . ."

"I'm afraid that, from now on, you're going to have to do that to yourself," she said, and hung up. She turned to Stone. "You heard?"

Stone nodded. "Not good."

"What am I going to do now?"

"I'm thinking, I'm thinking."

35

Stone and Holly were already having a drink at Elaine's when Lance arrived.

He settled himself at their table and ordered a drink. "So, how was sunny Florida?"

"Sunny," Stone replied. "I don't know how they stand it down there."

"Yes, it's a hard life. Holly, are you keeping the criminal elements of Orchid Beach in check?"

"Oh, that's not hard. It's mostly traffic and the occasional drug bust or burglary."

"Aren't you bored?"

"Funny you should mention that."

"Oh, really?"

"I've told Stone I'm thinking about making a change. God knows, life is good down there, but it's not very interesting."

"Perhaps I can be of help," Lance said. "Let me work on that."

"Sure."

Stone spoke up. "Actually, you can be of help on something else, Lance."

Lance smiled. "Trini?"

"Right," Holly said.

"I saw the news reports. When I heard that they'd taken Trini away in an FBI car I suspected they'd be hiding him. Is he back in the Witness Protection Program?"

"Yes," she said.

"Have you spoken to anyone at the FBI?"

"Yes, but I'm never speaking to him again."

"Holly, surely you know by now that the FBI is never going to stretch to help anybody in local law enforcement."

"I knew that, but it's been brought home to me afresh."

"Perhaps your best move would be to humiliate the FBI into turning Trini over to you."

"Humiliate them? That sounds like fun."

"Of course, you'd be burning your bridges. They'd never return another phone call of yours."

"Just tell me how to humiliate them."

"I know a well-placed reporter at *The New York Times*. I'm sure he'd like a story about how the FBI is hiding a mass murderer, keeping him from being prosecuted. Would you like to meet the gentleman?"

Holly grinned and opened her mouth to speak, but Stone threw up a hand.

"Hang on," he said.

"What?" Holly asked.

"This is a very big step."

"Well, yeah, I guess it is."

"I think you ought to give some thought to the consequences before you act on this. First of all, you're going to enrage the FBI."

"I'd like that," she said.

"You might not. Suppose you need them on an important case. I mean, you still have to use their lab, their computer databases, their expertise. You might find all that suddenly unavailable to your department—not overtly, just in small ways. They might 'misplace' your lab samples, or your computer connection might suddenly go down."

"Stone has a point, Holly," Lance said. "If you go to the *Times*, it would be like a declaration of war on the FBI, and they could make things uncomfortable for you."

"You still have to answer to your city council, don't you?" Stone asked.

"Well, yes."

"You wouldn't want key members of the council to start getting phone calls from highly placed people at the FBI, complaining about you."

"I guess not. Maybe I should just resign. That would fix all the problems you've brought up."

"But then a whole new set of problems might arise," Stone said. "God help you if you should ever get into some kind of trouble with the Feds."

"What kind of trouble?"

"Oh, I don't know. You might be caught up a tree, so to speak, and need the Bureau's help, or at least their inattention." He waited to see if the penny would drop about the tree. It didn't.

"What do you mean, 'up a tree'?"

"Just a figure of speech, but a pertinent one."

The penny dropped. "Oh," she said.

Stone turned to Lance. "Isn't there something else you might be able to do to help Holly locate Trini—something that could be accomplished without tossing a grenade into the Bureau?"

"I'd need more to go on than I have," Lance said. "If I had Trini's name in the Witness Protection Program, for instance."

Holly sat up straight. "Robert Marshall."

"What?"

"That's Trini's name in the Program. I got it from . . . a source."

"And how long have you known this?"

"Since not long after I came to New York."

Lance pulled out his cell phone and dialed a three-digit number. "Robert Marshall," he said. "New listing." He took out a notebook and wrote down something, then hung up. He ripped the page off the notebook and handed it to Holly. "Eighty-eighth Street," he said. "Two blocks east of here."

"You're kidding," Holly said.

"Nope."

"You've got a CIA thing that can give you that?"

"No, I called New York City information."

"Four-one-one?"

"Exactly."

Holly looked embarrassed. "Why didn't I think of that?"

"I don't know, why didn't you think of that?"

Stone began laughing. "All this time and trouble, and all we had to do was call information!"

"Well," Holly said, standing up, "let's go get him."

"Not until I've had dinner," Lance said, picking up a menu. "There are preparations to be made."

They ordered dinner, then Lance got out his cell phone again. "Write this down," he said when the phone was answered, and he read out the address. "I want a car and two men on the building now. Check the mailboxes for a Robert Marshall and figure out which apartment it is. Check the file on one Trini Rodriguez for a description. Call me back when you've got it nailed." He closed the cell phone. "We don't want to just go strolling in there, do we?"

"I guess not," Holly said.

36

As the waiter was taking away their dishes, Lance's cell phone went off. "Yes?" He listened for a minute or so. "Right. Soon." He hung up. "Your boy came home five minutes ago. So kind of him not to disturb our dinner."

Stone waved to a waiter for a check and signed it.

"Is everybody armed?" Lance asked. "Or do I have to think of everything?"

Stone and Holly nodded.

"Do you have cuffs, Holly?"

"Yep, two pair."

"Then shall we?" Lance pushed back from the table and led them outside to his car. "Take a left," he said to the driver, "then a block and a half straight ahead. One of our cars is there."

The driver did as he was told, and they came to a stop beside another black car. Lance rolled down a window and waved at the darkened windows. A man got out and got into the front seat of Lance's car.

"Tell me," Lance said.

"Your man came home ten minutes ago. He matched the file photo, ponytail and all. He lives on the top floor front; you can see his lights."

Lance looked out the window. "Mmmm, yes. The fire escape is on the front of the building. I'll want your partner at the bottom. Then there's the roof to deal with."

"I've had a word with the super and a look inside. There's a door and a stairway leading to the roof from the top floor."

"All right, you go up to the roof and wait for somebody to come running through that door, and for Christ's sake don't shoot one of us. My friends would prefer to take the man alive, but don't put yourself in peril to make that happen. We'll give you a three-minute head start, then we go in." The man got out of the car and went into the building.

"Here's what I'd like to do," Lance said. "The three of us go into the building and ascend the stairs to the top floor, front apartment. Holly, you knock on the door, then stand with your back to it, so he can see only the back of a woman's head through the peephole. As soon as he cracks the door, Stone and I rush in, with you right behind. We'll concentrate on Trini. It will be your job to keep anyone else who happens to be in the room from shooting Stone and me. That okay?"

"It's good for me," Holly said.

Stone nodded.

The three of them got out of the car, approached the building, and let themselves through the front door, which had had the bolt taped open. Lance put a finger to his lips, then led the way quietly to the fourth floor. He ducked under the peephole and took up a position on the left side of the door, while Stone took the right side. Lance nodded at Holly.

Holly rapped lightly on the door. No response. She rapped harder, then turned around.

"Who's there?" a muffled voice said from inside.

"Escort service," Holly replied, her back still to the door.

They could hear the rattle of the chain being undone, and the door opened an inch. "We didn't call for anybody," he said.

Simultaneously, Lance and Stone rushed the door, knocking the man off his feet. They ran into the room, guns at arm's length, with Holly behind them.

The man on the floor wasn't Trini, and there were three other men in the room, two of them pointing guns at Lance, Stone, and Holly. Trini was there, but he had no gun.

"Freeze, FBI!" one of the armed men shouted.

"Police!" Holly yelled, showing her badge. "I have a warrant for Rodriguez! Let's see some ID."

An agent reached for his ID without disturbing his aim. "Who are these two guys?"

Stone showed them his Orchid Beach badge.

"Fellow traveler," Lance said. "Can we all stop pointing guns at each other?"

The agents didn't move, and now the one they had knocked down was on his feet with a gun, too.

Holly got the warrant out of her purse and held it up for them to see. "This is a fugitive warrant from the State of Florida for Trini

Rodriguez. I'm taking him back for trial on multiple murder charges."

"Okay, everybody relax," the agent said. "Holster your weapons."

The FBI men did so, and Holly, Stone, and Lance complied.

"All right, lady," the agent said, "just hang on a minute. Can I see your ID again?"

Holly handed him the wallet with her badge and ID.

"Okay, Chief, I've got to make a phone call." He picked up a phone on the coffee table and dialed a number. "Put me through to Harrison," he said. He tapped his foot for a moment, then practically came to attention. "Mr. Harrison, this is Carson, at the Eighty-eighth Street apartment. I've got a lady cop here who's shown me a fugitive warrant for our guest."

Holly turned her attention to Trini, who was staring at her as though he'd like to strangle her. "You're all done, Trini," she said. "You're mine now."

Trini managed an evil smile. "We'll see," he said. "I'm going to kill you, after I've fucked you a few times, and I'm going to kill your daddy and your dog, too."

"I can't wait for you to try," Holly said.

"Yes, sir," the agent was saying. "I'll convey that to her." He hung up the phone and turned to Holly. "Your warrant is superceded by an existing federal warrant and national security considerations. I'll have to ask you and your people to leave."

"What do you mean, a federal warrant? Let's see it."

"It's on file in our New York office. I can have it faxed to you tomorrow, if you'll give me a number. In the meantime, my orders are to ask you to leave this apartment, and if you refuse, to arrest you for obstruction of justice."

"Now you listen to me," Holly said.

Stone spoke up. "Holly."

"What?"

"We have to leave."

"I'm not going anywhere."

"We have to leave, or we're going to end up in the federal detention center downtown."

"He's right, Holly," Lance said, taking her by the elbow and steering her toward the door.

Stone took her other elbow and they got her into the hall. The door was closed firmly behind them, and they heard locks turning.

"Thanks for the support, guys," Holly said.

"Stone is right, Holly. You're in a bad position legally."

They had started down the stairs.

"Holly," Stone said, "if you want him, you're going to have to go to a federal judge and get a court order vacating Trini's Witness Protection status and giving your warrant precedence."

"How long will that take?" Holly asked as they were leaving the building.

"The U.S. Attorney's office will fight it. There'll be a hearing—maybe more than one. Weeks, at least."

They got into the car.

"Or," Lance said, "you could just kill him."

Holly grinned. "You sure know how to make a girl feel better," she said.

37

The three of them sat in Lance's car, half a block from the building. They had been waiting for half an hour.

"Why do we think they're coming out soon?" Holly asked.

"Because they're not going to keep him in a place that's no longer safe from you," Lance replied. "They'll get him out as soon as they can arrange another location."

Another half an hour passed, then a dark van turned into the block and stopped in front of the building. There was a radio antenna on top. A moment later, Trini and the four FBI agents came out of the building, two of them carrying suitcases.

"You were right, Lance," Stone said. "They're moving him."

Lance spoke to his driver. "Follow the van, but stay well back."

The van pulled away, went around the block, and turned down Second Avenue. Traffic was fairly heavy. They followed it down Second Avenue to Sixty-sixth Street, where it turned right and drove west, continuing through Central Park.

"Looks like they're moving him to the West Side," Stone said. "I wonder why they still have him in New York? Why didn't they send him to Minneapolis or Seattle or someplace no one would think to look for him?"

"Because somebody as exotic-looking as Trini would stand out like a sore thumb in a white-bread city," Lance replied. "They'd send him to the Southwest. Except they haven't, of course."

The van left the park and continued west to Eleventh Avenue, then turned downtown.

"Maybe Chelsea?" Stone said.

"Maybe not," Lance replied. "Let's wait and see."

As the van approached Forty-second Street it moved to the left lane.

"They're headed for the Holland Tunnel," Stone said.

The van turned left, then right and went into the tunnel.

"Stay well back," Lance reiterated.

The van left the tunnel and got onto Route 3 West.

"This is starting to seem familiar," Stone said.

"What do you mean?" Lance asked.

"It's the route I take to Teterboro Airport."

"Ahhh," Lance said. "Maybe they're *really* moving him."

The van turned north on Route 17.

"Yep," Stone said.

A few miles along, the van turned right at the airport sign.

"Okay, which FBO?" Lance asked.

"The big ones are Atlantic, Millionaire, First, and Signature," Stone said. "They're all on the west side of the field."

"They're turning into Millionaire," Lance said.

"Better stop here. They'll check IDs at the gate. Driver, continue on to Atlantic Aviation."

"Why?" Lance asked.

"Because I can get us onto the field there," Stone said. He got out his NYPD badge and his Teterboro ID card, and in a moment they were being buzzed through the gate to the ramp. "Turn off your lights, turn right, and drive slowly south until you get to the Millionaire ramp."

They drove on for a hundred yards.

"Stop," Lance said, pointing. "Only one airplane ready for takeoff." He dug a pair of small binoculars out of the glove compartment and trained them on the airplane. "Can't see the registration number."

"Just wait," Stone said. "The airplane will turn right as it leaves the ramp, and you'll be able to see it."

The door to the jet closed, and it began to taxi. As Stone had predicted, it turned right.

"Got it," Lance said, jotting down the number. "Don't move the car, just let them taxi right past us." He got out his cell phone and pressed a speed dial number. "This is Echo 4141," he said. "I need the current flight plan for the following aircraft registration number." He read out the tail number. "It will be activated at Teterboro, New Jersey, momentarily. I need the destination and any stops in between." He put a hand over the phone. "They're logging on the FAA's Air Traffic Control computer now," he said to the backseat. "Yes? Thank you. I'd like a trace on the aircraft in case it changes destinations, and I'd like to know what time it is projected to land. Right." He hung up. "Their destination is Santa Fe, New Mexico," he said.

"I wonder why Santa Fe?" Holly asked.

"Trini will blend in with the large Hispanic population there. It sounds like a final destination, too. If they were going to put him on a commercial flight, they'd go to Albuquerque. Santa Fe has few commercial flights, and none late at night."

"Can you get someone to cover the arrival and follow them to their destination?" Stone asked.

"I'm afraid I can't stretch my authority that far, since I'm based in New York. I'm not even sure we have anybody on the ground in Santa Fe. Maybe Albuquerque, though."

They watched as the jet took off and turned to the southwest.

"We may as well go home," Lance said.

"Did they give you an ETA for Santa Fe?" Stone asked.

"They've flight-planned for four hours and ten minutes," Lance replied.

Stone looked at his watch.

"It's two hours earlier in Santa Fe. You know somebody out there?"

"I used to, but it's been a long time," Stone said.

"It's worth a try," Holly said.

"What the hell, I'll try," Stone said, getting out his cell phone. "I did some work once with a lawyer out there. If he remembers me, maybe he'll help." He dialed information. "A number in Santa Fe, New Mexico, for the residence of Ed Eagle," he said. "Please connect me." While the number rang, he turned to Holly. "You really want to chase him down?"

"More than anything."

"Hello," a deep voice said at the other end of the phone.

"Ed?"

"Yes, who's this?"

"Ed, this is Stone Barrington, in New York. We did a little work together a few years back."

"Of course, Stone. How are you?"

"I'm very well, thank you. I hope you are, as well."

"I can't complain. Business is brisk and life is sweet."

"Well, you can't ask for more than that. Ed, I need something done in Santa Fe, and I hope you can help me."

"I will if I can. What do you need?"

"I need a private detective, or just somebody smart, to meet a private jet that's going to be landing in Santa Fe in about four hours. There are three to five men aboard, and I want them followed to their destination."

"I think I know a fellow who can handle that," Eagle said. "Anything else he should know?"

"One of them is wanted in Florida on a fugitive warrant. The others are FBI agents, and they'll probably be met by an FBI car."

"A fugitive traveling with FBI agents?"

"It's complicated. I'll explain it when I get there."

"You're coming out, then?"

"I'll leave tomorrow morning in my own airplane; probably be there in time for dinner. Can you recommend a hotel?"

"How many are you?"

"Myself and a lady cop."

"Can you share a room?"

"You betcha."

"Then I insist you stay with me. Call me at

your fuel stop and give me an ETA, and I'll meet you."

"Thank you, Ed. If the destination of these parties is not local, then I'll need to know that. It might cause a change of plan."

"I'll call you by eight tomorrow morning, your time, and give you my man's report on their destination."

"Thank you, Ed. I'll speak to you then." He hung up and turned to Holly. "Okay, we're going to Santa Fe."

"Are you sure we shouldn't fly commercial?"

"I don't fly commercial, except overseas."

38

The following morning at 7:45, Stone had just finished packing when the phone rang.

"Hello?"

"Stone, it's Ed Eagle."

"Good morning, Ed."

"My man was at Santa Fe Airport last night when the jet in question landed and was met by a van with federal plates. He followed the group to a house out on the north side of town, in a semi-remote area. After a few minutes, the van left the house with three occupants, which indicates that your fugitive is in the house with at least two agents."

"That's great news, Ed. Thanks very much."

"Stone, I don't know if you've considered the ramifications of trying to arrest a fugitive who's already in federal custody."

"I'm just helping out a friend," Stone replied, "and I'm constantly reminding her of the difficulties involved, but she's determined to take this guy back to Florida for trial."

"We'll talk some more when you get here," Eagle said.

"Okay. We're refueling in Saint Louis, and I'll call you from there with an ETA."

"A word of advice. If you can stretch your fuel for landing at Wichita, it's a faster in-and-out."

"I'll keep that in mind. We'll have to see how the actual, as opposed to forecast, headwinds work out."

"See you tonight then."

"Thanks again, Ed."

Holly came into the room. "What's up?"

"They're in Santa Fe, and Ed's guy followed them to a house there, so it may be Trini's final destination."

"I'm ready to go when you are."

"Then let's do it."

Joan drove them to Teterboro, where Stone did a preflight inspection and got a clearance. They were rolling by nine o'clock.

Their route took them over Pennsylvania,

Ohio, Indiana, and Illinois, and the head-winds proved light enough for Stone to make Wichita for refueling. He called Ed Eagle from there and gave him an ETA of 9:00 P.M., Santa Fe time.

Ed Eagle was standing on the ramp when Stone taxied up to the Santa Fe Jet Center, and ten minutes later they were headed to Eagle's house.

"I've had a man watching the house all day," Ed said, "and nobody has left the place."

"Where is it?"

"It's about five miles north of the center of town, off Tano Road, on Tano Norte. The area has some new houses, but it's not all built up yet. There's a lot of empty land around it. I know the house, because I knew the guy who built it, and I went to a couple of dinner parties there."

"Can you describe it to me?"

"A single story—there are restrictions on building height out there—three bedrooms, a library, living room, dining room, kitchen, garage—about six thousand square feet. A subsequent owner built an elaborate wall along the road, so you can't see the house from the road."

"Does the wall go all the way around the house?"

"No. You could approach it on foot, but the terrain is a little rough—arroyos and ravines on the property. I did the closing when the original owner bought the property, and as I recall, he bought half of a twenty-five-acre tract. There are no other houses within, say, five hundred feet. There's also a swimming pool and cabana, a tennis court, and a guest house."

"Sounds pretty elaborate for somebody in the Witness Protection Program."

"I thought the same thing. It may just be a way point on the way to his final destination."

"Sounds pretty elaborate for an FBI property, too."

"Yeah. My guess is it's owned by somebody friendly to the Bureau—I'll have to check the property records to find out who—and that they've got your man stashed in the guest house. If that's the case, it might make him a little easier to get out of there. The guest house has its own access to the road."

"Can we take a look at it tonight?" Holly asked.

"You don't want to do that. You're tired, and you don't know the territory, and dinner's waiting for us."

"Relax, Holly," Stone said. "It doesn't sound like Trini's going anywhere."

"Oh, all right," Holly sighed.

Ed drove them through the village of Tesuque, north of Santa Fe, and up into the hills above the village, then turned into a driveway marked by a large stone eagle perched on a big boulder.

The house was spacious and comfortable, and the guest bedroom was inviting.

"Freshen up. There's a drink waiting for you, and dinner in a few minutes," Ed said.

Stone splashed some water on his face and brushed his hair. "You ready?" he asked Holly.

"You go get us a drink. I'll be along in a minute."

Stone found Ed in the kitchen, where there were sizzling noises coming from a skillet.

"Booze is over there in that cabinet," Ed said, pointing. "Help yourself."

Stone found a selection of half a dozen

bourbons and poured Holly and himself some Knob Creek.

"That lady of yours sounds hot for this guy," Ed said.

"That's putting it mildly. She's going at him with reckless abandon. We had the guy nailed in New York last night, only to find a bunch of FBI agents guarding him."

"How'd you find out he went to Santa Fe?"

"We followed them to Teterboro and a friend got a report on their flight plan. That's when I called you."

"Stone, I don't know what your relationship is to this lady, but I can guess. Are you sure you're not following your dick around?"

"No, I'm not sure," Stone replied. "I keep asking myself that question, but I just got caught up in this business, and I'd like to help her see it through."

"I'm happy to help you as much as I can, Stone, but see that I don't get mixed up in a kidnapping."

"Don't worry, I'll keep you out of it, Ed. How's life these days?"

"Life is very good. I got married a few years back, but she's at a spa in California this week, toning up and all that good stuff."

"I'm sorry I didn't get to meet her."

"Another time."

Holly joined them, and Stone handed her her drink. "Is there any way we can find out tonight who owns that house?" she asked. "That's been worrying me."

Ed picked up a phone and dialed a number. "Sharon? Ed Eagle. You remember the house you built out on Tano Norte? . . . That's the one. Any idea who owns it now? . . . No kidding? Since when? . . . Just curious. Thanks very much." He hung up. "That was the lady who was the contractor on the house. She says it's owned now by Byron Miller."

"Who's he?" Holly asked.

"He's the U.S. Attorney for our district, and I'd advise you not to try to take your man off his property. He could do bad things to you."

"Swell," Holly said, pulling on her bourbon.

39

Ed Eagle was waiting when Stone and Holly came into the kitchen for breakfast. "You're on the move early," Stone said.

"I've got a hearing at nine o'clock, and I didn't have time to prepare fully for it yesterday," Ed said. He spread a map over the kitchen table. "I want to show you exactly where the house on Tano Norte is," he said, pointing. "You go back into Tesuque, then take the main highway south. There's a lot of construction, and they've sealed off the old entrance to Tano Road, so you'll have to go this route and turn right at the first exit." He drew a line on the map with a Hi-Liter. "Tano Norte turns off Tano Road right here, and the house is another mile and a quarter down the road. You'll be able to see the house from a hill right here, but when you get to the place you'll just see a wall. My man is still out there, and I'm going to pull him off the surveillance this morning, unless you want to fork out three hundred bucks a day for his time."

"Pull him off, and I'll reimburse you for his time so far," Holly said. "My department has discretionary funds for this sort of thing."

"I'm just guessing, but I don't think Byron Miller is going to host a felon for very long. Either he wants something from the guy, or the place he's headed for isn't quite ready yet, but I think they're going to move him soon."

"What sort of guy is Miller?" Stone asked.

"A hard-ass. None of the lawyers I know like him, and he enjoys his reputation for being tough. If you cross him, he'll screw you first and ask questions later." Ed handed them a card and some car keys. "Here's my office number and the cell, too, and you can use the Jeep outside for as long as the wife is out of town, and she's not due back until next week. There are some binoculars in the center console. Have you got a cell phone?"

Stone wrote down both their cell numbers.

"Okay, have a good time," Ed said, and he was gone.

Stone and Holly followed Ed's directions, and Stone stopped the Jeep Grand Cherokee at the top of a hill. "That's the house out there," he said, pointing to an adobe-colored lump on the land nearly a mile away. "Let's get a closer look." He drove slowly down the road, enjoying the view to the north, until they came to a long wall.

"The place looks like a monastery," Holly said, pointing at the bell over the gate.

"We'd better turn around," Stone said, pointing at a sign that told them the road was a dead end. "We can't just camp out in front of the place." He drove back to the hilltop where they could see the house. "Anybody who leaves is going to have to come this way. There's no other road." He turned off on a dirt track that ended in a clearing, then pointed the car toward the house. "Good view," he said, rolling down the windows and taking the binoculars out of the center console.

"So we're just going to sit here?" Holly asked.

"We can't bust in there and take Trini," Stone said. "You know whose house it is." He trained the binoculars on the house. "Nobody's moving."

They sat for three hours, listening to a local radio station and watching the house. The day grew warm.

"This is really boring," Holly said.

"Sounds like you've never done a lot of stakeout work," Stone replied.

"No, I haven't, and now I know why. I like to keep on the move."

"Tell you what, why don't you drive back to Tesuque and get us some sandwiches? I'll stay here and keep an eye on the house."

"What happens if Trini moves?"

"I'll call you on your cell phone. You can head them off."

"And leave you sitting here?"

"I'll call Ed or a cab, if you have to follow somebody," Stone said, getting out of the car.

Holly got into the driver's seat. "What do you want?"

"A sandwich and a diet soda will do."

"See you soon." She started the car and turned back toward Tano Norte.

Stone settled himself under a piñon tree and took in the landscape. To the west a series of mountains rose, and from the map he figured out that was where Los Alamos was. The Rio Grande was supposed to be somewhere over there, but he couldn't see it. He picked out various spots on the landscape with the binoculars, occasionally checking the house.

He began to get drowsy and stood up to get his circulation going. What the hell was he doing out here in the high desert, watching a house, hoping Trini would move? He should be in New York, getting some work done, making some money, instead of letting this girl drag him all over the country.

Holly returned with their sandwiches, and they had just begun to eat when there was movement at the house.

"Some people down there," she said, grabbing the binoculars.

Four or five people had materialized from somewhere and were standing around a car, talking.

"Is one of them Trini?" Stone asked.

"I think so. It's hard to tell."

The people continued to talk, then they got into two cars and left the house, driving up the road toward them.

"They're moving," Holly said.

Stone started the car and drove the few yards back to Tano Norte. "Let's get a look in those cars." He turned into the road, then pulled over to one side and got out the map. "I'm going to pretend to be looking at this. You watch the car as it passes and see if he's inside."

"Okay."

Stone played the studious tourist, and a minute later the two cars overtook and passed him.

"Second car," Holly said. "Trini's in the backseat. Let's go!"

"Wait a minute. Let's not follow too closely." He gave the car a good head start, then got moving. As they reached the paved part of the road he pointed into the distance. "There it is."

"Don't lose it," Holly said.

Stone increased his speed to keep the car in sight. He followed it back onto the main highway, and they headed into the town. He followed the car until it turned into the parking lot of a large building only a short distance into town. He pointed at a sign. "It's the federal courthouse," he said. "They must be taking him to the U.S. Attorney's office."

"Or Trini is testifying in a case." Holly opened the door.

"Where are you going?" Stone asked.

"I'm going to follow them," she said. "You park the car."

"How will I know where you're going?"

"If Trini is testifying, they'll be going to a courtroom, won't they?"

"I can't argue with that." Stone found a parking place and followed her into the courthouse.

40

Stone stopped at the desk before the metal detector and showed his Orchid Beach badge. "I'm armed," he said.

"Sorry, Lieutenant," the guard said, "only federal officers can carry inside the courthouse. You'll have to check your weapon." Stone gave the man his Walther and got a receipt, then he walked through the metal detector and into a hallway.

His cell phone vibrated. "Hello?"

"It's Dino. Elaine's tonight?"

"Sorry, it's too long a drive."

"What?"

"I'm in Santa Fe, New Mexico."

"What the fuck are you doing way the hell out there?"

"I'm with Holly. It's the Trini thing; we followed him out here."

"You've gone out of your fucking mind," Dino said pleasantly. "I mean, I can see fooling around with this thing to get the girl in the sack, but . . ."

"Dino, this has nothing to do with sex."

"Yeah, sure."

"Well, not much. I share her outrage that the Feds would let this guy take a walk, that's all, and it worries me that she's doing this alone."

"Well, you're going to worry yourself right into a federal prison, if you're not careful. Lance told me about your attempt to bust this guy. You've been warned off. Why are you still in this?"

"To tell you the truth, I'm getting near the end of my rope. I'm ready to come back to New York."

"Call me when you get in. We'll have dinner, and I'll straighten you out." Dino hung up.

Stone put the phone away and looked up and down the hallway. No sign of Holly. He found a courtroom and peeked inside. It was half full of people, but there was no judge on the bench, yet. Holly was sitting in the back row of seats. He went in and joined her.

"What's happening?"

"Trini and two FBI agents are sitting in the first row, behind the prosecutor's table," she said, nodding. "The guy at the table must be Byron Miller."

Stone looked at the two men sitting at the table, their backs to him. "If the U.S. Attorney himself is trying a case, then it has to be an important one."

A bailiff stood up and shouted the name of a judge, and the crowd stood until he was seated.

"Mr. Miller, call your next witness," the judge said.

Miller stood up and called Trini, then waited while he was sworn and sat down. "Mr. Rodriguez," he said, "were you, until recently, a member of organized crime?"

"Yes," Trini replied. "Until late last year I worked for a family in Florida."

"By 'family' do you mean a Mafia family?"

"Yes."

"What were your duties?"

"I arranged loans for applicants and took care of collections."

"Loans from the Mafia family?"

"Yes."

"Were these loans made to people who

could not obtain them from conventional banks?"

"Yes."

"Were these loans made at very high interest rates?"

"Yes."

"Was this, in fact, an illegal loan sharking company?"

"Yes, it was."

"Did you attend a meeting of organized crime figures on June tenth of last year in Miami, Florida?"

"Yes, I did," Trini said.

"What was the purpose of the meeting?"

"Some people from New Mexico wanted to get financing for a new racetrack."

"Was anyone in this courtroom besides yourself present at this meeting?"

"Yes."

"Could you point out these people?"

Trini pointed at the defense table. "Those two gentlemen right there."

"Let the record show that Mr. Rodriguez is pointing to the two defendants, Roberto and Chico Rivera." Miller turned back to Trini. "Did the organization you worked for make a loan to the Rivera brothers?"

"Yes, we did."

"In what amount?"

"Two million dollars."

"And what were the funds intended for?"

"To bribe public officials in New Mexico to pave the way for their getting a license to build the racetrack."

"Did you ever learn if they were successful in bribing public officials in New Mexico?"

"Yes. We learned that they had been successful."

"Thank you, Mr. Rodriguez." He turned to the defense table. "Your witness."

The defense attorney stood up and began to bombard Trini with questions.

Holly leaned over to Stone and whispered, "How long do you think this is going to go on?"

"My guess would be not long. Let's go outside."

They got up and went out into the hallway.

"We could take him when he leaves the courthouse," Holly said.

"Not on federal property," Stone replied. "Your warrant has no force here, unless you get a federal judge to sign off on it."

"Then I'll go to the judge in this case where he's just testified," Holly said.

Stone shrugged. "You can try."

They went back into the courtroom.

"Thank you, Mr. Rodriguez," the judge said. "We'll take a fifteen-minute recess before continuing with the next witness." He stood up and left the courtroom.

"Let's go," Holly said. She approached the bailiff and flashed her badge. "I'd like to see the judge, please."

"On what business?"

Holly produced her paperwork. "I have a fugitive warrant for a witness in this case."

"Just a minute." The bailiff took the warrant and disappeared through a door. Five minutes passed, then the bailiff came back, approached the prosecutor's table, and spoke with Byron Miller, who rose and followed him toward the judge's chambers. The bailiff beckoned Holly and Stone to follow.

The judge was sitting at his desk eating a sandwich, his robe thrown over a chair. "You're Chief Barker?" he said to Holly.

"Yes, Your Honor, and this is my associate, Stone Barrington."

"This is the United States Attorney, Mr. Byron Miller," the judge said, nodding toward Miller. "Everybody sit down."

They sat.

"Mr. Miller, this police officer has presented me with what seems to be a properly executed fugitive warrant for your witness, Mr. Rodriguez, on charges of murder."

"That's twelve murders, Judge," Holly said.

"Are you all done with Mr. Rodriguez?" the judge asked Miller.

"Yes, Judge," Miller said, "but Mr. Rodriguez has been certified by the Attorney General for the Witness Protection Program. He has recently played an important role in breaking up a terrorist ring in New York, and the FBI have informed me that he will be testifying in other trials to come. It's important that he remain in federal custody until the government is done with him."

Stone spoke up. "Your Honor, the fact that Mr. Rodriguez has been placed in the Witness Protection Program indicates that, even when the government is done with him, they have no intention of returning him to the Florida jurisdiction for trial on these murder charges. They're going to let him walk."

"Is that the case, Mr. Miller?" the judge asked.

"I can't speak for the attorney general in this matter, Judge."

"Well, you've been speaking for him up until now. Why are you getting so shy all of a sudden?"

"Your Honor, I can only tell you that this witness is crucial to more than one case against defendants who are far worse than he is, and that he needs to be kept in federal custody until he has finished testifying."

"And how long do you anticipate that will be?"

"I can't say, Your Honor, since the cases are spread over more than just this jurisdiction."

The judge flipped through the warrant again. "Well," he said, "I don't like the sound of this at all. These are heinous crimes, and the government ought not to be able to ignore them and give this witness protection from being brought to justice. I'm going to authorize Chief Barker to serve her warrant, take Mr. Rodriguez into custody, and return him to her jurisdiction for trial. If the government wants him to testify in further trials, they can apply to the judge in the state case for temporary custody."

"Thank you, Judge," Holly said, beaming at him.

"Of course, your order will apply only to this jurisdiction, Your Honor," Miller said smoothly.

"Yes," the judge replied. He stamped Holly's warrant and signed it. "All right, let's get my court back into session and continue with our trial."

Everybody stood up and left the chamber.

Holly walked over to the prosecution table, where Byron Miller was talking on his cell phone. "Mr. Miller, where is Rodriguez now?"

"I'm afraid I don't know," Miller said.

"He's staying at your house. Can I find him there?"

"I'm on the phone here," Miller replied. "Now if you'll excuse me."

The bailiff called the case again, and the court stood for the entrance of the judge.

"Let's get out of here, Holly," Stone said.

"What have they done with him?" Holly asked when they were in the hallway.

"I don't know, but we'd better find him before he leaves the jurisdiction," Stone replied.

41

Stone and Holly went out to the parking lot and looked for the car that had brought Trini to the courthouse. It was nowhere to be seen.

"Let's go to Miller's house," Holly said. "Now that we have a valid warrant, we can get in."

"Right," Stone said. He retraced his route to Tano Road and turned down Tano Norte. "I can't believe we've finally got a legal handle on this guy. You said you brought cuffs?"

"Two pair," Holly said. "I'll truss him up like a Thanksgiving turkey."

They arrived at Miller's house and found the gates still closed. Stone reached out the window and pressed the button on the intercom.

"Yes?" a woman's voice responded.

"This is the police. Please open the gates."

There was a buzzing noise, and the gates swung slowly open. Stone parked the car, and they walked to the front door and rang the bell. A moment later a Hispanic woman came to the door.

"Yes?"

"I have a warrant for the arrest of Trini Rodriguez," Holly said.

"There's nobody here," the woman replied.

"How about the guest house?"

"No, I just cleaned it. The three men staying there went to the airport."

"How long ago?" Holly asked.

"Maybe ten, fifteen minutes."

"How do I get to the airport?"

"You go back to Tano Road, then turn right at the intersection, then right again on the four-lane highway. That takes you straight there."

They ran for the car and sped back toward Tano Road, then found the divided highway. Stone was shortly doing a hundred miles an hour.

Holly sat grimly in the passenger seat,

clutching her warrant. "I wish we had a siren," she said.

"I don't think this thing would go any faster if we had a siren."

They followed the signs to the airport, left the car, and ran into the Santa Fe Jet Center, straight through the building and out onto the ramp. The jet they had followed from Teterboro was taxiing away, and Holly started to run after it.

"No, no!" Stone yelled after her, and she stopped. "He's going to be doing twenty or thirty miles an hour on the ground." He pointed at the tower. "That's where we need to go."

They ran the short distance to the main terminal building and up the stairway to the control tower. At the top they found a locked door and an intercom. Stone rang the bell.

"Yes?"

"This is the police. We have to stop an airplane from taking off."

The door buzzed open, and the single occupant of the tower stood up. "Let's see some ID," he said.

Stone and Holly flashed their badges. "It's the jet that's taxiing now," Stone said.

He ran to the window and pointed. The jet was just taxiing onto the runway.

"I just got their IFR release and cleared them for takeoff."

Stone grabbed a microphone and called the airplane.

"Yes, tower?"

"This is the police. We have a warrant for one of your passengers, Rodriguez. Enter a left downwind for two zero and return to the airport."

"Stand by, Santa Fe." There was half a minute's silence, then the pilot came back. "Sorry, Santa Fe, the FBI has given me orders to continue my flight. Good day."

"Shit!" Stone said.

"What can we do?" Holly asked.

The tower controller spoke up. "I can call Albuquerque Center on a land line. That's their handoff controller."

"It wouldn't do any good," Stone said. "They'd get the same answer we did."

"So we're screwed?" Holly asked.

"That's about it," Stone replied. "Thanks for your help," Stone said to the controller.

"Don't mention it."

"Can you check their flight plan for their destination?"

The controller picked up a tape and consulted it. "Teterboro, New Jersey. Time en route is three hours and fifty minutes."

"Thanks very much."

They left the tower and walked back to the car. "So we go back to Teterboro?"

"Yes, but they're going to be hours ahead of us. Our flight time back is going to be about seven hours, including a fuel stop."

"So we've lost him again."

"Maybe not completely." Stone got out his cell phone and called Dino.

"Bacchetti."

"Dino, it's Stone."

"You still in Santa Fe?"

"Yes, but we'll be heading back today. I wanted to ask a favor."

"So what else is new?"

"A jet just left Santa Fe with Trini Rodriguez aboard." He gave Dino the tail number.

"You want me to shoot it down?"

"Not quite. It's going to be landing in Teterboro in about three and a half hours, stopping at Millionaire. Can you get somebody to meet the jet and follow the occupants to wherever they're going?"

"I certainly can't send a cop to New Jersey to do that, but I guess I can do it my-self."

"I'm going to owe you for this one."

"You sure are. The next four dinners at Elaine's are yours."

"Done. You can reach me on my cell phone." He hung up and started the car. "Dino's going to meet the flight and see where they take Trini."

"That's great news."

"Let's go back to Ed's house and get our clothes, then we'll follow."

They drove back to Ed Eagle's, went into the house, and started packing.

Holly lay down on the bed. "I'm ex-hausted," she said. "Can we take a nap first?"

Stone lay down beside her. "So am I."

They were still sound asleep when Ed Ea-gle walked in and woke them up. "How'd it go?"

"We both fell asleep," Stone said.

"You've got altitude sickness," Ed said. "Everybody feels lousy for the first twenty-four hours in Santa Fe. The city is at seven thousand feet of elevation, and my house is at a little over eight thousand. Come have some dinner."

"We've got to get back," Stone said, trying to clear his head.

"I'm not letting you fly out of here in your condition," Ed said. "You wouldn't get there until dawn, anyway."

Stone's cell phone vibrated. "Hello?"

"They're on the ground," Dino said. "I'm on it."

42

They departed Santa Fe Airport early the following morning, feeling better but still tired, having thanked Ed Eagle profusely for his help. They followed the same route back, but stopped at Terre Haute, Indiana, to refuel, and it was starting to get dark when they set down at Teterboro. A car service took them back to the city, and they met Dino at Elaine's for dinner.

"So where did you follow them to?" Stone asked, when they had ordered a drink.

"To an apartment a couple of blocks from here, on Eighty-eighth Street."

Holly groaned. "Not again. We've traveled, what, a couple of thousand miles, and we're back where we started?"

"So, why don't you go over there and get him?" Dino asked.

"We tried that before, and we were met by three or four FBI agents with drawn guns."

"Oh, yeah, Lance mentioned that."

"Stone," Holly said, "why can't we do in New York what we did in Santa Fe?"

"You mean go to a federal judge?"

"Yes. It worked once, didn't it?"

"To tell you the truth, I was astonished that it worked."

Dino spoke up. "You mean you got a federal judge to sign off on your warrant?"

"That's right," Stone said.

"I'm astonished, too."

"I think what we would have to do is to force the FBI to show cause why they shouldn't release him to you. Then there'd be a hearing, where the U.S. Attorney in New York or his staff would argue the motion, and they'd probably win. I think it would be a waste of your time and mine, and speaking of my time, I've got to go back to working for a living, instead of chasing Trini Rodriguez all over the country."

"So you want me to go back to Orchid Beach with my tail between my legs?" Holly asked.

"I wasn't suggesting a position for your tail, but I think you might have better luck with a federal judge in your own jurisdiction."

"I think I like Lance's suggestion better."

"What, kill Trini?"

"I didn't hear that," Dino said.

"I'd love to, really I would," Holly said brightly.

"Maybe Lance's other suggestion would be more effective, without getting you put in jail."

"The New York Times?"

"Right."

"You said that could make trouble for me and my department."

"And you said you were tired of it anyway. Want to go out in a burst of glory?"

"Or down in flames?"

"Same thing."

Dino spoke up again. "Could I just remind you both that the last time you annoyed Trini there were very serious attempts on both your lives? Talk about going down in flames!"

"There is that," Stone said. "They might get luckier next time."

"The *Times* idea is looking pretty good right now."

"Think about it," Stone said. "Suppose you convince the *Times*, and they run a big story. Then you'll have a media horde camped on your doorstep—rather, *my* doorstep—clamoring for interviews. *America's Most Wanted* will be after you, as will every supermarket tabloid in the country. You think that will help?"

"I don't know," Holly said. "I'm so tired. I feel like I'm still in Santa Fe, with altitude sickness."

"So am I," Stone admitted. "Why don't we think about this tomorrow?"

"Just like Scarlett O'Hara," Holly said, downing her drink. "Let's get out of here."

Stone and Holly were sound asleep in his bed when there was a loud noise in the bedroom. Stone sat up. "What was that?"

A very bright light blinded him. "That was the sound of your body hitting the floor," a man's voice said.

"What's going on?" Holly asked, sitting up and clutching the sheet to her breast.

"Now your little quest is at an end," the voice said.

"It's Trini," Holly said to Stone.

"Swell."

There was the sound of a semiautomatic pistol having its action worked.

"Could I just point out something?" Stone asked.

"Be quick. I want to kill you, then go to bed."

"You haven't committed a crime since you've been in the Witness Protection Program—at least not one they can hang on you."

"They can't hang this one on me, either," the voice said.

"Oh, yes they can. The New York City Police Department knows about you, knows where you live. You kill us, and your federal protection will evaporate like the morning mist. You'll be a fugitive from the Feds as well as the Florida authorities. Your picture will be all over television, all over those most-wanted shows, and there'll be a big reward out for you. You'll never have another day's peace for the rest of your life."

There was a long silence, then the voice spoke again. "This is your last warning.

Next time, you both die, and you know I can do it." Suddenly, the light went out, and footsteps could be heard on the stairs.

"Now's my chance," Holly said. "If I can kill him before he leaves the house, it'll be a good shooting."

Stone grabbed her wrist. "Hang on. You don't know if he has somebody with him. They could be guarding the stairs until he's out of the house, and you're not going to have any night vision for a few minutes after having that light in your eyes. Let it go."

Holly sat down on the bed. "You're a pretty good lawyer," she said. "You talked him out of killing us."

"Next time, he'll have an alibi, and he'll kill us."

"Next time, set the burglar alarm, will you?"

"Yeah, I did forget that."

"You're forgiven, since I'm still alive, but if you forget again, I'll *never* forgive you."

Stone got up and went to his safe.

"What are you doing?"

"I'm getting the Walther out of the safe. He could change his mind."

"You think you could set the alarm now?"

And he did.

43

Stone was scrambling eggs when Holly came downstairs, wrapping a robe around her naked body.

"Good morning," he said.

"No, it isn't. That son of a bitch would have killed us last night if you hadn't talked him out of it."

"Okay, okay, I'll do the alarm every night."

Holly picked up a phone and dialed a number.

"Who are you calling?"

"A certain cell phone." She waited, tapping her foot. "Grant? Listen to me: Your star witness got out of his cage last night, came into my bedroom with a gun, and threatened to kill me. I'm filing a formal complaint with the NYPD about this. . . .

What?" She put her hand over the phone and turned to Stone. "Turn on the TV."

Stone switched it on. "What are we looking for?"

"Try CNN."

He switched to CNN. A reporter was standing in front of Trini's apartment building on East Eighty-eighth Street. "So one FBI agent is dead and another wounded, apparently by a man being held as a material witness. We don't have a photograph yet, but his name is Trini Rodriguez, also known as Robert Marshall. He is in his mid-thirties, six feet two inches tall, one hundred and eighty pounds, and of Latin and Italian extraction. We expect to have a photograph of him later this morning."

"So," Holly said into the phone, "you got one of your people killed and another hurt? . . . Of course you did it! You're responsible!" She held the phone away from her. "He hung up."

"So, Trini is on the streets?" Stone asked.

"Since early this morning," Holly said. "Grant couldn't tell me anything more than CNN did."

"You and I go armed everywhere," Stone said.

"Too right. Where do we start looking for him?"

"Let me call Dino." Stone dialed Dino's cell phone number. "I hear our boy is off his leash," he said.

"And in a big way," Dino replied. "We're taking a backseat to the Feds on this, since killing an FBI agent is a federal crime."

"So you're not actively looking for him?"

"Oh, sure. We've sent a photograph to all precincts and issued an APB."

"You have any clues to his whereabouts?"

"If I did, he'd be in a cell right now."

"Will you keep me posted?"

"Sure, that's my only job, isn't it?"

"Thanks, Dino." He hung up. "The NYPD is on it, but the Feds are taking the lead. He'll turn up."

"You don't understand," Holly said. "*I* want to turn him up. I want to find him before they do."

"And how do you expect to do that?"

"Call your Mafia friend again. Ask him what he knows."

"I'll call him, but he won't know anything. He can put the word out, and if anybody is sheltering him, he might call me."

"Then we'll know something the NYPD and the Feds won't."

"If we're lucky."

"It's about time we got lucky."

Stone couldn't disagree with that.

"Let's go to Little Italy," she said.

"After breakfast and a shower."

Hungry and unshowered, Stone drove slowly up and down the narrow streets of Little Italy. He stopped the car in front of a deli. "Go in and get us a roll and coffee."

"Keep driving," she replied.

"This car isn't moving until I've had breakfast."

"Oh, all right," she said, getting out and slamming the door. She came back shortly with a paper bag and two cups of coffee.

Stone dug in. "This is when it happens," he said, looking around the street.

"When what happens?"

"When we see him. When I'm right in the middle of eating. Remember last time? I never got lunch."

"Oh, stop your bitching," she said, sipping her coffee. "We've got a real chance of catching this guy now."

"I don't think you want to catch him."

"*What?*"

"You just want to go on hunting him. You enjoy it."

"I do not."

"Yes, you do. You've already admitted that you're bored stiff in your job. You just want to get out of that little town in Florida and see some of the world, and Trini Rodriguez is your ticket."

"That's ridiculous," she said, but less heatedly.

"If we catch the guy it's going to be a real downer for you, assuming you survive the experience, which, if the events of last night are any indication, you may not."

"Oh, I'm going to survive. Don't you worry about that. Trini's chances are not so hot, though."

"Let me tell you what to hope for."

"What?"

"Hope the NYPD catches the bastard, because they just might honor your warrant as a way of pissing off the FBI, which they love to do. Also, hope Trini doesn't kill a cop in the process, because if that happens, they'll never release him to you *or* the Feds."

"I hope I see him on the street, so I can get just one clear shot at him."

"Holly, this is not the O.K. Corral, and you are not Wyatt Earp. This is New York City; millions of people live here, and most of them are on the street every day."

"Don't you think I know that?"

Stone sighed. "I hope to God you do."

"Did you call your friend Eduardo?"

"And when would I have had a chance to do that?" Stone put his empty cup into the paper bag and handed it to Holly. "All right, I'll do it now." He got out his cell phone and dialed the number. Pete answered and connected him.

"Good morning, Stone," Eduardo said. "Have you had any luck finding this Trini fellow?"

"No, Eduardo, and this morning he killed an FBI agent who was guarding him and wounded another."

"This man must be stopped," Eduardo said.

"He's on the run now, and I'd be grateful for any help you could give me in locating him."

"I'll make some calls," Eduardo said. "Are you at home?"

"No, I'm on my cell phone." Stone gave him the number, and Eduardo hung up.

"Happy?" he said to Holly.

"Deliriously," she said grumpily.

A man in a raincoat walked up to Stone's side of the car. "Excuse me," he said.

Stone turned and looked up at him, only to find himself looking into both barrels of a sawed-off shotgun.

"I've got one over here, too," Holly said.

"What can I do for you?" Stone asked, placing his hands on the steering wheel.

"You can do what you're told," the man said.

"Shoot," Stone replied. "No, scrub that—I mean, your wish is my pleasure."

"You got a good attitude," the man said. "Get out of the car."

44

They were marched across the street and down the block by the two men wearing raincoats and carrying shotguns. As they moved down the street a pair of steel doors opened ahead of them and a freight elevator appeared.

"Hop on," one of the men said.

They got on, the platform descended into the darkness below the sidewalk, and the doors closed above their heads. Before their eyes could become accustomed to the gloom, hands searched them and removed their weapons. Then they were shoved along a basement filled with crates of canned food and bottles of olive oil to a storeroom at the rear, where they were shoved rudely inside. The door was closed and bolted.

"All right, what now?" Holly said.

Stone couldn't see her, or his own hand in front of his face. "You think I have a solution for this problem?"

"You're resourceful. Think of something."

"It's your turn."

She sighed loudly. "You want to just wait around here until Trini arrives and shoots us?"

"You think that's the plan?"

"Well, I don't think those two guys were with the FBI or the NYPD, do you?"

"Come to think of it, I don't believe either of those groups ordinarily arms its people with sawed-off shotguns."

"Well, that's an astute observation."

"It's the best I can do in the dark."

A light came on. It was a tiny flashlight, and Holly was holding it.

"You always carry a flashlight?"

"It's on my key ring," she said, aiming it around the room. All four walls were brick, and the floor concrete, with a large drain in the middle. Along the ceiling was a row of meat hooks.

"Uh-oh," Stone said.

"What?"

"Nothing."

"Don't tell me 'nothing'; *what*?"

"Turn off the light and save the batteries for when we need them."

"Need them for what?"

"For seeing."

"We need them now for seeing."

"There's nothing to see."

"There's those hooks. I don't like the look of them."

"Me, either. That's why I said, 'uh-oh.' "

"Oh."

"Yeah."

"We've got to get out of here," she said.

"I'd appreciate your thoughts on just how to do that."

There was a long silence.

"Well?"

"I'm thinking about it," she said.

Stone put his hand against the door and pushed. "Solid oak," he said. "Firmly bolted."

"Maybe if we both put our shoulders against it?"

"We'd bruise our shoulders quite badly."

"What would you suggest?"

"We can wait for somebody to unbolt it, *then* put our shoulders against it. We might surprise them."

"*Fuggedaboutit!*" said a voice from outside the door.

Holly reached out and grabbed for Stone, then put her lips close to his ear. "I think they can hear us."

"I think so, too," Stone whispered back.

"Maybe we'd better shut up."

"Good idea."

"Don't stop thinking, though."

"I'm still thinking."

A long silence.

"You come up with anything yet?" she whispered.

"Not yet."

Another loud sigh. She switched on the light and turned it on some crates against the wall. "We can sit down," she said.

They sat down.

"There's even room to lie down," she said.

"Are you sleepy?"

"No, I'm horny."

"At a time like this?" he whispered.

"Well, it looks like we're not going to live very long. It might be our last chance."

"I don't think I could rise to the occasion," he whispered.

She put her hand on his thigh and felt for his zipper. "I'll bet you can."

"Holly."

"What?"

"Not now."

"If not now, when?" She got the zipper undone and began to feel around.

"You have a point," he said, reaching for her.

45

Something woke Stone, and when he opened his eyes he was dazzled by the light from a single bulb in the ceiling. He shook Holly.

"Again?" she asked.

"Not right now. Look." He pointed toward the door. A bottle of wine with the cork half removed and a paper bag were on the floor near the door.

Stone got up and retrieved them. Inside the bag were two paper cups, a large slice of Parmesan cheese, and a loaf of Italian bread. They fell upon the food.

"What time is it?" Holly asked, her mouth half full.

Stone consulted his watch. "A little after eight. Man, this is good cheese."

"Bread, too," she said. "Night or morning?"

"I don't know. Night, would be my guess. More wine?"

"Please."

He poured it for her, then gulped. "I just had a thought," he said.

"Share it."

"Last meal?"

"Stop sharing."

They heard a noise coming from outside the door, steel clanking against concrete. It went on for some time, then it changed to the sound of a pick and shovel in dirt.

"I don't like the sound of that," Stone said.

"Maybe it's construction work."

"Somehow, I don't think so."

"I told you to stop sharing."

Stone walked over to the door and listened. The sounds were clearer and even less encouraging. He could hear two men grunting at their labor. "Why would they feed us, then kill us?" he asked.

The answer came back from the other side of the door. "Because I'm a romantic."

"You've been listening to us, ah . . ."

"Screwing? Yeah. How could I help it?"

"Well, thanks for the food and wine."

"Don't mention it. Nice Chianti, huh?"

"Very nice," Stone replied. He went and sat by Holly.

"I think that answers your question," he whispered.

"More wine," she said.

Stone poured for both of them.

"You're taking this a lot better than I am," Holly said.

"No, I'm not. I'm just . . ." Stone stopped and listened. "The digging stopped," he said.

"Oh, shit. More wine."

Before he could pour, the door opened and a man stepped inside holding a shotgun.

"Okay, let's go," he said.

Stone recognized the voice from the other side of the door. "I wonder if we could talk about this for just a minute?"

"Nope. You're all out of time." He waved the shotgun toward the door.

Stone and Holly got up from their crates and walked out of the room. The lights were on in the cellar. They were led between rows of stacked goods to the other end, where two sweating men with shovels stood by a large hole. Two bags of lime sat next to the hole.

The smells in the cellar were of cheese, fresh fruit, and fresh earth. These were the last scents they would ever smell. "I wonder if I could get you to make just one phone call before you do this?" Stone asked.

"Nope." He shoved them so that they were standing at one end of the hole, then he and another man with a shotgun took up positions a few feet away.

"You've got my cell phone. The call is to Eduardo Bianchi," he said.

The men stared at him dumbly.

"I think Mr. Bianchi probably has an unlisted number."

"All you have to do is push *send* twice, and you'll be connected. He was the last person I called, and the number is already in there."

Nobody moved.

"I really do think it would be in your best interests to speak to Mr. Bianchi before you do this."

The man finally spoke. "You know Eduardo Bianchi?"

"I know him very well," Stone said. "I was nearly his son-in-law."

"Dino Bacchetti is his son-in-law."

"Dolce and I were engaged, before she . . . got sick."

The man stared at him for a long time. "You understand it would be very embarrassing for me if I called Mr. Bianchi and he didn't know you or want to hear from you?"

"I assure you, you won't be embarrassed."

"If I'm embarrassed, then I'm going to hurt you before I kill you. The lady, too. You understand?"

"I understand perfectly."

The man held out a hand to one of his colleagues. "Gimme his phone."

The man handed him Stone's phone.

"Just press *send* twice," Stone said.

"Yeah, yeah, I got it." The man pressed the button twice and waited. "Nobody's answering," he said.

"He was there earlier, just before you, ah, invited us in here."

"Hello?" the man said, then he started speaking Italian.

Stone caught the words "Don Eduardo."

He stopped speaking, then started again, apparently speaking to Eduardo, then he stopped. "What's your name?" he said to Stone.

"You were going to kill me, and you don't even know who I am?"

"I know who the lady is; that's enough."

"My name is Stone Barrington."

The man repeated this into the telephone. "*Sì. Sì. Sì. Grazie,* Don Eduardo." He closed the phone and handed it to Stone. "Don Eduardo knows you," he said.

Stone breathed an audible sigh of relief.

"He says to kill you anyway."

Stone stopped breathing.

"Just kidding," the man said, then burst out laughing. All the men laughed with him.

"I may die anyway," Holly said to Stone.

"I know how you feel."

When the man had gotten control of himself he held out a hand to Stone. "My name is Vito."

Stone shook the hand.

"Don Eduardo says to take you back to your car."

"Good."

"But I gotta kill the lady."

"Now hang on a minute," Stone said.

"Yeah," Holly echoed, "hang on!"

Vito burst out laughing again, and the

others followed suit. "Come on," he said finally, waving them toward the elevator. "I'm just kidding again." His shoulders were shaking, and tears were rolling down his cheeks.

"So, we dug this hole for nothing?" one of the men with a shovel said to Vito.

"Don't worry about it, it'll get used," Vito replied.

He rode up in the elevator with Stone and Holly and handed them their guns. "You can find your car from here?" Vito asked.

"Yes, we can," Stone replied. "One more thing. We want Trini Rodriguez."

Vito rolled his eyes. "*Everybody* wants Trini," he said.

"Don Eduardo would like us to find him."

Vito looked at him doubtfully.

"No kidding."

"Trini is with the fuckin' towelheads some-where," he said.

"Towelheads?"

"Yeah, the Ayrabs."

"And where are the Ayrabs?"

"Around somewhere."

"I thought all the Ayrabs got arrested when Trini pulled off his little deal with the FBI."

"The FBI, what do they know?" Vito said, laughing.

"Will you be speaking to Trini?" Stone asked.

"Yeah, I guess. He'll want to know how you died." Vito began laughing again.

"Do me a favor, Vito. Tell him something he'll like to hear."

"Yeah, okay. I'll make him happy."

Stone handed him a card. "Then find out where he is and call me."

Vito took the card. "You gonna cap Trini?"

"No, the lady is going to arrest him and take him back to Florida to be tried for killing a dozen people at a funeral."

"Trini did that?" Vito looked amazed.

"He did."

Vito said something to himself in Italian. "It'll be a pleasure to rat him out," he said. "*Buona sera.*"

Stone and Holly walked down the dark street toward where they had left the car.

"As long as we're down here, you want to get some dinner?" Stone asked.

"Thanks," Holly said, "I already ate. I just want to get into bed, assume the fetal position, and suck my thumb for a couple of days."

46

When they got home, Holly did exactly what she had said she was going to do, except she didn't suck her thumb.

Stone was tired, but oddly alert. He called Dino.

"Bacchetti."

"It's Stone, but it almost wasn't."

"Huh?"

"Some of Trini's buddies from the Italian side of the equation stuck a shotgun in my ear in Little Italy and walked Holly and me to a nearby cellar, where they proceeded to dig a grave for the two of us."

"Are you speaking to me from the grave? Because if you are, I want to record this conversation."

"Fortunately, no. I was able to persuade the leader of this merry band of men, a guy

named Vito, to call Eduardo before he un-
loaded his shotgun in our direction."

"And Eduardo called them off?"

"Yes. Fortunately, he was at home."

"You want me to arrest somebody?"

"No, after all, they only scared us half to
death, and anyway, Vito might be able to
help us locate Trini."

"I thought you were ready to give up on
Trini."

"Oddly enough, my near-death experience has renewed my interest in finding the
son of a bitch. In fact, I think I want to be a
witness at his execution, if I don't actually
do it myself."

"Funny, when the two guys on the motorcycle had a go at you, all you felt was bad
about killing them."

"Looking down the barrels of two shotguns concentrates the mind wonderfully."

"I expect it does."

"What's the latest on Trini? Why did he
shoot the two FBI guys?"

"Well, from what I hear on the grapevine,
the two agents tried to get him out of bed
too early in the morning, and it irritated him,
so he shot them both."

"Are you serious?"

"Absolutely. He just went nuts, according to the agent who's still alive."

"Well, since he was standing at the foot of my bed in the middle of the night, threatening to kill me, I guess he missed some sleep. Some people are just grumpy if they don't get their eight hours."

"So, what's your next move?"

"Vito says he'll be talking to Trini, who will want the details on how we begged for our lives."

"Did you beg for your lives?"

"No. I concentrated on getting Vito to call Eduardo before he spread us around the cellar. But Vito is going to give Trini details that will please him and then call me and tell me where Trini is, if he can find out. He says Trini is with his Arab friends—or towelheads, as he prefers to call them."

"I thought the FBI arrested all the towelheads."

"So did I, but apparently there's an abundant supply of them."

"I think I'd like to talk to the towelheads," Dino said.

"Tell you what: We work together on this,

you take the towelheads, and we'll take Trini."

"What are you going to do with him?"

"Take him back to Florida and get him tried."

"That's a sweet idea. I hope it works for you."

"You going to help?"

"Okay, you get me a location on Trini and his buddies and I'll supply a SWAT team. I'll get a judge to honor Holly's warrant, and you three can hotfoot it to the airport. I'll take the towelheads home with me."

"You've got a deal, but no FBI."

"Why would I want those guys around to take the credit?"

"Why, indeed?"

"Dinner tomorrow?"

"You're on."

"And you're still buying, remember?"

"I remember."

Dino hung up, and Stone called Eduardo.

"Stone, are you all right?"

"Thanks to your help, I am, Eduardo."

"I want to apologize for these people of ours."

"No apology necessary. You can't be expected to know everything."

"I'm glad they called me."

"So am I."

"Have you had any luck in finding this Rodriguez fellow?"

"I'm working on it. One of the men who, ah, detained us says he may be speaking to him, and he'll try to find out where he is. There are some Arab gentlemen involved, apparently."

"I have heard of these people, and I would be pleased to see them caught and put into prison."

"If we can get a location on them, that could very well happen. I'd be grateful to hear of any information that might come your way."

"Of course. I'll call you."

"Thank you again for saving our lives, Eduardo."

"Please, I was happy to."

They both hung up, and now Stone was tired. He went upstairs, got undressed, and got into bed with Holly, who was sleeping as if drugged. Soon, he was, too.

Stone got up at mid-morning the following day and found Holly still sleeping. He reached out to give Daisy a pat, then remembered she was in Florida with Ham. Then he sat up in bed, wide awake.

He got into a robe, went downstairs, and called Ham.

"Hello?"

"Ham, it's Stone Barrington."

"How you doing, Stone?"

"I'm okay, and so is Holly. She's still asleep."

"What's up?"

"We've had a brush with Trini, and I think you ought to be on the lookout for his people around your place."

"Yeah?"

"Yeah. I think maybe you might think about changing locations. Why don't you move into Holly's place until we can nail this guy?"

"You really think he might be a threat to us here?"

"I do."

"What does Holly think?"

"I don't want to wake her to ask, but I think she'd agree with me."

"All right, we'll throw some things in a bag and go over there."

"Thanks, Ham, I'd feel better if you did. Please give my best to Ginny."

"Sure thing. Bye." Ham hung up.

Stone went back upstairs, feeling he had done all he could for the moment.

47

Ham walked into the kitchen where Ginny was cleaning the fish he'd caught early that morning. One of the reasons he loved her was that she would clean his fish, something he hated doing himself. Daisy was asleep on the floor beside her.

"How would you like a little vacation?" he asked.

"Would I have to clean fish?"

"Nope."

"I'd love it. Where you want to go?"

"Why don't we get in that airplane of yours, and you fly us out to the Bahamas."

"Where in the Bahamas?"

"You know them better than I do. Where's the fishing good?"

"Ah, ah, ah," she said, wagging a bloody finger.

"Oh, right; no cleaning fish. Where can we go that somebody else will clean the fish?"

"I know a little resort on Cat Cay that has its own airstrip. You could give your fish to the restaurant and let them worry about the cleaning."

"Sounds good to me. Why don't you stick those fish in the freezer and throw your toothbrush and a bikini into a bag, and let's get out of here."

"Right now?"

"Right now."

"I never knew you to be so spontaneous. Who was the phone call from?"

"Just a guy."

"C'mon, Ham, what guy?"

"It was Stone."

"And Stone suggested we take a vacation?"

"Sort of."

Ginny began wrapping the filets for freezing. "I want to know the whole story, Ham."

"What whole story?"

She put the fish in the freezer and came and put her arms around his waist. "You know, you've been working on that poker face of yours for so long you think you can fool anybody, but you can't fool me."

"Why not?"

"Because I can see right through your eyes into your brain, and right now I see deception."

"Not much deception. After all, can it be so bad if I'm offering you a trip to the Bahamas?"

"Seems to me I've heard you say more than once that the Bahamas are boring, all that sun and sand."

"Not if I can fish."

"And what do I do while you're fishing?"

"I don't know, what do you do here while I'm fishing?"

"That's right, you wouldn't know, would you?"

"Well, I'm not here when I'm fishing, am I?"

"I get naked and do witchcraft incantations."

"You can do witchcraft incantations in the Bahamas, can't you?"

"No, I'd frighten the natives."

"You'd frighten the natives here, if I'd known what you were doing. I like the naked part, though."

"You would, wouldn't you?"

"I sure would. You gonna get packed?"

"Not until you tell me why we're going."

"Stone thought it would be a good idea."

"Why did Stone think that?"

"He had a little brush with Trini Rodriguez."

"He said 'a little brush'?"

"Sort of."

"And what do you think he meant?"

"Well, usually, having a little brush with Trini involves a death experience, but he was still talking, so I guess he and Holly are all right."

"So now he thinks we're going to have a death experience?"

"I think he wants us to avoid that."

"By going to the Bahamas?"

"No, he just wanted us to move into Holly's house for a while. The Bahamas was my idea."

"So you're more worried than he is?"

"No, I just thought the Bahamas would make a nice change until somebody shoots Trini in the head."

"Okay, you talked me into it. I'll go pack." She gave him a little kiss and turned toward the bedroom.

Ham caught a movement out of the corner of his eye; somebody outside. He'd only seen a shoulder and an elbow. "Don't do that right now," he said.

"What?"

He went into the living room, opened his gun safe, and took out an Ithaca riot gun he'd had for years. He handed her the shotgun and a box of shells. "Take this into the broom closet and load it," he said. "Take Daisy, keep her quiet, stay down low."

She regarded him calmly for a moment, then took the shotgun and went back into the kitchen.

Ham took his Beretta 9mm from the safe, shoved a loaded magazine into it, and worked the action. He put two more magazines into his pocket, then took out the Browning automatic shotgun that he used for bird hunting and loaded it, putting extra shells into another pocket. He went to a closet in the living room where he kept his fishing clothes and got inside, leaving the door ajar so he could see the front door. He tuned out the birds in the trees outside, tuned out the cars crossing the bridge over the Indian River half a mile away, and listened to everything else.

He heard the tiny creak of a board from

the back porch; he heard the scuff of a shoe sole from the front porch. He heard the squeak of a hinge on the screen door to the back porch. He knew they were listening, too, and they weren't hearing voices any- more. He thought about saying something, but the closet door he stood behind was flimsy and would not stop a round. He held the shotgun in his left hand, ready to bring up the barrel, and the old automatic in his right.

Then he saw the shoulder and elbow he had seen out the window, and they were at- tached to a head and a neck. The man was short and stocky, and he held an Uzi in his hands.

Why do these yahoos think they need machine guns? he asked himself.

The man stopped just inside the front door and, looking toward the rear of the house, held a finger to his lips, then waved for his companion to approach.

That's it, Ham said to himself. You two fellows just get a little closer together.

The first man was making hand motions now, directing his friend toward the kitchen. No more waiting.

Ham kicked open the closet door.

"Freeze," he said, but he knew they wouldn't. The short barrel of the Uzi was swinging around, and he fired the shotgun at it once, while pointing the Beretta 9mm at the other man.

The first man and the Uzi parted company, and he flew backward, landing on and smashing the mahogany coffee table. The second man dropped his weapon and threw his hands into the air.

"Good evening," Ham said in a low voice. "How many more of you?"

"None," the man said. "Let me out of here, and you'll never see me again."

"That's a possibility," Ham said, "but not until I get some answers. Lie down on the floor." He didn't call Ginny out yet, because he wasn't sure there weren't others.

48

Stone was at his desk, working his way through a pile of work he had dictated days before, when the phone rang.

Joan buzzed him. "Ham Barker on line one, and he wants to talk with both you and Holly."

"Buzz Holly in the bedroom," Stone said. He watched the lights on the phone blinking, then turning red again. He picked up the instrument. "Ham?"

"Yeah, Stone. Holly's on the line, too."

"What's up?"

"Well, we were about to start packing for a little vacation when we had a couple of visitors."

"Are you both all right?"

"Oh, yeah, we're fine. One of our visitors is suffering from being dead, though, and the other one is taped to a kitchen chair. Don't you just love duct tape?"

"Ham," Holly said, "was this a good shooting?"

"Well, if you think having an Uzi pointed at you with intent is a good reason for a shooting, then it's a good shooting."

"Have you called the station?"

"Not yet. I wanted to have a little chat with the other one first."

"Don't wait too long," Holly said.

"Oh, I'm about ready to call now. I just wanted to let you and Stone have the results of our chat first."

"Okay, what are the results?"

"Well, the fellow was a little reluctant to talk at first, until we made him take off his pants and then taped him to the chair and then told him about how Daisy was trained to eat genitals, how they're her favorite thing."

Holly burst out laughing. "I've got to remember that one."

"After that, and after Daisy stood in front of him and showed her teeth, he got real talkative."

"And what did he have to say?" Stone asked.

"Trouble is, he doesn't really know all that much. Turns out he works for some bad people in Miami, and he and his former buddy had traveled up here at the request of your Mr. Rodriguez. That didn't come as much of a surprise."

"No," Holly said, "it wouldn't."

"What did come as a surprise was exactly what Trini wanted them to do to Ginny and Daisy and me when they got here."

"Do I want to hear this, Ham?" Holly asked.

"Probably not. Suffice it to say that he wanted to cause us all some pain before we shuffled off this mortal coil."

"Tell my cops about this in detail," she said.

"Wilco. Now I thought you might have an interest in how this fellow got his instructions from Trini."

"Oh, yes," Holly said.

"It seems Trini called him on his cell phone."

"Oh, good. That means the calling number might still be in the phone."

"Funny you should mention that," Ham said. "I've got the last number, which is where Trini called from, and nine other numbers, four of them in New York. Seems Trini has been moving around the past day or so."

"I've got a pencil," Stone said.

Ham read off the list of numbers in reverse order. "I expect you know somebody who can run down those numbers."

"You bet I do," Stone said.

"Stone, you still think we should vacate the premises for a while?"

"Yes, I do. Trini may be persistent."

"Okay. Soon as we're squared away with the cops, we'll be on our way. Holly, you can reach us on our cell phones."

"Okay, Ham, and you tell Hurd Wallace at the station to call me if he needs any help dealing with your visitors."

"Wilco, baby. You take care of yourself, and Stone, too." Ham hung up.

"Stone, you still on the phone?" she asked.

"Still here."

"Who are you going to get to run down those numbers?"

"Dino would be best."

"Couldn't you get it done more . . . privately?"

"Holly, listen to me: You and I are not go-

ing to go after Trini all by ourselves, and neither are you going to do it alone, even if I
have to hog-tie you."

"Well, being tied up is an interesting
thought, but what do you think that Dino
could do that you and I couldn't do just as
well?"

"Well, just for starters, he can conjure up
a SWAT team, who stand a much better
chance of success than you and I busting
into some room full of well-armed Arab terrorists, without getting somebody besides
them shot."

"You're such a sissy, Stone."

"That's why I'm still alive," Stone replied.
"I learned as a cop not to bust down doors
myself when I could get a dozen guys in
black body armor to do it for me."

"Oh, all right, call Dino."

"My very thought. Bye-bye." He hung up
and dialed Dino.

"Bacchetti."

"It's Stone."

"Hey."

"Two of Trini's hoods tried to kill Holly's
father and his girlfriend this morning, down
in Florida."

"Everybody okay?"

"One of the shooters isn't, and the other gave up a cell phone with ten numbers in it, four of them in New York, at least the last one from a call made by Trini himself."

"Shoot."

Stone read off the numbers.

"I'll have addresses on these in five minutes, and we'll raid all five."

"Great, but Holly and I want to come along on the raid on that last number, the one Trini called from."

"Stone, you know I can't do that. If one of you got hurt, the chief of detectives would fall on me from a great height."

"Listen, we're both sworn officers of a Florida police department, and with a fugitive warrant. You can make a case for us being entitled. And we'll stand in back of your team. I think that after what Holly has been through with this guy, she's entitled. Trini gave his hit men instructions to torture Ham and Ginny and the dog, too, before they died."

"Oh, all right, but you're both going to have to dress up in body armor, helmets, the whole thing, and you don't fire any shots at all. You got that?"

"I've got it, and I'll explain it forcefully to Holly."

"Okay, then. I'll call you back when I've got an address and a team assembled. Give me an hour." He hung up.

Stone trudged upstairs to explain to Holly that she wasn't going to get to personally remove Trini's liver. Not yet, anyway.

49

Stone stripped down his Walther, inspected it, wiped the parts with an oiled rag, reassembled it, loaded a round into the chamber, shoved in a full magazine, put the safety on, and stuck it into his shoulder holster.

Holly had been watching him. "How good a shot are you?"

"Pretty good. Dino is Deadeye Dick."

"Yeah?"

"Twice—at least twice—he's saved my ass by killing somebody with a difficult shot. Most cops I know have never fired their weapons, except on the range. How about you? How good a shot?"

"Very good indeed, but not a patch on Ham. He's the best I ever saw, maybe the best shot alive—and with any weapon. He has this gift, and of course, he's worked hard at it. I've seen him explode a cantalope at a thousand yards with a sniper rifle, and he unerringly hits moving targets with a pistol."

"Like you say, it's a gift; genetic."

"Unfortunately, I got only half his genes."

"I'd say you got some pretty good ones."

She smiled. "Thanks. You think we're near the end of this?"

"God, I hope so. I'm not sure how much longer I can do it."

"I could do it forever."

"I know. Reckless abandon and iron will are a powerful combination. I'm glad you're not hunting me."

"What makes you think I'm not?"

"Uh-oh."

She laughed. "Don't worry about it. I won't threaten your precious bachelorhood."

"What makes you think it's so precious?"

"Well, you've created this perfect existence for yourself. You'd never let anybody disturb that, would you?"

"You've created a pretty perfect existence for yourself, too."

"Yeah, but since Jackson's death, it

hasn't been the same. And I've already told you I'm bored with the work."

"So what are you going to do?"

"Lance has offered me something."

"What? When?"

"At Elaine's, the last time, when you were in the john and Dino was on the phone."

"What did he offer you, exactly?"

"He was vague but intriguing. He said I'd have to do some training at a place called the Farm, in Virginia. Four months, probably."

"I thought those guys recruited from the bottom."

"You mean, not middle-aged, retired soldiers and policemen?"

"Middle-aged, you?"

"Sure. You, too."

"Well."

"It might be fun."

"The training would be a pain in the ass."

"I like that sort of thing. I did a lot of it in the army, training and retraining, then passing the training on to others."

"Maybe you're cut out for it then. But would the work be fun?"

"Lance seems to enjoy it."

"Sometimes I think he enjoys it too much."

"I know what you mean. Still, he's serving his country, so what does it matter if he enjoys it too much?"

"I hope I never find out. So, you want to go work in an embassy somewhere?"

"No, the work he's talking about is domestic and mostly urban. The Agency has a new role in homeland security now, and the change has made them understaffed. The money is no better than decent, but I've got my military pension, and I'm fully vested in my police pension, too. Plus what Jackson left me."

"Sounds like I should marry you for your money."

"I'm not ever going to marry."

"You sound very sure."

"I am. It just isn't out there for me. You're a catch, but you're too much like me. Jackson was a wholly different person, calm and wise and funny. He wasn't brilliant, but he knew how to do the right thing in any situation."

"That's as much a gift as Ham's shooting."

"You're right, and he cultivated it every

day. But he's gone, and there's nothing I can do about it."

"Did they ever catch the people who did it, that cult group, or whatever they were?"

"No, but Lance says I'd have a better chance with the Agency. I could never run them down in law enforcement. Either I'd have a department to run, like now, or I'd be caught up in a bureaucracy with some supervisor's shoe on my neck. I don't think it would be like that with Lance."

"Maybe not."

"I could always quit, if I didn't like it."

"I suppose."

The phone rang and Stone picked it up. "Hello?"

"It's Dino. The address is less than two blocks from your house."

"Jesus." He got a pencil and wrote it down. "We'll meet you there."

"No, come here. We've got the building plans on the way, and we need to plan this well."

"We'll be there in fifteen minutes."

"Bring your weapons and Holly's warrant."

"Will do." He hung up.

"Got your warrant?" he asked Holly.

"You bet your ass."

"Then let's go."

On the way uptown, in the cab, Stone reached out for Holly's wrist and felt her pulse.

"What are you doing?"

"It's about ninety," he said. "You want to calm down. Take some deep breaths. It's going to be at least a couple of hours before we go in."

"I want to do it now."

"I know, but you have to be patient."

"No, I don't," she replied.

"You'll do a better job if you pace yourself."

"Maybe."

"Certainly."

She began taking deep breaths, and her heart rate started to come down.

"That's better," he said.

"No, it isn't," she replied.

50

The team met in a conference room at Dino's precinct. There was a pile of equipment near the door, and men, and a couple of women, were milling around, talking.

"Okay, everybody, settle down," Dino said, setting a blowup of a floor plan on an easel. A blown-up photograph of Trini Rodriguez was pinned to a wall.

People took seats or leaned against the walls.

"We're lucky on this one. The building's under renovation, so current floor plans were filed for the new building permit. What we've got is a five-story walk-up, just like the ones on either side, with a fire escape down the back. We're lucky, too, that the fire escape on our building has been removed, pending replacement, so there's no way down, except the main staircase.

"The phone number we tracked down belongs to the top-floor apartment, though there's not supposed to be anybody living in the building while the fire escape is down, but the neighbors say there are still people living there. The building is owned by a Muslim charity, and the tenants appear to be Muslim, too, so we should treat anybody inside as noncooperative but not hostile, unless they behave that way.

"It's possible that, if the occupants see us going up the stairs, they might give the alarm, and that would make this work more dangerous, so anybody who sees us should be hustled inside his apartment and told to shut up. Anybody who tries to give the alarm should be arrested and gagged until we're done.

"We've got a twelve-man team. I want four on the roof—you can access it from the building to the east—and eight going up the stairs. We've got two officers from a Florida department who have a fugitive warrant for Rodriguez, and they'll be bringing up the rear, so I'll keep them with me.

"According to the neighbors across the

street, there are a lot of people living in each apartment, so you should expect there to be as many as half a dozen people in the apartment. They should all be immediately restrained, unless they point weapons at officers, in which case you should respond with armed force. Any questions?"

"Yeah," said a burly young man sitting at the table. "You have any idea what they might be armed with?"

"My best guess is handguns, but you should be ready to deal with automatic weapons."

"If automatic weapons are a possibility, then I suggest we use a stun grenade before going in."

"Negative," Dino said. "There may be women or even children in there, and since that incident last year when the woman died of a heart attack after a stun grenade was used, we can use them only in dire emergencies when we're certain who's in there."

"Have we used any listening devices on the place?"

"We've pointed a mike at an upstairs window from across the street, but the blinds are drawn, and all we've heard is a kind of low muttering, which we take to be men's voices, and not much of that. We think they may be sleeping."

The man nodded.

"Anybody else?"

The SWAT team leader walked to the easel and pointed. "Going in, try to confine any shooting to this direction, to the east, because we've got a double brick wall there. If possible, avoid shooting toward the walls, here and here, that have windows. Even though we're using frangible ammo, I don't want any rounds going through an open window and flying around the neighborhood. Clear?"

Nobody said anything.

"Is the search warrant here yet?" the leader asked Dino.

"It's on the way," Dino replied. "We won't go until it's in hand. It's for the whole building."

"Do we have arrest warrants for anybody but Rodriguez?"

"Not specifically, but anybody in the apartment should be arrested for harboring a fugitive."

"Women, too?"

"Yes. There'll be a couple of people from

Children's Services on hand to take charge of any children in the apartment, and one of them is an Arabic speaker."

"One of my people speaks Arabic and Urdu, too," the leader said, pointing at one of his men. "He'll do all the talking until we've established who speaks English."

"Trini Rodriguez speaks English," Holly said.

Everybody turned to look at her.

"He might pretend not to, and I'd suggest that if he's armed and he's slow obeying commands in English, somebody shoot him."

"This is Chief Barker from the Orchid Beach, Florida, PD," Dino said. "She's had considerable experience with Rodriguez. Anything else to offer, Holly?"

"He's a stone killer," she said, "and he'll do anything to avoid being arrested, including shooting police officers. He won't hesitate, and neither should you."

"Okay," Dino said. "We've got four detectives in the block observing the house, two in the building across the street on the same floor as our target apartment. We'll be in two vans, and we'll stop on the avenue and check with them before moving in." He looked around the room. "You guys look ready to me. Let's go!"

The men picked up their equipment and filed out.

Dino walked over to a pile next to the door. "This is our stuff," he said. "Let's suit up. We're aiming for entry at six P.M."

51

It was hot in the van in which Stone, Holly, and Dino were riding, and the heavy equipment made things worse. It was past 6:00 P.M. A few of the SWAT team were exchanging macho banter, but most were quiet. Stone wiped sweat from his forehead. "I'm going to need a shower after this."

"Me, too," Holly said.

"Hey, driver!" Dino called out. "Crank up the AC, will you?"

"It's going full blast, Lieutenant," the man called back.

A minute later, the van pulled to a stop, and Dino picked up a handheld radio. "Ricardo, you there?"

"Yes, Lieutenant."

"What's happening inside?"

"Some women in Muslim dress went into

the building carrying groceries, but I couldn't tell what floor they went to."

"Anybody leave?"

"No, sir."

Dino looked at the SWAT team leader. "We're good to go."

"Okay, everybody," the leader said, "fast across the sidewalk, slow up the stairs. I want complete silence from everybody except me and Lieutenant Bacchetti, and we're using earplugs with the radio."

Somebody opened the door, and men from both vans spilled onto the sidewalk and ran up the stairs to the front door, while four others ran to the building next door to gain roof access. Somebody defeated the lock to the street door, and everybody crowded inside, with Stone and Holly bringing up the rear. Stone and Holly had earplugs for their radios, and they could hear any conversation between the SWAT team leader and Dino.

The first element of the team made their way slowly up the stairs, being as quiet as possible, but there was some noise— equipment brushing against the banister, the occasional slip of a boot. They climbed the stairs like a giant caterpillar, snaking around the landings and making their way inexorably upward.

Stone and Holly, right behind Dino, were on the fourth-floor landing when the team leader spoke.

"Stop," he breathed into the radio. "Dino?"

"Right here," Dino whispered.

"There are two doors on the fifth floor."

"What are you talking about?"

"Could be two apartments."

"That wasn't in the plans."

"I know."

"Then let's go in both doors."

"We've only got one ram to take out the doors."

"How tough do they look?"

"Heavy, brand-new, only got primer on them."

"Okay. Knock on one door, say it's the plumber. As soon as somebody cracks it, knock down the other one and go in both."

"Okay. Hang on, one of my men will have to unsuit so he'll look okay through the peephole."

"Okay."

They waited as patiently as they could on the landing, and then they heard a knock.

"Plumber," a male voice said. "I gotta turn off the water for a few minutes." A pause. "Look, pal, the landlord says I go in there right now. You aren't even supposed to be in the apartment, so let me in."

They heard a chain rattle, then the door opening, then all hell broke loose. They heard the ram hit the second door.

"Police! On the floor, everybody!" Other voices added to the din. Shots were fired, then the shooting stopped.

Dino ran up the stairs, followed by Stone and Holly. Both doors were open, one off its hinges, and the hallway was empty. Dino ran through the second door.

Stone and Holly were right behind him. The scene that presented itself was of half a dozen men, all dressed in white, lying on the floor with their hands secured behind them with plastic strips. One man lay faceup on the floor, his chest a mass of blood and holes. He didn't appear to be breathing.

"Is he here?" Holly asked.

"Hang on a minute," Dino said, "we got another door."

A team member was swinging the heavy ram toward what appeared to be a bedroom door. The steel tool struck the door and bounced off, leaving a dent.

"We got a steel door," he said, "and it's braced."

"Keep at it," the team leader yelled.

The man continued to batter the door, then gave up the ram to a second, fresher man.

"This ain't working," the team leader said. "Bring up the saw."

A team member carrying a large black nylon bag unzipped it and produced a battery-operated radial saw. He went to work on the walls around the door, slicing through the timber studs, then he stood back.

"Once more with the ram," the team leader said.

A man picked up the ram and swung it at the door with all his might. The door skidded off the timber bracing it and fell into the room, creating a cloud of dust, and the team poured through the opening, shouting. A moment later, the shouting stopped.

"What's happening?" Holly yelled, pushing her way into the room, followed by Stone and Dino.

"Holy shit," somebody said.

They were all standing around a hole about eighteen inches in diameter that had been punched through the outer wall and into the building next door. Men were stripping off their armor so they could squeeze through.

"Put that equipment back on!" the team leader shouted. "Nobody goes in there without armor!" He held the radio to his lips. "Roof team, start down and search every apartment on the way!"

"Hang on," Dino said, "our warrant doesn't cover the building next door."

"I want four men on the front door of the building next door," the team leader said, pointing to men, and they ran out of the apartment.

"I'm going through there," Holly said, pushing her way forward.

"You don't want to do that, Holly," Dino said. "You want a good bust out of this. We'll have the building sealed in a minute, then we'll send for another warrant."

"It's hot pursuit, Dino. You don't need a warrant to pursue."

"Okay," Dino said to the team leader. "Let's get that hole made bigger and get some men through it. We can't search the other apartments, but we can search the one on the other side of the hole and the hallways."

SWAT team members went to work with tools left in the apartment, and ten minutes later, they were able to get men in armor through the hole.

Stone and Holly followed them and emerged into an empty apartment under renovation.

"Who was on the roof?" Holly asked.

Two men raised their hands.

"Did you see anybody come onto the roof from this building?"

They looked at each other sheepishly. "We had our backs to it," one of them said, "watching the exit from the other building."

"Is there a fire escape on this building?" Holly asked.

"Yes, ma'am."

Holly turned to the SWAT team leader. "Then let's get going. We have to pursue."

"Hang on, Holly," Dino said. "The guy's been gone for, what, fifteen minutes? All he had to do was catch a cab. He's gone for now. We've still got a city-wide APB out on him, and we'll get his picture on the news.

That's all we can do for now, and all you can do is wait."

"Shit, shit, shit!" Holly said.

"My feelings exactly," Dino replied.

"Let's go home," Stone said.

52

Holly, Stone, and Dino trooped disconsolately down the stairs and out into the street, still wearing their body armor. As they hit the sidewalk a television van pulled into the block, and a reporter sprinted toward Dino.

"Lieutenant Bacchetti!" she was hollering. "Give us a minute?"

Dino stopped. "What can I do for you?"

"What just went down here?"

"Call information services, they'll give you a statement."

"Yeah, sure," the woman said.

"Why don't you talk to Chief Holly Barker of the Orchid Beach Police Department?" he suggested, grabbing Holly's arm and dragging her forward.

"Chief Barker?" the woman said. "Who did you arrest here?"

"I'm afraid we didn't arrest anybody," she said. "I'm in New York with a fugitive warrant for one Trini Rodriguez. We entered this building with the help of the NYPD, believing him to be here, but he apparently had a well-planned escape route, and we missed him."

"Isn't that the man wanted for killing an FBI agent and wounding another?"

"Yes, it is, but I want him for a dozen murders committed in the state of Florida."

"We interviewed Special Agent Grant Harrison from the FBI's Miami office less than an hour ago, and he's posted a one-hundred-thousand-dollar reward for Rodriguez. If he's caught, who gets him?"

"I suppose that depends on who catches him," Holly said.

"If you catch him, are you going to hand him over to the FBI?"

"If I catch him, I'm going to take him back to Florida and see him tried."

"What about the FBI?"

"What about them?"

"Don't they have precedence?"

"Says who?"

"Says Agent Harrison."

"Well, he would, wouldn't he? Excuse

me." She went to the van where Stone was waiting and stripped off her equipment. "Let's get out of here."

When they arrived at Stone's house, he switched on the TV and saw Holly's interview on the all-news channel.

"You did very well," Stone said.

"Hang on," Holly said, "here comes Grant."

"In an interview five minutes ago, Special Agent Grant Harrison of the FBI's Miami office disagreed with Chief Barker," the anchorman was saying.

"Chief Barker apparently doesn't understand procedure in this case," Grant said. "The FBI will take custody of Mr. Rodriguez when he's caught, and he'll be tried in federal court for the murder of a federal agent and the attempted murder of another."

"But the NYPD has an all-points bulletin out for this man right now," the reporter said. "Do you think they'll give him up if they capture him?"

"We've already seen an example of how the local department works," Grant said. "They made an attempt to arrest Mr. Rodriguez today. They failed, and now he's at large again. They should have left this to us."

"We understand that it was Chief Barker and the NYPD who tracked Mr. Rodriguez to the East Side address," the reporter said. "Did the FBI know his whereabouts?"

"That's all I have to say at this time," Grant said. "We're offering a one-hundred-thousand-dollar reward for information leading to the arrest of Trini Rodriguez."

The anchorman came on-screen again with a photograph of Trini.

"The reward is going to do it," Holly said. "Somebody will turn him in to the FBI for the money, and I'll be back where I started when I came to New York."

"They seem to have overlooked the fact that the NYPD arrested half a dozen terrorist suspects and killed one in the raid," Stone said. "That must have pissed off Grant."

"I want a nap," Holly said.

"We're having dinner with Dino," Stone said. "I'll wake you in time."

They arrived at Elaine's to find Dino already sitting with Lance Cabot.

"Good evening," Lance said.

"Hi," Holly managed.

Stone and Lance shook hands.

"I was just congratulating Dino on bagging four men who are at the top of our most-wanted list," Lance said, "and two others who would have been, eventually."

"Yeah, a lot of good it did us with the press," Dino said.

"Dino," Stone said, "you had an opportunity to tell the TV people about the arrests today. Why didn't you?"

"I hate talking to those people," Dino said.

"That's why you're not the chief of detectives," Stone replied.

"I wouldn't have the job. I'd never see my wife and kid."

"You never see them now," Stone pointed out.

"What do you mean? I'm home for dinner almost every night."

"You're in here almost every night," Stone said.

"Hey, fellas," Holly interjected, "can we have a drink in peace?"

"Don't worry," Lance said. "You'll bag Trini. He's running out of places to hide, and his picture is all over TV."

"Can you help?" Holly asked.

"I've got a few ears to the ground."

They ordered drinks, and they had hardly arrived when Herbie Fisher appeared at their table, like an imp from a magic lantern.

"Hey, everybody," Herbie said brightly. "Hey, Stone, Holly, Lance, Dino."

"It's Lieutenant Bacchetti to you," Dino said.

"Can I have a drink?"

"No," Stone said. "Go away."

"But I've got some information for you," Herbie said, sounding hurt.

"Shoot him, Dino," Stone said.

"I want the reward," Herbie protested.

"Then go see the FBI," Dino said. "It's their reward."

"But don't you want Trini Rodriguez?"

"Herbie," Dino said, "if you don't get out of here, I'm going to call a patrol car and have you arrested."

"For what?"

"For annoying the police."

"Then maybe you better take a look at

this," Herbie said. He tossed a five-by-seven photograph on the table.

Lance picked it up. "Where did you get this?"

"I processed it."

Holly looked at the photograph. "It's Trini."

"Where did this come from?" Stone asked, looking at the picture.

"A guy brought two rolls of film into the store this afternoon. This negative was on one of them."

"Who was the guy?"

"I have his name and address," Herbie said slyly, rubbing his fingers together in a fashion indicating he wanted money.

"You still want me to shoot him, Stone?"

"Not until he gives us the name and address," Stone replied.

"So, do I get the reward?"

Stone clapped him on the back. "Sit down, Herbie, and have a drink. Good to see you."

53

Herbie took a sip of the twelve-year-old Scotch he had requested. "Looks like I'm getting more popular," he said to nobody in particular.

"It's an illusion," Stone said. "Who brought the pictures in?"

"This guy."

"Which guy?"

"This Italian guy."

"How did you know he was Italian?"

"You think I don't know a goombah when I see one?" Herbie took another sip of Scotch. "And he had an Italian name."

Stone took out his notebook and a pen. "Spell it for me," he said.

"G . . ." Herbie blinked. "Hey, what about the reward?"

"It's like this, Herbie: The FBI said on television that they were offering a reward for the arrest of Trini Rodriguez. They didn't say that *they* had to arrest him."

"So, they'll give me the reward even if Dino arrests him?"

"Well, that is certainly what I inferred from their announcement. Do you have any reason to think differently?"

Herbie scratched his head. "I don't think so."

"Well, there you are."

"Where?"

"There."

"Where's there?"

Stone sighed. "Herbie, do you know what obstruction of justice is?"

"Sort of, I think."

"Well, if you don't give me the name, Dino will arrest you for obstruction of justice."

"Why give it to you? You're not a cop, Dino is."

"Then give it to Dino."

"Dino, if I give you the name, do you promise I'll get the reward?"

"Herbie, if you give me the name and address of the guy who brought the film in for processing, I promise I'll do everything in my power to get you that reward. I'll even

write the FBI a letter, saying you're the guy
who deserves the reward."

Herbie brightened. "Okay."

"That's *if* we arrest him and on your information," Dino said. "If he's not at this guy's
address, there's no reward."

"Yeah, that seems fair," Herbie said.

"So, give me the name."

"And I'll be a hero?"

"Herbie, you're going to be a *dead* hero if
you don't give me the name right now."
Dino stuck his hand under his jacket, as if
reaching for his gun.

"Okay, okay," Herbie said, raising his
hands. "The name is Galeano—G—"

"I know how to spell it," Dino said.
"What's his first name?"

"Vito."

"Hey, wait a minute," Dino said. "I know
that guy. He runs a numbers operation, and
God knows what else, out of a grocery
store in Little Italy."

"That's the address he gave me," Herbie
said, taking Stone's pad and pen and laboriously writing out the address.

"What's he doing getting film processed
in Brooklyn?" Dino asked.

"He lives in the neighborhood. I'm not

sure exactly where. He comes in all the time with his wife's pictures."

"Stone and I are acquainted with the gentleman, too," Holly said, inspecting the photograph. "Oh, oh, take a look at this, Stone," she said, pointing. "I think this nails down the location, don't you?" She handed him the photograph.

Stone inspected it carefully. "Aha," he said, "I believe that's our grave in the background."

"Your grave?" Dino asked. "What the fuck are you talking about?"

"Didn't I tell you about that? Mr. Galeano and his friends dug this hole in the basement of his grocery store especially for Holly and me."

Dino took the picture and looked at it closely. "So, why aren't you in it?"

"Because I persuaded him to call your father-in-law first. Eduardo suggested he not do it."

"When did he dig the grave?"

"Yesterday," Stone replied.

"So we know Trini was there yesterday."

"Right."

"And how do we know Trini isn't in the hole?"

"Because he was at that apartment to-day."

"Did you actually see him?"

"No, but one of the SWAT team identified him just before he slammed the escape door in their faces."

"When do I get the hundred grand?" Herbie asked.

"Herbie," Dino said, "do you remember the conditions attached to the reward?"

"Sort of."

"Let me review them for you: Number one, we have to arrest Trini on the information you supply. Number two, the FBI has to sign off on it."

"Yeah, but you're going to write them a letter."

"Herbie, as eloquent as I am on department stationery, not everybody does everything I ask them to. Especially the FBI."

Herbie frowned. "I don't think I like the sound of that."

"Gee, I'm sorry," Dino said.

"Can you find out where Vito lives?" Stone asked Dino.

"Yeah, sure, but Trini's more likely to be at the grocery store than at Vito's house.

Those guys never bring business home to the family, especially business like Trini."

Stone's cell phone vibrated. "Hello?"

"Is this Stone Barrington?"

"Yes. Who's this?"

"This is Vito. You remember me?"

"Vito! How could I ever forget?"

Vito chuckled. "Yeah, I guess you wouldn't, in the circumstances."

"Have you got a line on Rodriguez?" Stone asked.

"I think I might," Vito said. "You want to meet me down at my place of business in the morning?"

"I have to wait until morning?"

"Well, I'm not going to be able to do anything for you until midday, at best, but if you want to spend the night in my basement . . ."

"No thanks, Vito, I've seen enough of your basement."

"Okay. Come down tomorrow morning about eleven, and I'll see what I can do. You remember the address?"

"Oh, yes."

"See you then." Vito hung up.

"Herbie," Stone said, "I'm afraid there's been a little hitch in getting you the reward."

54

Herbie finally seemed to take a hint and left.

Lance watched him walk out of Elaine's. "You know, that is one of the densest human beings it has ever been my misfortune to meet."

"I have to agree," Stone said. "And he's one of the most annoying, too."

"Then why do you keep messing with him?" Dino asked.

"I don't keep messing with him. He keeps messing with me."

"You, too, Lance," Dino said.

"I know, I know. He was there when I needed him for a photograph, and now I can't get rid of him. He's convinced that he'd be perfect for Agency operations."

"Can't you find a suicide mission to send him on?" Stone asked.

"Herbie is the kind of guy who'd walk into a suicide mission and walk out with a smile on his face and everybody else dead, and he wouldn't have had a thing to do with it."

"How the hell did you ever come up with him?" Stone asked.

"An operator I know gave him to me; Herbie's his nephew."

"You, too? You know Bob Cantor?"

"*You* know Bob Cantor?" Lance responded.

"He works for me all the time."

"Well, he has more than one client."

"No wonder he's busy when I call him these days," Stone said.

"Okay," Dino said, "what's the deal with the phone call you just got?"

"It was Vito."

"I got that part."

"He says he may be able to put his hands on Trini tomorrow. He wants us to come down to his grocery store tomorrow morning."

"You'd better take this seriously," Dino said. "Vito Galeano is a serious guy."

Holly spoke up. "He certainly seemed serious when he was about to shoot us and bury us in his cellar," she said.

"Believe me, he was," Dino replied. He turned to Stone. "What made you think to ask him to call Eduardo?"

"If I'd asked him to call the mayor, it wouldn't have worked," Stone said. "Come on, Dino, who else do I know who's connected?"

"You could have told him to call me."

"A guy's about to shoot us, and I should tell him to call a cop?"

"I've known Vito since we were kids. He's a coupla years older than me, but we went to the same school. He pulled a bunch of bigger kids off me once and slapped them around, so I always felt I owed him. Once, when he was in a tight spot, I had a chance to help, and he's been grateful. Here's some advice: If you know him now, next time you get in trouble with some wise guys, tell them to call Vito, instead of Eduardo. Not one in a hundred of them knows Eduardo, but they all know Vito, and they don't mess with him."

"I guess that's good advice," Stone said. He turned to Lance. "I hear you're trying to recruit Holly to your organization on a more full-time basis."

"*Stone!*" Holly hissed.

"It's all right, Holly," Lance said. "Stone's family."

"I am?" Stone asked.

"You signed up, didn't you?"

"I guess I did at that. Holly, maybe Lance is the guy to help you with your little money problem."

Holly turned red. "Stone, you'd better shut up right now."

"Are you in need of funds, Holly?" Lance asked, sounding concerned.

"No, I am not," Holly replied.

"Far from it," Stone chipped in.

"I don't understand," Lance said.

"It's better that way," Holly replied.

"Come on, Holly," Stone said, "who better than Lance?"

"Yes," Lance said, "who better than me? If you have a problem, I'd like to help."

Holly looked around the table.

"Maybe I'd better go to the john," Dino said, half rising.

"Sit down, Dino. All right, I'll tell you about it." Holly went through her story. Everyone was rapt, except Stone, who seemed to have trouble not laughing.

When she had finished, Lance patted her

hand. "Don't worry about it, my dear, we'll think of something."

"Think of what?" Stone asked.

"Yes, what?" Holly echoed.

Lance looked around to be sure he wasn't being overheard. "You have a large sum of money obtained from an illegal operation—money you didn't report. You want to get rid of it in a, shall we say, profitable manner?"

"I suppose."

"This is called money laundering, and there are a number of ways to do it."

"I'll bet," Stone said.

"All of them carry a certain amount of risk," Lance explained. "Perhaps the safest thing to do is for you to get the case to me, and I'll deal with it. After a little time has passed, you'll have a sizeable sum deposited in an overseas bank account. You'll receive a credit card in the mail, and from then on, you charge whatever you wish to the card. You'll have to keep track of what you spend in your head, because you don't want the mailman bringing a monthly statement, do you?"

"That's it?" Holly asked.

"That's it."

"It sounds too simple."

"Well, you'll have to pay a service charge on the original deposit, say, ten percent."

"To whom?"

"It's better you don't know. But you'll still have more than five million in the bank, should you ever need it, and it would be invested in any manner you wish."

"So, I'd be earning money?"

"I should think at least an eight percent return."

"Nice."

"Of course, you'll owe taxes on what you earn, but you can invest in tax-free municipals. You can buy just about anything with a credit card these days—a car, for instance—but you'd want to stay away from buying anything that would create a legal record, like a house."

"A car creates a legal record," Holly said.

"Not an important one. It wouldn't show up on your credit report, for instance, if you didn't finance it."

"There you are," Stone said. "Problem solved."

"Not exactly," she replied. "I've still got to get it to Lance."

"Put it in your car and drive it up here," Stone said.

"Or in your airplane."

"Forget that. I'm not getting involved. I have a law license to protect."

"Do it while you've still got a badge to flash," Lance said, "in case you're stopped by a highway patrolman who wants to search your car."

"I'll think about it," Holly said. She turned to Stone. "Can we go home now?"

"Sure."

Dino spoke up. "I want to go with you to Vito's place tomorrow."

"Why?" Stone asked.

"You'll be better off with me there."

"Okay, sure."

"Good with me," Holly said.

"And don't you go into that store until I say so."

55

Stone and Holly were having breakfast the following morning.

"I don't like this," Stone said.

"What don't you like?"

"Before, when we went into that apartment with Dino, we had a SWAT team ahead of us, and there was shooting. Now we're just supposed to walk into Vito's grocery store and walk out with Trini? It doesn't add up, and if it did, I still wouldn't want to go in there like that."

"What do you suggest?"

Stone called Dino.

"Bacchetti."

"I don't like it, Dino."

"Who's this?"

"It's Stone, dummy. You don't recognize *my* voice after all these years?"

"What don't you like?"

"I don't like walking into that grocery store with no SWAT team and no backup."

"Vito's your backup."

"The last time I saw Vito he was backing me into a freshly dug grave."

"You don't trust him?"

"Why should I trust him? Because he didn't kill me?"

"That's a start."

"That was because he was afraid of Eduardo."

"Because he *respected* Eduardo."

"Whatever. He didn't back off because he'd suddenly taken a liking to me."

"Maybe he liked Holly."

"He was going to kill her, too."

"You got a point."

"Of course I do. The point is, what's going to happen when we walk in there? *If* we walk in there."

"You'll be with me."

"You're not big enough to hide behind."

"He respects me."

"Why, because he saved your skinny little ass from bullies when you were ten?"

"No, because I saved his fat ass from a long time upstate, and he appreciates that."

"Okay, that takes care of you. What about Holly and me?"

"It's transferable."

"What?"

"The respect."

"Look, these goombahs are murdering people they respect all the time, you know? The respect seems to kind of vary from day to day—one day you're a prince of a guy, the next you're in a fifty-five-gallon drum of lime in a New Jersey swamp, waiting for Judgment Day."

"Stone, I don't think I've ever seen you so nervous."

"I don't think I've ever had more reason to be nervous. I've been threatened and shot at and dragged all over the country, and—"

Holly broke in. "I did *not* drag you all over the country," she said. "You came voluntarily."

"That was only because I wanted to get you in the sack."

"You had already gotten me in the sack. How soon you forget!"

Dino broke in. "You wanted to get me in the sack?"

"Oh, shut up. You know I was talking to Holly."

"How do I know who you're talking to? I can only hear you."

"We've got to have a plan, Dino."

"What sort of plan?"

"The kind of plan where men in black suits and body armor with automatic weapons and stun grenades go in first and let us know when they've got Trini handcuffed."

"You don't understand. Vito has a certain standing in his community, you know? He would not respond well to assault teams running up and down the aisles of his grocery store, tossing stun grenades. It would not reflect well on him in his neighborhood."

"Well, we need *some* kind of a plan," Stone said.

"What kind of plan do you want?"

"Suggest something."

"I don't know what to suggest. I'm okay with just going in there and talking to Vito."

"How about you send a few undercover people in there to do some shopping and reconnoiter?"

"Oh, sure, and they're not going to stick out like tourists from Alabama? The whole neighborhood would know."

"Well, think of *something*, Dino."

"I'll call you back," Dino said, then hung up.

"Hey!" Stone shouted down the phone. "Don't hang up on me!"

"He hung up?" Holly asked.

"He hung up; said he'd call me back."

"So, he'll call you back."

"You heard me voice my concerns?"

"I heard. I don't really see what the problem is. Vito said just to come down there."

"So now *you* trust Vito? The guy who was going to put two in your head and bury you in his cellar?"

"I kind of like him."

"He's a fucking mafioso, and you kind of like him?"

"Well, your friend Eduardo is a fucking mafioso, and you like him."

"First of all, he's not a fucking mafioso, he's more of . . . an elder statesman of Italian-American diplomacy."

"He's a fucking mafioso."

"And I've had a lot more experience of Eduardo than you've had of Vito."

"Granted. Why don't we just wait to hear what Dino has to say?"

The phone rang, and Stone picked it up. "Hello?"

"Okay, listen . . ."

"Who is this?"

"Now *you* don't recognize *my* voice?"

"What is it?"

"I talked to Vito, and it's okay."

"That's your plan? You talked to Vito, and it's okay?"

"That's my plan."

Stone sighed. "Okay, what do we do?"

"Vito suggested we come in my car, since yours is getting to be a little too well known in the neighborhood, so I'll pick you up at ten-thirty."

"Okay." Stone hung up.

"He talked to Vito, and it's okay?"

"Yeah."

"And that's the plan?"

"Yeah."

56

Stone led Holly upstairs to his safe and opened it. "I'm not comfortable going after this guy with your Sig-Sauer and my Walther," he said, rooting around in the safe. "They're both .380s, and we need more stopping power."

"What did you have in mind?" Holly asked.

Stone handed her a gun. "This is a Sig P239," he said. "It's a little larger than your P232, and it's nine millimeter."

"I own one. What are we using for ammo?"

He rooted around some more and came up with a magazine. "This is loaded with MagSafe ammo. You know about it?"

"Sounds familiar; remind me."

"Instead of a lead slug, it's epoxy with

fairly large buckshot encapsulated. It will penetrate soft body armor, but the great thing is that even if it goes all the way through a body, it won't ricochet, and it won't kill some bystander. Makes a big wound in the original recipient, though."

"Why doesn't everybody use it all the time?"

"Because it costs something like three bucks a round. It's best saved for special occasions."

"And what are you carrying?"

Stone handed her a pistol. "It's a Sig Pro. Guy I know sent it to me. Got a fifteen-round magazine."

"I want this one," she said, tucking it into the belt of her jeans.

"Oh, all right, I'll take the P239." He handed her the Pro's magazine and closed the safe. "Let's go."

"Okay," Dino said as they headed downtown at mid-morning, "here's what Vito told me. You ready?"

"We're ready," Stone said.

"He's luring Trini down to the store with a really good story."

"What's the story?"

"The story is, a truck is going to make a delivery to Vito's grocery store, and half of the truck is given over to a compartment rigged up as a room. It's air-conditioned, it has a bed and a chair and lights and a chemical toilet and a lot of dirty magazines. The truck actually exists, according to Vito."

"What's the truck got to do with this?" Holly asked.

"Vito has told Trini that they're going to take him to Florida in the truck, two guys driving nonstop. He's got food and water and the magazines in the back, and they're there in twenty-four hours."

"Trini wants to go back to Florida?"

"He says he can get lost among his home-boys down there, and then he'll get a ship out somewhere. Anybody stops the truck, the rear part is stacked to the ceiling with cartons of Italian foodstuffs. Pretty slick, huh?"

"Pretty slick," Holly admitted.

"So that's how Vito knows for sure Trini will be there today?"

"Right. He's due at noon."

"And Vito is just going to hand Trini to me?"

"That's the idea."

"I don't get it," she said.

"What?"

"What's in it for Vito?"

"He makes Eduardo happy."

"Eduardo is still in this?" Stone asked.

"Up to his ears, apparently, and Vito always likes to make Eduardo happy. In his business, you make Eduardo happy, good things happen to you."

"This is just crazy enough to work," Holly said.

"Wait a minute," Stone said.

"What?"

"Trini was behind Vito's kidnapping us, right?"

"Right, I guess," Dino said.

"Well, I'd like to know what Vito told him."

"Why can't you just relax and let this happen?"

"Oh, all right, I suppose Vito could tell him *something*."

"You bet your ass he could."

"What's the plan when we get there?"

"Vito will tell us then."

57

The three walked into Vito Galeano's grocery store at eleven sharp. The place was not terribly big—four rows of shelving running up and down the space, a counter at the rear, and, up half a flight of stairs, a loft office from which Vito had a view over half glasses of the entire store. It was old-fashioned and fragrant with hanging sausage and spices. Vito came down the stairs, checking each of the half-dozen customers in the place, and finally, checking out Stone, Dino, and Holly.

"*Buon giorno,*" he said to Dino.

"*Buon giorno,*" Dino replied.

"How you doin'?" he said to Stone and Holly.

"Good," they replied simultaneously.

"This is Gino," he said, nodding at the

aproned man behind the counter, who nodded at them all.

Vito reached under the counter, pulled out an apron, and handed it to Dino. "Here's how we're going to do this," he said. "Dino, you're the only one who looks like he could work here, so you put on the apron and stand behind the counter with Gino. Pay attention to the way he works while we're waiting, so you won't look stupid when Trini comes in."

"Right," Dino said. He took off his jacket and tie, rolled up his sleeves, and put on the apron.

"You were born to this," Stone said.

"Aw, shut up."

"You two," Gino said, nodding at Stone and Holly, "get over to one side of the store, so the shelves will hide you. Trini comes in, he'll walk down the center aisle, like everybody. When that happens, Gino, Dino, one of you sing out, 'Vito, gimme a price on a whole Genoa salami!' That means Trini is in the store." He looked out to the street. "Here comes the truck."

They all turned to see a beautifully painted black truck pull up to the curb. Painted on the side was the legend "Gaetano Galeano & Sons, Premium Provisions" in a florid style.

"Beautiful truck," Stone said.

"Thanks," Vito replied. "My old man designed it before the Genoveses got to him on the bocce court at the coffeehouse."

"Sorry about that," Stone said.

Vito shrugged. "It's our game," he said. "Anyway, Trini comes down the center aisle, you hear the thing about the price of salami, and you two come around the shelves into the aisle behind Trini. You're carryin'?"

They nodded.

"Don't shoot nobody, okay? Except Trini, if you have to."

They shook their heads.

"There'll be a man up in my office with a shotgun. Dino and Gino are carryin'; Trini's bracketed." He looked at Holly. "You got cuffs?"

She nodded. "Three pair."

"You frisk him and cuff him, then we hustle him over to the stairs." He nodded to his right, where a door led to stairs to the basement.

Stone didn't want to think about the basement. "Then what?"

"Then we talk."

"What's to talk about?" Holly asked.

Dino held up a hand. "You'll talk."

Holly shrugged. "We'll talk." She shot a glance at Stone that meant she didn't like this.

Stone shook his head slightly; this was no time to argue.

"Is the truck real?" Holly asked.

"What, real?" Vito asked. "You never seen a truck?"

"I mean, does it really have the hidden compartment?"

"Comes in handy from time to time," Vito replied. Then he looked at Dino. "You already forgot this, right?"

"Yeah, yeah," Dino said.

"Anybody hungry?" He took a tray of sliced salami and olives from under the counter. "We got free samples."

Everybody took something to be polite, except Stone, who took it because he was hungry.

"Okay, spread out, and let's do this," Vito said.

Dino hopped over the counter and took up his position. Stone and Holly moved to where they had been told. They couldn't see the store entrance.

"What's your plan?" Stone asked.

"What Vito said," Holly replied.

"I mean after we've taken him. What are you going to do with him?"

"I haven't given it much thought," she said, taking the Sig Pro from her purse and pumping a round into the chamber.

"It's time you did," Stone said. "In a few minutes you're going to have a dangerous criminal on your hands, and you'd better figure out how you're going to handle him."

"I'm going to take him home," she said.

"How?"

"Airlines?"

"Think about how much trouble Trini could make on an airplane with a couple of hundred civilians watching. Then you've got to get him to Orchid Beach."

"We'll get a flight to Palm Beach, and I'll have a squad car meet us."

"I've got a better idea."

"What?"

"I know a guy out at Teterboro who can produce a jet charter on demand—something light, like a Lear or a CitationJet."

"What's it going to cost?"

"A guess? Eight, ten thousand."

"I can spring for that. My department's

got a discretionary fund for emergency ex-
penditures."

"That's our best bet. We bundle Trini into
Dino's car, drive him to Teterboro where the
jet's waiting with the engines running. Two
and a half, three hours and you're home."

"You coming?"

"Once he's on board, you won't need
me," Stone said.

"Oh, I need you," she said, leering at him.

"I thought we satisfied that need last
night."

"Only temporarily."

"We'll work on that."

"Vito!" Dino yelled suddenly, "gimme a
price on a whole Genoa salami!"

"Trini's in the store," Stone whispered.
"Here we go."

58

Stone peeped around the shelves and saw Trini walking toward the counter, with a large semiautomatic pistol stuck in his belt in the small of his back. Stone motioned to Holly, and they fell in behind him.

Dino was waiting for him with half a smile on his face. "*Buon giorno*," he said.

"Yeah, yeah, where's Vito?" Trini responded.

Dino reached behind him, produced a weapon, and stuck it in Trini's face.

Trini reached for his gun, but Stone grabbed his wrist, shoved it up between his shoulder blades, while Holly grabbed the gun and snapped handcuffs onto Trini's wrist.

Holly hit him in the back of the head with the heel of her hand. "Bend over the counter, stupid, and give me your other hand."

Stone put some pressure on the hammerlock for emphasis. "Do as the lady says."

Reluctantly, Trini offered the other wrist, and he was now handcuffed.

Holly stuck her gun in her bag and went over him thoroughly—front, back, and crotch.

"Hey, you want to eat that, baby?" Trini smirked as she felt him up.

"Don't worry," she replied, "there'll be a lot of guys who'll want it where you're going, and you'll find yourself on the receiving end, too. You'll end up as some big guy's bitch."

Trini began kicking and spitting at her, until Stone hit him in the crotch. Then he became more manageable.

"Did I mention," Holly said, "that you're under arrest and that you have the right to keep your mouth shut?"

"Let's get him downstairs," Dino said.

Two of Vito's men materialized and hustled Trini down to the basement. Vito beckoned Dino into a corner, and the two men began to talk earnestly. Holly and Stone were left at the counter.

"I can't believe it," Holly said. "Just like *that*"—she snapped her fingers—"and it's over."

But Stone was watching Dino and Vito as their conversation, though whispered, became more animated. "Maybe it's not over yet," he said, nodding toward the two men.

Holly watched them for a moment. "What's going on?"

Dino turned and began walking toward them.

"I have a feeling we're about to find out," Stone said.

Dino looked embarrassed. "There's a problem," he said.

"What problem?" Holly asked.

"A problem about Trini."

"What, do they want to put him in that grave downstairs?" Stone asked.

Dino shook his head. "No, they want him alive. They want the reward."

"What reward?" Holly asked.

"The hundred grand the FBI is offering for Trini."

Holly seemed to be hyperventilating.

"Hey, wait a minute, Dino," Stone said, "we had a deal."

Dino looked away. "Apparently, we don't have a deal anymore."

Holly found her voice. "Dino, you tell Vito . . ." She stopped. "Never mind, I'll tell him myself."

"Holly . . ." Dino made a grab for her arm, but she shook him off and walked toward Vito, who didn't seem glad to see her coming.

Stone steered Dino away from them. "Let her try. It can't hurt."

"No, I guess it can't hurt. I'm really embarrassed about this."

"It's not your fault."

"Vito says we didn't close the deal; we never shook on it."

"Shook on it? What is this, high school?"

"Apparently. Anyway, the hundred grand seems to overrule any argument I could make."

Stone glanced at Holly and Vito, though he couldn't hear them. They were talking earnestly, but Holly wasn't waving her arms or shouting. "Look at that," he said.

Dino looked toward the two. "She seems

awfully calm," he said. "I was afraid she'd shoot him."

"Now she's smiling."

"Vito is smiling, too."

Then, to the mutual astonishment of Stone and Dino, Holly and Vito shook hands.

Holly walked back to where they stood. "Let's get out of here," she said.

They walked back to the car, and Stone waited until they were inside before he began talking. "What the hell was that all about?" he asked.

"Yeah," Dino echoed, "what did you two have to say to each other?"

Holly looked smug. "I made him an offer he couldn't refuse."

Stone and Dino, who were in the front seat, looked at each other.

"What the fuck?" Dino said.

"Dino, would you do me a great big favor?" Holly asked, digging her cell phone out of her purse and dialing a number.

"Sure, anything."

"Would you take me by Stone's house, wait while I throw my stuff into a bag, then drive me to LaGuardia?"

"Why not?" Dino said.

Holly began talking to an airline reservations clerk.

Stone looked at Dino. "Do you have any idea what's going on?"

Dino shrugged. "I think the lady is sick of you, and she's going home."

"Holly," Stone said, "what's going on?"

She waved him quiet. "I'm on the phone," she hissed.

59

The following evening, back in Orchid Beach, Holly left her office at dusk and drove north on A1A, with Daisy in the passenger seat, her nose out the window, sniffing the damp Florida air.

Holly turned left down a side road and, after half a mile, came to the rear gate of the real estate development that had once been called Palmetto Gardens, and later, Blood Orchid, and which was now in federal hands. She stopped and, leaving the motor running and the lights on, got out and went to where the gate was chained and locked. She knew the combination to the lock because she had locked it herself. A moment later, she took off the chain, then drove her car inside. She locked the gate behind her and bore to her left, along a road that ran alongside the golf course.

The course looked good, since the Feds had kept on the grounds crew until they could sell the place. The auction was scheduled for a week hence, and they had been working hard to make the grounds look good.

Holly pulled into a dirt road and drove fifty yards, then stopped the car, switched off the engine, and got out, followed by Daisy. Using her SureFire tactical flashlight, she walked purposely through the woods, switching on the light a second at a time to find her way. Daisy ran ahead, scaring up rabbits and sniffing at everything.

She came to a live oak tree about thirty feet tall, then stopped. She stood quietly for a few minutes, letting her night vision develop and looking around for other human beings. The property seemed deserted, and as she waited, a full moon rose in the east, making the flashlight unnecessary.

She put the light back into its holster, took off her heavy gun belt, and began climbing the tree, while Daisy watched, baffled. A little more than halfway up, at about twenty feet, she stopped. The case was still there, though it was covered in pine pollen. She looked down. "Daisy," she said, "go over there." She pointed, and Daisy followed her instructions. "Sit." Daisy sat. "Stay." Daisy stayed.

What the hell, she thought, it was a sturdy case. She took it by the handle, dangled it for a moment, and let go. The case hit one limb, slowing it, then it fell unimpeded to the pine straw–padded floor of the woods. It bounced once, then fell on its side, intact.

Holly climbed down the tree, picked up the case, and put it into the trunk of her patrol car. Then she got Daisy back inside, let herself out the gate, and headed toward town.

She drove into the basement garage under the police station, parked the car, and got the case out of the trunk. It was heavier than she had remembered, and it was something of a struggle to get it upstairs and into her office. There were only two people in the squad room, a duty officer handling the phones and radio and a detective catching up on his paperwork. The rest of the night shift was on patrol.

She got the case into her office, dampened some paper towels, and wiped the pine pollen off the case, making its black aluminum surface look nearly like new. Then she hoisted the case onto a table and opened it. She was greeted with the sight of rows of hundred-dollar bills, sorted into stacks of one hundred, each secured with a heavy rubber band. She counted out twenty of the stacks and packed them into a small zippered duffel from her locker. Then she counted out another ten stacks, dropped them into a Federal Express envelope, and wrote out a note on her stationery. She put the note into the envelope, sealed it, filled out a FedEx waybill, and stuck it to the envelope.

Then she picked up the heavy case and took it into the darkened evidence room. She went through the procedure for setting the combination locks on the case, then locked them and looked around for just the right spot. She found a place among some filing boxes that had been seized during a drug raid, and set it there. Then she got an evidence sticker, put her name on it, and fixed it to the side of the case. If anyone came across it, they wouldn't be able to open it, and if they asked about it, she could say she'd forgotten to log it in.

She went back to her office, picked up the duffel and the FedEx package, and set them on her desk, looking at her watch. It was nearly ten. The call should come soon. She switched on her desk light, picked up a law enforcement magazine, put her feet on the desk, and started to read. Twenty minutes later, her cell phone vibrated on her belt. "Yes?"

"Hey, you ready for us?"

"Yes." She asked where he was, then gave him directions, then she hung up, picked up the duffel and the FedEx package, and walked down to the garage with Daisy clicking along on the tile floor behind her.

She got some gear out of her car, then waited in the garage for another twenty minutes, until headlights appeared outside. She walked out and held up a hand for the truck to stop.

Two men got out. "Hey, how you doin'?" the passenger said.

"I'm good. You got my package?"

"Sure. You got *my* package?"

She handed him the duffel. "It's in stacks of one hundred hundreds. Count it."

He counted it carefully. "It's good," he said, and he led the way to the rear of the vehicle.

Holly watched as the two men removed a dozen boxes from the back of the truck. Then one man climbed in and walked forward a few steps. He knocked on something. "Hey, man, we're here," he called. "You ready to come out?"

Holly switched on her flashlight, illuminated the inside of the truck, and pulled out her gun.

"Here we go," the man said, opening the door.

Trini Rodriguez stepped out into the bright glare of the tactical light, holding up a hand to spare his eyes. He would be effectively blind for a minute or two. He followed the other man forward, then hopped down from the truck. "Hey, what's with the light?" he said.

Holly held the light so that it illuminated her gun, which was pointed at his head. "Lie down on the ground," she said.

"What?"

"You see the gun? Lie down on the ground, or I'll shoot you where you stand."

Trini prostrated himself.

"Is he clean?" Holly asked the men.

"Oh, yeah. We didn't let him have a piece."

"What the fuck is going on?" Trini asked.

Holly handed the belt to one of the men. "Put this on him," she said, "buckle to the rear." She watched as they buckled the belt on him and rolled him over. Then she handed them the cuffs. "Run these through the ring and handcuff him, hands in front," she said, and they did. "Now get him on his feet."

They stood him up, then stepped back.

"Guard, Daisy," she said, pointing at Trini.

Daisy took up a position in front of him and bared her teeth, making a low growling noise.

"You keep that dog away from me!" Trini hollered.

"Behave yourself, or I'll show you how she's been trained to eat genitals," Holly said. She turned to the two men. "Gentlemen, our business is concluded. Please thank Vito for me, and give him my very best."

They bade her good night, got into the truck, and drove away.

"Now," she said to Trini, "you're under arrest. We're going to pretend that I read you your rights, and I hope that, between here and the cell that's waiting for you, you'll give me an excuse to set the dog on you and shoot you in the head. Now turn around and march."

Trini turned around and marched.

Ten minutes later, Trini was secured and logged in. "He's being arraigned tomorrow morning," she said to the duty officer who had helped her. "The paperwork is all done. Put him down for some breakfast."

Trini looked at her sullenly through the bars. "I'm gonna get you," he said.

"Trini," she replied, "you're all through getting people, and you've just spent your last day on earth as a free man. All the rest of your days, which are numbered, you'll be looking at the world through bars, right up until the moment they put the needle in your arm."

On the way home, Holly stopped at a FedEx box and dropped her package into it.

"Now let's go home and get some dinner," she said to Daisy.

Daisy made a little noise in anticipation. She knew what "dinner" meant.

Holly drove home with a wonderful sense of satisfaction. Now her only worry was what to do about Lance Cabot's offer of work. In her head, just for fun, she began composing a letter of resignation to the city council of Orchid Beach.

60

Stone was sitting at his desk when Joan came in with a Federal Express package.

"This just came for you," she said. "You want me to open it?"

"I'll do it," Stone said, glancing at the return address on the label. He ripped open the package and dumped the contents onto his desk as his secretary watched.

"Holy shit," Joan said, uncharacteristically.

Stone picked up the note among the bundles of cash. " 'For services rendered,' " he read aloud.

"Those must have been some services," Joan said.

Stone laughed.

"What's so funny?"

"I never thought she'd use the cash," he said.

"Who?"

"Holly Barker. Log this in, put it in the safe, and include the taxes in the next quarterly payment to the IRS."

"Yes, boss," Joan said, sweeping the money back into the envelope. She left his office.

Stone took out a sheet of his stationery and began writing.

Payment received. I don't know what you've decided to do about Lance's offer of work (and of assistance with foreign banking), but I hope your decision brings you back this way soon. It would be fun to know you without the burden of chasing somebody else. Best to Ham, Ginny, and Daisy.

Fondly,
Stone

He addressed and sealed the envelope, got his jacket, and dropped the envelope on Joan's desk on his way out.

"Where you going?" she asked.

"To look at Porsches," he said, closing the door behind him.

ACKNOWLEDGMENTS

I want to express my gratitude to my editor, David Highfill, and all the people at Putnam who work so hard to get my work to its readers.

I'd also like to thank my literary agents, Morton Janklow and Anne Sibbald, and all the people at Janklow & Nesbit for their fine representation over the past twenty-two years. Their fine work is much appreciated.

AUTHOR'S NOTE

I am happy to hear from readers, but you should know that if you write to me in care of my publisher, three to six months will pass before I receive your letter, and when it finally arrives it will be one among many, and I will not be able to reply.

However, if you have access to the Internet, you may visit my website at www.stuartwoods.com, where there is a button for sending me email. So far, I have been able to reply to all of my email, and I will continue to try to do so.

If you send me an email and do not receive a reply, it is because you are among an alarming number of people who have entered their email address incorrectly in their mail software. I have many of my replies returned as undeliverable.

Remember: email, reply; snail mail, no reply.

When you email, please do not send attachments, as I *never* open these. They can take twenty minutes to download, and they often contain viruses.

Please do not place me on your mailing lists for funny stories, prayers, political causes, charitable fund-raising, petitions, or sentimental claptrap. I get enough of that from people I already know. Generally speaking, when I get email addressed to a large number of people, I immediately delete it without reading it.

Please do not send me your ideas for a book, as I have a policy of writing only what I myself invent. If you send me story ideas, I will immediately delete them without reading them. If you have a good idea for a book, write it yourself, but I will not be able to advise you on how to get it published. Buy a copy of *Writer's Market* at any bookstore; that will tell you how.

Anyone with a request concerning events or appearances may email it to me or send it to: Publicity Department, G. P. Putnam's Sons, 375 Hudson Street, New York, NY 10014.

Those ambitious folk who wish to buy film, dramatic, or television rights to my books should contact Matthew Snyder, Creative Artists Agency, 9830 Wilshire Boulevard, Beverly Hills, CA 90212-1825.

Those who wish to conduct business of a more literary nature should contact Anne Sibbald, Janklow & Nesbit, 445 Park Avenue, New York, NY 10022.

If you want to know if I will be signing books in your city, please visit my website, www.stuartwoods.com, where the tour schedule will be published a month or so in advance. If you wish me to do a book signing in your locality, ask your favorite bookseller to contact his Putnam representative or the G. P. Putnam's Sons Publicity Department with the request.

If you find typographical or editorial errors in my book and feel an irresistible urge to tell someone, please write to David Highfill at Putnam, address above. Do not email your discoveries to me, as I will already have learned about them from others.

A list of all my published works appears in the front of this book. All the novels are still in print in paperback and can be found at or ordered from any bookstore. If you wish to obtain hardcover copies of earlier novels or of the two nonfiction books, a good used-book store or one of the online bookstores can help you find them. Otherwise, you will have to go to a great many garage sales.